SAFE
HOUSE

SAFE HOUSE

JO JAKEMAN

Harvill *Secker*

LONDON

1 3 5 7 9 10 8 6 4 2

Harvill Secker, an imprint of Vintage,
20 Vauxhall Bridge Road,
London SW1V 2SA

Harvill Secker is part of the Penguin Random House group
of companies whose addresses can be found
at global.penguinrandomhouse.com

Penguin
Random House
UK

First published by Harvill Secker in 2019

A CIP catalogue record for this book is available from the British Library

www.penguin.co.uk/vintage

ISBN 9781787300880 (hardback)
ISBN 9781787300897 (trade paperback)

Typeset in 12/16 pt Bembo Std
by Integra Software Services Pvt. Ltd, Pondicherry

Printed and bound in Great Britain by Clays Ltd, Elcograf S.p.A.

Penguin Random House is committed to a sustainable future for
our business, our readers and our planet. This book is made
from Forest Stewardship Council® certified paper.

MIX
Paper from
responsible sources
FSC
www.fsc.org   FSC® C018179

For Danny and Alex.
My heart. My home.

PROLOGUE

Interview Room 3

Wednesday, 28 November 2018, 10.18 a.m.

Conor Fletcher slams the palm of his hand on the table between them and says, 'I knew something like this would happen!'

DC Naz Apkarian covers a yawn with the back of her hand. The long night had turned into a slow morning.

'Yeah? I'd love to borrow your crystal ball one day, Mr Fletcher.'

Conor shakes his head. 'Funny,' he sneers. 'But your incompetence led to a woman's death.'

He looks towards the door. Naz can see he's itching to get out of here. *You and me both*, she thinks. He's not under arrest. He can leave whenever he wants but he needs to understand what happened just as much as Naz does.

Naz's partner, DC Angus Harper, sits in silence. He's an imposing man. Though he uses words sparingly, his presence is all that's needed to shut people up, or to make them talk. He folds his arms, knowing this makes the fabric of his shirt strain around his biceps.

'Go on then,' Naz says. 'I'm all ears. Why don't you tell us where we went wrong?'

Conor glares at her. His cold blue eyes are too close together. On instinct Naz dislikes him. She doesn't appreciate being criticised – especially before she's had her first caffeine hit of the day. He's not really angry, he's defensive. In this job it's important to recognise the difference.

'I think you know,' Conor says.

'I'm not sure I do.' Naz turns to her colleague and asks, 'What about you, Harper? Any idea what he's talking about?'

Without taking his eyes off Conor, Harper shakes his head. 'Not me.'

'Nope. See?' Naz says. 'We're clueless, Mr Fletcher. You'd be doing us a favour if you'd care to share your thoughts with us. We're just trying to understand what happened, and it seems you have all the answers.'

She waits.

Naz knows Conor Fletcher has plenty to say. She can see it in the twitch of his cheek and the set of his jaw. The words on the tip of his tongue are desperate to be heard.

'She tried to warn you,' he says at last. 'You should've known someone would come looking for her. She told you she wasn't safe, but you wouldn't listen, would you? You should have done more to help.'

'If you knew that she was in danger, Mr Fletcher, it begs the question, why you didn't do something to help her yourself?'

'Don't try to shift the blame on me. I did everything I could. Can you honestly say the same?'

'You're saying this was inevitable?' Naz asks.

Conor folds his arms and laughs, though there's no humour in his voice. 'It was only a question of who was going to get to her first.'

CHAPTER ONE

Charlie Miller

Friday, 5 October 2018

Charlie's new life began today. Luckily, she never much cared for the old one.

With one hand on the steering wheel and an eye on the road, she checked her reflection in the rear-view mirror and barely recognised herself. The darker hair still took her by surprise. The tips were almost ginger where 'chocolate brown' supermarket dye had fought the blonde, and lost.

She looked back to the empty lane that was narrower than it had any right to be and still dark with overnight rain. Puddles captured sections of blue sky, as if it had fallen from the heavens. She had missed the tangy smell of a world washed clean by rain. It was the scent of new beginnings.

Fear and excitement battled it out for supremacy in her stomach. The cautious part of her – which was both sizeable and used to getting its own way – thought about turning the car around, going back the way she'd come, but there was nothing waiting for her there. Her old life didn't exist any more.

Charlie's new life could be so . . . well, it could be so *safe*.

Her mum used to accuse her of 'playing it safe', as if *safe* was something to be avoided. She could never understand why Charlie didn't apply for a better job – but who would want the extra responsibility and the paperwork? And, of course, she never took risks. What kind of fool would willingly expose themselves to danger? Her mum said that Charlie was stuck in her ways and Charlie supposed she had a point – until the day before yesterday she had the same hairstyle she'd had since she was twelve.

Safe. Yes, Charlie played it safe on a semi-professional level. And until two years ago she thought she was doing a fine job of it.

The road ran parallel to a river that dipped towards the glimmering sea in the distance. She thought back to family holidays where they'd spend what felt like an eternity in the car before she'd shout from behind Mother's headrest, 'I can see the sea!', as if being the first to spot it deserved a prize. She didn't have a family any more and no one to share a car journey with. Funny how much could change in such a short space of time.

The Buttery was waiting for Charlie on the other side of the river. The name made her think of thick stone walls and homely fires. Old-world charm and heavy wooden doors. If she couldn't get a moat and a drawbridge, a cottage at the crumbling edge of Cornwall was the next best thing to keep the world at bay.

The automated female voice coming from her phone told her, *Take the first turning on the left,* but it was only a twist in the road that dipped beneath a few inches of water and popped up again on the other side. She half expected to be washed downstream in an elaborate game of Poohsticks. As she inched towards the sign for Penderrion the phone told her she was, *Arriving at destination.*

The houses here were trim and expensive. Set back from the lane, they had lawns that would be perfect for warm-evening G&Ts and a game of croquet. They represented a life that Charlie would never be part of.

She slowed the car as the road began to peter out. The neat lawns melted away, replaced by a bank of trees and unruly hedges. She glanced in her rear-view mirror. Had she missed the house? Gone too far? But then she saw the *Sold at Auction* sign poking from beneath a huddle of trees that bowed and bobbed in the breeze. Beyond it, she turned down an overgrown track that was dense with wizened brambles – nature's barbed wire – telling her to *Keep Out*. As she pushed the car forwards, a rabbit lurched from the undergrowth and kicked its heels at her to lead the way.

Charlie brought the car to a halt behind the cottage. She turned off the engine and pulled herself out of the car. Hands on the base of her back, she stretched and groaned. Though she'd seen pictures, this was the first time she'd seen The Buttery with her own eyes. Phrases like 'investment opportunity' and 'in need of modernisation' were euphemisms that should have told her everything she needed to know, but still she'd set her expectations too high.

'You've got to be joking,' she said, though her words were tugged from her mouth and blown to the top of the trees like discarded litter before they could reach her ears.

The roof bowed like a washing line of bedsheets, and the kitchen window was missing its glass. A lot of work would be needed to turn this house into a home, but Charlie had come prepared.

She looked at the upstairs window where a limp curtain fluttered and fell. Did she see, or just imagine, a figure in the shadows? She took a slow step backwards.

5

The curtains swayed again but there was no one there. They were curled by the tender caress of the wind. Nothing else. She unclenched her hands that she didn't realise were in tight fists by her side.

'Idiot,' she muttered.

There's no danger here. There couldn't be, because no one knew where she was. This was her fresh start.

She could be anyone in the world – anyone she wanted – except Steffi.

If she wanted to stay safe, she needed to make sure everyone forgot that Steffi Finn had ever existed.

CHAPTER TWO

Steffi Finn

Thursday, 28 December 2017

Day 37 of sentence

'Cold out,' said Prison Officer Manning. 'Didn't think my car was going to start this morning.'

Though Steffi appreciated the attempt at normal conversation she found it difficult to sympathise with anyone who was able to sleep in their own bed, drink tea out of their own mug and drive their own car to work.

'Any snow yet, Miss?' she asked.

'Some up in the Peaks,' Manning said. 'They've shut the Snake Pass and the Cat and Fiddle Road again.'

Steffi loved the sound of places she'd never seen. She tucked the words away for later when she'd be alone and could let the roads take her mind out of here.

HMP Hillstone was generally considered to be less harsh than some of the other prisons she could have been sent to. With seven wings and two hundred inmates, there was never a quiet moment, and Steffi looked forward to being locked back in her cell, which, for now, she didn't have to share with anyone else.

Steffi looked back to the newspaper on the table. As long as she kept her eyes down, and folded herself small enough so she was almost invisible, the prison officers and the other inmates left her alone. She was no fun if she didn't fight back.

This period between Christmas and New Year fell flat whether you were locked-up or not. The prison had made ineffective attempts to provide some Christmas cheer. There'd been roast turkey and carols, and the women had been allowed to watch *The Polar Express* in the afternoon lull. There were paper-chain decorations made by the inmates. Some of the women seemed excited, happy even. Steffi supposed that, for some of them, this was better than the alternative.

Steffi's only acknowledgement of the day came in a Christmas phone call to her mum and dad but she wished she hadn't bothered. It was too painful for all of them. They couldn't bring themselves to sit around in paper crowns when their daughter was in prison and Steffi couldn't bring herself to pretend that she was anything but miserable.

It could be worse. There was more than one way to lose a daughter. For the parents of Katy Foster and Anna Atkins, a daughter in prison was a luxury. They'd be visiting a graveside and setting an empty place at the dinner table. Steffi wondered whether her parents ever wished that she was dead. Instead of shunning them, the neighbours would give them extra hugs and invites for mulled wine and mince pies.

Once a week the inmates were allowed to visit the prison library. It was the time Steffi looked forward to the most. It wasn't just the uniformity of the straight spines or the neatness of the shelves that mesmerised her like a moth to a light – it was the newspapers. They were her link to the outside, proof that the world hadn't stopped as soon as she was sentenced. She sat and read each one, cover to cover, no matter how big or small the story.

The front pages showed chaos on the roads and queues for the post-Christmas sales. She wondered whether she'd be less materialistic when she got out, or more. She'd appreciate the value of simple pleasures, sure, but she also wanted to be able to buy a new lamp, a pair of pyjamas or a bar of chocolate whenever she wanted.

The papers didn't mention Steffi any more. There was part of her that found the omission disappointing. Hurtful even. She wanted them to print the truth about her, but she knew that'd never happen. Instead, she read that women in party dresses were 'flaunting their curves'. Saw that the picture to accompany a story about a woman sexually assaulted showed her posing in a bikini on holiday and the associated story detailed what she'd been drinking that night.

Until she'd become a victim of the tabloid press Steffi hadn't noticed the language they used and how it had seeped into her consciousness. If it hadn't been for the differing ways in which she and Lee had been portrayed by the media she might never have noticed.

Steffi wondered what Lee's prison was like. Was it bigger or louder? Did he have a better gym, better food or better books in the library? Did he get extra perks for serving a double life sentence? She still thought of him every day. It was difficult not to. She was sure that he'd be thinking of her, too. Even if his appeal was successful, Lee Fisher would remain in prison for many more years yet. How long could he hold a grudge? She was willing to bet it was longer than any number of life sentences. The Lee she used to love would have forgiven her in a heartbeat, but the real Lee – the one he'd kept hidden – was capable of unspeakable acts of cruelty.

She flicked through the paper. Every time Steffi read that 'a reliable source said . . .' or 'a source close to the actress confirmed . . .' she scoffed out loud. She'd had plenty of those when her case went to court. She still had no idea whether they were real or completely made up by the journalists. Were they allowed to do that? She'd accused Conor of talking to the papers. They'd been best friends since school, dated for a while, and then his legal firm agreed to represent her. Now they were arranging for the sale of the home that she would never set foot in again. She wished she didn't have to rely on him so much. In an ideal world she wouldn't rely on anyone.

He'd looked sheepish when Steffi asked if his girlfriend – God, what was her name? – was leaking information to the press. Conor had been seeing The Girlfriend for eighteen months but Steffi hadn't met her. Conor said she was an actress, though he never mentioned her actually starring in anything. Lee had met The Girlfriend – no, seriously, what *was* her name? – at Max's birthday party. He went to great lengths to describe how fascinating she was, how beautiful, amusing, so slim and tall. 'Could have been a model,' he'd said. 'And she was so attentive.'

Each one of these compliments felt like they were a direct insult to Steffi. And maybe she was just the tiniest bit jealous that this woman had shown such interest in Lee. Wasn't Conor enough for her? Of course, with the benefit of hindsight she wished that Lee had eloped with the actress on the spot. It could have saved Steffi a lot of trouble.

Steffi had never liked parties and Lee didn't approve of alcohol. There was nothing he hated more than a drunk woman. Steffi had been a social drinker when they'd met but Lee had asked her to give up alcohol and, in turn, he said he'd give up smoking for her. It had been a deal she'd been happy to make. She'd thought that Lee was perfect in every way except for the smoking. And then she discovered that smoking hadn't been his worst habit after all.

Lee had been remanded in prison following his arrest. Steffi used to think that he was the lucky one – at least he hadn't had to live a half-life in the real world, like she had. He wasn't spat on and intimidated. But then he ended up in hospital with a fractured jaw. It turned out prison wasn't the safe haven Steffi thought it was.

Her solicitor – not Conor, but one of his colleagues – was the one who advised her to accept her sentence quietly. In the grand scheme of things, ten months was little more than the blink of an eye, he'd said. But that was easy for him to say. She bit her lip. It wasn't that difficult to do, she'd always been quiet. She'd quietly stood by as Lee Fisher lied to her. She'd spoken softly behind closed doors and drawn curtains but remained tight-lipped in the face of questions from journalists when Lee had tried to pin the blame on her. She declined to give an interview in response to their claims that she knew more about the murders than she was letting on. She let the lawyers, the papers and the angry mob say what they liked about her. Steffi had been confident that the truth would come out at the trial if she bided her time and waited to clear her name. Patience. An underrated virtue.

By the time she was in the dock, she'd lost her voice completely.

So far Steffi hadn't had any visitors in prison. Her mum was sick again, and Steffi had never had much to say to her dad even before she was arrested. Conor had offered to come but she didn't want him to see her like this. If she saw him now, she would go to pieces. She used to have friends, didn't she? But prisons didn't feature in their lives so it was easier for them to forget Steffi existed.

But just in case she worried that no one remembered who she was any more, she still received plenty of letters. Vile letters. Hateful letters. She'd given up hoping to find a message of support among the noise. They believed the lies that Lee had told. They believed that she knew what Lee was doing and that she'd covered for him. Some even went as far as to say she'd driven him to it. It wasn't true.

Or was it?

If she hadn't gone against her word and drunk too much that day, if she hadn't chosen to believe every word Lee had told her . . .

It was something the prison counsellor, Hester, talked about a lot. Why did Steffi consider her needs to be secondary to those of the men in her life? Why didn't she respect herself enough to walk away from toxic relationships? Why did she believe Lee in the face of all the evidence?

Hester kept coming back to the men in Steffi's life.

'Let's talk about your father,' she said.

'Let's not,' Steffi answered.

Steffi had been in prison for a little over five weeks. It was hardly a long time, but it was excruciating in its loneliness and the speed – or lack of speed – with which each day passed. Steffi hadn't felt warm since she'd arrived. She tried to imagine lying on a sunlounger, the water's edge only a quick, light-footed skip over baking-hot sand. She thought of long lunches and cold beers, and the tightness of reddening skin.

Summer would have risen and fallen by the time Steffi got out, but she'd make up for it next time around. Renovate an old house? Maybe. Take up pottery again, learn to ballroom dance? No, not dancing. She wasn't the dancing sort. She needed something she could do on her own without relying on a man. Something solitary. She was aware of how pathetic this sounded, but she wouldn't be dragged down by anyone ever again.

If there was anything the previous year had taught her, it was that she was a terrible judge of character. She'd trusted too easily, always keen to believe the best of people. Naïve was the word that Conor had used.

When Lee told her that the police were trying to frame him, Steffi believed every word. It was so reasonable, the way he explained it. If the police wasted their time on trying to fit him up for the murders, the real killer would be out there waiting to kill again. Lee had been accused of kidnap and assault years before though no charges were ever brought. He told her that that was the only reason the police were viewing him as a suspect. She thought she was doing the right thing by saying she was with him that evening. And she really did want to do the right thing.

Lee had patiently explained to her that some people might say that it was her fault he didn't have an alibi in the first place. And if she hadn't made him so mad, if they hadn't argued, he wouldn't have been anywhere near that pub. If she really loved him, she would know he wasn't capable of such a thing. She did love him, didn't she?

So when the police asked her where Lee was on the night of Friday 1 July, she didn't hesitate for a second when she said, 'He was with me, all night.'

And those six words made it possible for him to kill again.

CHAPTER THREE

Charlie Miller

Friday, 5 October 2018

She liked it.

Charlie stood in the middle of the room with her hands on her hips and nodded. At the very least, the cottage had character.

More than one season had blown in through the broken kitchen window. Crumpled leaves huddled in corners alongside crisp packets that had skittered across the tiles. She'd have to board up the window if she was going to get any sleep tonight but, on the whole, it could have been worse. It could have been prison. It could have been the bottom of a canal.

Mould crept into corners and paper was coming away from damp walls like blisters. The terracotta kitchen floor was smooth with age, a slight concavity showing decades of footsteps through the back door, but there was little else to see. The rooms were stripped bare and there weren't even any cupboards in the kitchen. No carpets, no furniture, no light bulbs, no warmth.

The removals company had packed up the fragments of Charlie's life and delivered everything she'd kept in storage, pushing the spare set of keys through the letter box. Now, she held all the keys. It was an important distinction. Charlie could set her own hours and decide when to come and when to go. She'd decide when to lock or unlock a door. When she'd been in HMP Hillstone, Charlie imagined leaving every door open, never to be shut up like an animal again. But now that she had her freedom, she preferred the idea of keeping everything secure. Locks kept people in, but they also kept people out. They kept you safe.

Cardboard boxes were stacked on top of her old table. Black bin liners stuffed below. She didn't know what had happened to the rest of her furniture. Charlie's old house was still on the market, though it was empty now. The estate agents were overwhelmed by interest in the beginning. Scores of people queuing to look around the place, but they were only nosy neighbours and idle gossips. Several items went missing. Charlie wondered if she'd find her knickers and her knick-knacks for sale on eBay. She was only worth something as a hate figure. Notoriety had value.

Before she went to trial, Charlie didn't pack away her clothes, wrap her cups in newspaper or cosset her glasses in bubble wrap. She, quite simply, didn't believe she would be sent to prison. It wasn't that she thought herself to be free from blame, but she'd done her research into similar cases. Other women had been given suspended sentences, community service. Those women's lies were worse than hers. They knew their men were guilty. Charlie didn't.

Well, not straight away.

Her lawyers told her not to worry. They thought that a suspended sentence was the likeliest outcome. Charlie had voluntarily changed her statement, done whatever she could to be helpful, and alerted the police to a case that they hadn't yet linked to Lee. But then the media got involved, and they questioned how she knew so much to begin with.

And then the world found out that Anna Atkins had a young family. That Anna was a teacher. That Anna put up a brave fight. That if Charlie hadn't perverted the course of justice, Anna would still be alive today.

Charlie's parents packed up some of her personal effects and got rid of the rest. They tried to give some of it to charity shops, but nowhere would take anything that had been tainted by Lee's hand. In the end, her parents had to hire a skip, which was full at nightfall yet half empty by dawn. The neighbours couldn't get enough of keepsakes from the twisted couple who lived up the road.

Charlie had been in prison for less than a year but, in waiting for the case to come to court, her life had been on hold for almost two. She'd watched as the few friends she still had became too busy for coffee. Charlie's boss, Tina – who she once considered a friend – started to get red blotches on her neck every time she walked into the office.

'Why don't you go home, love?' she said eventually. 'Until it all blows over.'

But the wind didn't stop blowing, and Charlie was out in the cold.

In the days that followed, a woman slapped her across the face in the newsagent's and a child stamped on her foot.

'P'raps it'd be for the best if you shop somewhere else,' the shopkeeper said. And Charlie's world became that little bit smaller.

She shook off the memories of her old life and went upstairs, treading carefully on the wooden boards. The first of the two bedrooms was just big enough for a single bed, with a window that was dirty both inside and out. There was a hole in the ceiling where plaster had fallen from wooden struts. The floor was bare and there was a dark brown stain, the colour of old blood. Charlie stepped away from it and held on tightly to her imagination in case it took her to places she didn't want to go.

In the bathroom the light barely crept between thick ivy tendrils at an open window, but it was enough to see crucifixes all over the wall. Some were ornate, some simple, and some had Christ hanging limply from them.

Charlie shuddered and put her hand to her neck.

If anything was to give her an unfavourable view of the previous inhabitants it was this room. Everyone was peculiar, had their foibles, but most knew when to hide them. Their strange taste in bathroom décor had scared off any other buyers at auction. She really should have been thankful, and, she told herself, once she got over the initial shock, she would be.

Charlie dreamed of having calming baths, with candles flickering gently, making shapes on the ceiling, while she drank tea and sang along to old country music, but there was no way she could relax with those *things* on the wall. For a symbol that was meant to signify hope, they did a good job of appearing sinister.

She pushed and pulled at the nearest cross, wondering how much effort it would take to remove it, but it didn't budge. Perhaps she should work on this room first. It wasn't as if she could avoid it for ever. She'd seen outbuildings – there might be a toilet out there – but, no, she'd take crosses over spiders any day.

She heard a creak behind her. A floorboard resisting weight. And again, but somewhere else. A different tone. A different floorboard.

Charlie turned her head and froze.

She waited but, as is often the way, the noise refused to be pinned down now that she was giving it her full attention. She shook her head. It was just the old house settling about her, making way for the new owner. Still, Charlie's skin prickled.

She slowed her breathing. In through the nose, out through the mouth. Charlie had to be rational. No one could have found her. Not yet. Not ever. She'd been so careful. There was nothing to link her to this house or to Cornwall. If anyone wanted to find her, this was the last place they'd look.

She walked out on to the landing, taking slow steps on the balls of her feet. Nothing there. No more sounds. She peered over the railings, but the stairs were empty. Even if someone was in the house with her, it would be a naughty teen, a nosy rambler, it would have nothing to do with what she'd done.

'Hello? Is anyone there?' Charlie called.

Nothing. Her shoulders relaxed a little but she still had to take a minute for the pulsing in her ears to dull. She went back into the bathroom to close the window. The breeze was strong, no wonder the house was creaking. The ivy stopped the window from shutting so she pushed it roughly to the side. A movement in the lane caught her attention. There was a tall figure dressed in a black jacket and hat. He was walking slowly down the path behind the cottage and, as Charlie watched, he whipped his head around to look straight at her. She snatched her hand away, letting the vines fall and settle.

'No one knows where I am,' she told herself. 'I'm safe here.'

CHAPTER FOUR

Pinchdale Telegraph

Saturday, 21 July 2018

JUDGE RULES FINN DOES NOT DESERVE LIFELONG ANONYMITY

Former GP's receptionist Stephanie Finn is set to be released after serving her ten-month sentence for perverting the course of justice in a case that gripped the nation. But her request for anonymity has been denied.

Stephanie Finn was convicted of providing a false alibi for Lee Fisher when he murdered Katy Foster in July 2016. The police had initially ruled Lee Fisher out of their inquiries when Miss Finn claimed he had been with her all evening. In fact, the couple had rowed and spent the night apart, leaving both of them without an alibi for the night in question.

Finn claimed she had mistakenly thought Fisher to be sleeping in the spare room after their argument. It wasn't until later that she said he didn't come home when he said he did.

However, Finn only came forward with her suspicions after the disappearance of 30-year-old mum-of-two Anna Atkins in Edinburgh. It also came to light that

Finn cleaned their car of evidence, though the court failed to convict her of assisting an offender.

Finn was 24 when she met 32-year-old Fisher in Sheffield in 2014. She was living with her childhood sweetheart at the time but dumped him for the pharmaceutical salesman. Said to be besotted with her, Fisher moved in to Finn's house three weeks later and friends say the couple were inseparable.

Amid concerns she would be attacked on release from HMP Hillstone, Finn asked for a new identity and police protection. While four former UK prisoners have been granted lifelong anonymity, their cases were seen to be higher profile than that of Finn's and all had received numerous death threats. The judge ruled that he did not believe Finn's life was at risk and, therefore, she does not require a new identity.

This will come as a blow to Finn's legal team who insist that her life will be in danger when she is released.

CHAPTER FIVE

Ben Jarvis

Saturday, 6 October 2018

Morning was straining at the curtains. The only other light came from Ben's laptop. He'd sold everything else to pay rent on the shitty bedsit that had been his home for the last twelve months. The lease was up and the landlord wanted him out. Fuck him. It was a travesty what he charged for this dump. Ben's only regret was selling his car. Now he'd have nowhere to sleep.

How could he have missed Steffi Finn getting out of prison? They must have bundled her out under the cover of darkness. He knew they wouldn't announce the date and time of her release, but he'd been monitoring her case so carefully he thought that he would've heard whispers.

He looked at the knuckles on his right hand. They were still sore but at least they'd scabbed over from where he'd put his fist through the wall. He wouldn't be getting his deposit back.

Ben picked up a beer can from the side of the bed and shook it gently. He wasn't proud of the relief he felt when he realised there was some left. He drained it and let his head fall back on to the wall behind him. So bloody tired.

He'd been up all night scouring the internet for a trace of Finn but, since she'd been released from Hillstone, there'd been no word of her. Not yet. Every online news article that mentioned her was historic, going back months.

He reread every one of them, searching for something he might have missed. A clue to where she might have headed after coming out of prison. He clicked on an article about the death of Finn's mother, Margaret. He read her age, where she'd lived, the school she'd taught at, where she died, what kind of cancer took her life, and what her only child was convicted of. It was all laid out as if she was public property. And that's exactly what she was.

'The apple doesn't fall far from the tree, Margaret,' he muttered.

He searched for the Flintside School website, and found an *In Memoriam* page for the sorely missed teacher who had first begun teaching there thirty years ago. Old pupils, grown now with children of their own, remembered her fondly, back when she was still known as Miss Miller. He sneered. If Miss Margaret Miller was such a saint, how had her daughter become embroiled in murder and lies?

Ben had spent the evening hanging around the internet chat rooms. There were a number of vigilante groups that made it their mission to track down those who'd been released without having been adequately punished, but Steffi Finn wasn't on their hit list. They were more interested in paedophiles and child killers. For now, he was on his own.

'Come out, come out, wherever you are,' he growled into his laptop.

Finn would break cover eventually, but, for now, it was as if she'd disappeared into thin air.

Lee Fisher was the one Ben really wanted. As long as Fisher was inside, he was protected. For the right price, an accident could be arranged, but Ben didn't have that kind of cash. Besides, he still had something Ben wanted and until then, he was safe.

Finn was a different story. Though all she'd been convicted of was providing a false alibi, she knew more than she was letting on. Ben didn't buy her innocent act because there was no way she could have lived in the same house as Lee and not known what he was up to. Ben's soon-to-be ex-wife used to know if he was lying about how many pints he'd had with the lads on a Thursday night. She'd know if he'd eaten a packet of biscuits at his desk. No, Steffi Finn was as much to blame as Fisher was.

Ben rubbed his eyes with the heels of his hands. He'd not been sleeping. The insomnia came and went but it was particularly bad at the moment. A busy mind wasn't conducive to a peaceful night's sleep.

There had to be a way to find her. He wouldn't be surprised if she was living under a false name now. He probably wasn't the only one who wanted to track her down, so she'd have gone into hiding until it was safe to come out again.

He knew that she had no living relatives and it was unlikely that she would return to her home in Pinchdale. Still, it was worth a try.

He slapped his cheeks hard.

It was time to focus.

CHAPTER SIX

Charlie Miller

Saturday, 6 October 2018

Charlie snaked an arm out of the sleeping bag and swiped at the electric heater until she found the 'on' switch. She'd slept in her clothes, complete with gloves and hat. The temperature had dropped overnight to a level that had seemed beyond Charlie's limits yet, somehow, she'd survived the night without frostbite or hypothermia.

She would've left those three golden bars on all night long if she could've done so safely, but she didn't know enough about the house's electrics to trust them yet. It'd be such a shame to survive a murderous boyfriend, two attacks in prison and the hatred of a nation, only to be felled by faulty wiring.

With no curtains at the low bedroom window Charlie could see the blushing early-morning sky. There was a mist hanging in the valley below, making eerie stick men of the trees. A seagull cawed three times and another answered with irritation. Charlie sat up and the camp bed creaked and groaned. Her coat slid off the sleeping bag with a hiss. Today she was going to shop for a hot-water bottle, blankets and, if she could afford them, the thickest curtains she could find.

She squinted at the display on her mobile and saw it was six forty-five. Unfortunately, that was the only thing the phone was good for, as the display also showed there was *no service*. She'd bought the phone for emergencies but would have to hope that they only happened when she had a couple of bars of coverage.

It was Saturday and her treacherous mind told her it was still two hours until *unlock*. On weekends even prisoners were allowed a lie-in and the prison officers would open the cells at an indulgent, slovenly, eight forty-five. During the week, however, it was eight on the dot. Rules like these didn't apply to her any more, but the memory of how she'd had to live for the past ten months was like a callus on her mind. It was too hard for her to ignore.

Charlie had taken all the practical courses, like plastering and woodwork. She knew she'd need to work when she got out and she'd find it difficult to get references without exposing who she used to be. She loved using her hands to create and to build. When she'd been young enough to believe that she could do a job that made her happy – rather than one that paid the bills – she'd wanted to be an artist. But that was the whimsical dream of a girl with no grasp on reality.

She'd been a good inmate, if there could be such a thing. Neat and unobtrusive. She didn't cause fights, rarely spoke. Ever the people-pleaser, Charlie had hoped the prison staff would applaud her for how well she took her sentence. But, when she left, they just turned her mattress and got ready for the next one.

Technically, she was free now. No prison officers to watch her in the bathroom, no cameras to chart her movements, no inmates waiting to get her on her own. She could do anything she wanted to do, even run around the house in her underwear, but first she'd wait for the heating to kick in.

She'd had a productive evening. There were now energy-efficient light bulbs in all the rooms. The kitchen was clean, and the kettle and toaster were ready for action. She'd covered the broken kitchen window with a board she'd found in the outbuildings. And then she'd bleached, polished, swept and vacuumed as if she was expecting important visitors for tea.

Charlie wiped under her eyes, an old habit from the days when she wore make-up to sleep in. Lee didn't like to see her bare-faced. He said it was a fright that he could do without. He told her that he wasn't trying to hurt her feelings, it was just that she looked so pretty in make-up it was a shame not to use it more often. She used to attempt to wake up before him so she could sneak into the bathroom to fix her face and brush her teeth.

She kicked the bed with her heel. She didn't know who she was angriest with – Lee, for making her feel like she was *almost* good enough, or herself, for buying in to all his crap. How could she have thought that her happiness depended on his? Why was his mood the indicator for how their day would pan out?

Now the most important aspect of her appearance was that she didn't look like the woman she used to be. Her hair was no longer in a blonde bob, she'd lost twenty pounds, and she tried to walk with more purpose than she used to. It didn't matter if her hair was straightened, nor if her roots had been touched up every five weeks. It made no difference to her if her legs were shaved, and it didn't cross her mind whether her clothes were in style or in season. Right now, she only wanted to be warm and comfortable. And safe. She wanted to wrap herself in layers to protect herself from prying eyes and the piercing cold. If there was such a thing as heated bubble wrap, she'd roll herself up in it.

She thought it was meant to get warmer the further south you got. Didn't Cornwall have palm trees? So why had she never felt so cold in her entire life? She'd slept in the extra-thick walking socks she'd bought with a pair of hiking boots – kit that she could run in, climb in, scramble to safety in. They were among the few items she'd bought brand new.

Until her house in Pinchdale sold, money was going to be tight. She'd picked up some clothes and kitchen essentials from a charity shop in Bristol on the way from the supported housing unit they'd placed her in. She'd stuffed the clothes she'd worn in HMP Hillstone into a bin outside Gordano service station when she'd stopped to grab a coffee on the M5. Even the smell of the prison washing powder in their seams brought back the crushing feeling in her chest and she didn't want any reminders of her recent past. She wouldn't go back to prison, not even in her mind.

Charlie yawned and her jaw clicked. Tension had knotted the tendons in her neck and she felt an ache up the side of her face into her temple. She was sure that she was grinding her teeth in her sleep again.

It was no surprise that she hadn't slept well in the unfamiliar house. There was a scratching in the walls that she took to be mice, a screaming outside that she took to be foxes, and a shaking of the windows that she took to be masked intruders. She'd unzipped her sleeping bag three times in the night to check that the window was still boarded up, that neither wind nor axe-wielding maniac had found a way into the house. At some point, in the minutes that crept past two o'clock in the morning, she'd fallen into a shallow and peace-less sleep.

Usually the first thing she'd hear upon waking would be the other prisoners shouting, laughing, crying. Now it was the unfamiliar sound of seagulls that greeted her, as harsh and insistent as an alarm call.

Charlie considered the person she was now and contrasted it with the person she used to be. She put them side by side as though they were two separate people and she was somewhere in the middle. She'd picked the name Charlie because she thought it sounded friendly. It was the kind of name that could be dressed up or down depending on the occasion. Charlotte for job interviews and meeting the in-laws, Charlie for every day, and Char for laughs between friends.

She'd known a girl called Charlie in junior school, a kind and popular girl who they'd all been drawn to. All the kids knew, even then, that she was destined to live life just that little bit brighter than the rest of them. The name came with positive memories and a promise that if she could grow into the name, she would instantly become a better person.

The surname Miller was a gamble, only a small one, but it was important enough to her that it was worth the risk. It had been her mum's maiden name and something she could cling to when there was no other trace of her in Charlie's life. Her mum was the first person she wanted to call when she was released from prison, and still the only person she wanted to call for advice. She would do anything to hear her voice once more.

The world had turned too fast and, when Charlie was finally granted her freedom, it was to a world that didn't contain either of her parents. Charlie would never be called by the name that her mum had carefully chosen for her when she'd first held her as a baby. The least she could do was, in turn, choose a name that reminded her of her mother. It was the only way she could think of to honour her mum.

The name Miller suited Charlie's frame of mind better than Finn ever did. Finn had been her father's name. It was a harsh name, a cold name. It had been a name that she'd never been able to live up to.

CHAPTER SEVEN

Steffi Finn

Wednesday, 24 January 2018

Day 64 of sentence

She thought she'd experienced loneliness before, but she was wrong.

Steffi had never been surrounded by so many people and yet she felt so utterly isolated. It hadn't gone unnoticed that she didn't get any visitors. The other inmates took that as further proof, as if any were needed, that she was worthless. Other women seemed easy in each other's company, sure of their place. There was laughter, jokes, smiles, but Steffi couldn't tell if they were really able to find joy in their days or whether they believed that showing any other emotion would make them an easy target. Steffi held her feelings close to her chest. Fear, boredom and anxiety all looked the same on her pale features. She remained courteous but silent. She sought out shadows and edges to conceal and to protect her.

As the cell door closed behind her for the evening, Steffi felt her hands unclench. There were crescent moons on her palms where her nails had been digging in. She rolled her head from side to side, stretching the taut tendons in her neck. It took effort to not look at someone the wrong way or not breathe too loudly. Steffi had never known such hostility. She'd been mistaken in thinking that she would find common ground with some of the other women in here but had learned it was safer to keep her head down and her mouth closed.

As soon as she met Lee she'd started to drift away from her friends; by the time she went to prison the rift was absolute and she had no one left to turn to. She hadn't noticed it at first and even when she did, she didn't mind. *Life moves on*, she thought, *and so do people*. When she and Lee were together they didn't need anyone else. On the few occasions when she was going to meet up with friends, Lee would get ill or forget and make other plans for them. Tickets, non-refundable.

And then there were the comments, along the lines of, 'Have you ever wondered if they only invite you so that you can be the designated driver?'

And then, when she finally reached out, they were too busy for coffee, and calls became shorter and shorter. There'd be the, 'Oh God, sorry, I'm just on my way out.' And, 'Sorry, Steff darling, the kids aren't well. Call you later, yeah?'

She'd had to change her number to stop the hate calls but the girls never responded when she sent them her new details. It was to be expected, really.

Only Anita had been honest with her. 'This is more than I can cope with. It's doing my head in. I've got journos stalking the kids at the school gates wanting to know what kind of a godmother you are.'

'What did you tell them?'

'What do you think I told them? I said that you never forgot a birthday. That you let them plait your hair, and put make-up on you. Said you were the salt of the fucking earth and worth ten of them and if they ever came near me and my family again . . .'

Once the initial frenzy of the reporters had subsided, Steffi had gone back home. She managed a few months of lying low, of keeping the curtains closed, but as the date of her trial neared – due to start the week after Lee's – the coverage began again and so did the attacks.

They came for her in droves. They didn't even wait for the night to cover their tracks. They were brazen, wanted her to see. Door bells ringing, excrement pushed through the letter box. There was name-calling and narrowed eyes – and that was just from her neighbours.

She'd heard their sniggers through her closed curtains, heard the scuff of their feet behind the windows. She couldn't say what came over her to make her do it, but one day she just snapped. She jerked open the front door and ran into the driveway.

'Come on, then!' she called. 'Where are you?'

The paint canister rolled across the footpath and dropped into the gutter. She could feel the high and mighty deep in their houses, watching from the shadows, pleased she was getting her dues at long last.

She didn't blame them for hating her. There were some days when she couldn't stand to look at herself in the mirror. Her life had been ripped apart and she'd lost everything, but that was nothing compared to what had happened to Katy and Anna.

Steffi grabbed the canister and shook it like she'd seen in the films. She appraised the red writing across her brickwork. Giving the can an extra shake, she flamboyantly daubed a slanting 'W'.

'There.' She stepped back and put her hand on her hip, nodding. 'If you're going to call me a whore, at least spell it right.'

The papers knew all about it by the next day. Complete with a photo taken from the upstairs window of number twelve. Funny how they didn't catch sight of the kids who'd vandalised the house, only of her losing her mind. Looking like a crazy woman. They didn't capture her screaming into a cushion with tears rolling down her face, or her vomiting into the sink with despair.

She'd called Naz Apkarian, the detective who'd so patiently interviewed her. She was quick to come round.

'So, your fingerprints are on the spray can?' she asked.

'Yes, but only because—'

'And you're responsible for the graffiti?'

'I only corrected their spelling.'

Naz had sighed and flicked a mint into her mouth. 'You just can't help yourself, can you?'

Steffi left the house that night knowing that she would never return. Even if she was given a suspended sentence, she'd have to go where she could start again. They'd keep coming for her until they felt she'd paid the price. For some of them, it would never be enough.

Conor had been tasked with finding her somewhere to live for when she got out. He'd been a conveyancer at Hunt, Fellows & Bartlett since returning to Sheffield, and had offered his help gladly, which was more than anyone else had done and more than she deserved from him. He assured her that he wouldn't let anyone know where she was going to be living, though he told her she was being paranoid and no one would care by the time she got out. He said that Anna's family were upset when they shouted that they'd kill her, and that emotions were running high in court. They would have calmed down by the time she was released in October.

She almost believed him.

CHAPTER EIGHT

Charlie Miller

Tuesday, 9 October 2018

Charlie was unpacking the boxes marked *kitchen* on the floor of the living room. Deep blue skies contrasted against the pure white clouds like a children's painting and cast a broad square of gold upon the floor.

She ran her fingers over glasses and mugs. Too many were broken, chipped or stained and would be thrown in the bin. She lived alone, with little expectation of ever having visitors – she only needed a mug, a bowl and a plate – yet it still seemed wasteful to get rid of these items. It had been a long time since she'd cooked a meal but the pans might be of use one day, if only to catch leaks from the roof.

Food was associated with nurture and love, neither of which she was in a mind to direct at herself. With no one else to cook for she was unlikely to stretch her menu beyond cup-a-soup and bread. She hadn't got a fridge yet so it'd be unwise to buy fresh food anyway.

Before she'd even finished unwrapping the largest of the mugs, she knew it was Lee's favourite: the one that he'd got with an Easter egg one year. Typical that, of all the mugs, this was the one that escaped unscathed. Images, unbidden, of Lee at the breakfast table, pushing the butter dish out of her reach with a sad smile and a shake of his head in case she reached for another slice of toast.

Charlie dangled the mug by the handle. Sturdy this one, it could last for a long time. Wouldn't it be a shame if . . .

She spun it into the fireplace, where it broke into three pieces.

'Oopsie,' she said.

She was looking forward to the day she could light a fire in here but, for all she knew, seagulls nested in her chimney. She'd never had an open fire before and would have to ask around to find someone who could sweep chimneys. Charlie readjusted her scarf and rubbed her hands together.

Even with the heating on full blast and every door in the house closed, she couldn't seem to hold on to the heat. It danced around and swirled up to the eaves, laughing as it went and leaving her shivering. She hated the boarded-up window in the kitchen, not just because it kept out the light and failed to hold on to the heat, but because she didn't feel secure enough. Anyone could get inside her house if they had a crowbar and ten minutes to spare. Replacing the window was a priority.

She heard footsteps outside the window and an elongated shadow marched across her floor. Charlie scrambled to her feet in a panic. So far, she'd not met any of her neighbours, but then it was hardly likely when she'd not ventured out of the house yet. She was scared to unwrap her new identity and try it out in front of others who might see straight through her. What if they recognised her? What if they asked questions that she didn't know the answers to? Worse than that, what if the answers gave her away?

Looking out of the window she saw, with a contradictory mix of disappointment and relief, that it was only the postman with a parcel under his arm. Charlie considered ducking under the window, ignoring him, but he raised his hand when he saw her and it was too late to pretend that she wasn't in.

'Morning,' Charlie said as she opened the door. 'I'm Charlie.'

She was attempting to keep the nerves from her voice but she noticed the slight tremble. She wanted to appear friendly and definitely not give the impression of having just got out of prison.

'Charlie,' she said again, with an outstretched hand. 'Charlie Miller.'

She looked the postman in the eye, hoping he wouldn't doubt for a minute that it was her real name. She was still trying it out for size but it seemed to fit her well enough.

'Hiya, I'm Peter,' he said. 'Just moved in, have we?'

Instead of shaking her hand he placed a parcel in it. It was too cold for shorts, yet he wore them anyway. His unzipped jacket and rosy cheeks mocked Charlie for wearing her scarf indoors.

'Yes, I moved in on Friday,' Charlie said. 'Still surrounded by boxes, though.'

Her thoughts were so loud she hadn't registered his name when he'd spoken. Ordinarily she wouldn't have minded, but this was a fresh start and she was desperate to fit in, play nice. The nature of the postman's job meant that he had access to every person in Penderrion. A well-placed compliment would determine how easily Charlie was accepted.

Charlie looked at the brown Jiffy bag in her hand. It had to be from Conor because he was the only one who knew where she was. Strange, though, because they'd agreed to have the minimum contact in case . . .

'It's for the chap down at the bungalow,' said the postman.

'Oh. So it is.' She could see now that it was addressed to Aubrey Hollingsworth, Chi Lowen, Penderrion. This was a village that didn't do house numbers. God help anyone who needed an ambulance, or even an Amazon delivery.

Through the trees she could see a grubby-looking bungalow. He was her closest neighbour but she'd not seen any movement since she'd moved in.

'He's got a note on his door saying to leave it here,' the postman explained.

'Are you sure? But he doesn't know me.'

'Can't tell you what's in his head. He's harmless enough but a bit . . . Well, you'll see what I mean when you meet him. You don't have to take it for him. I could leave it behind his bin and pop a note through his door if you like?'

The bungalow had a house-of-cards look about it. It was anyone's guess how it was still standing after the recent storm. There was a makeshift conservatory to the side with a corrugated roof. It was green with moss and leaves. The windows were speckled with dirt and grime accumulated over years of determined neglect. The garden, however, was immaculate. Neat borders, low hedges, tight clumps of plants.

'No, no. It's okay. Thanks, I'll take it for him. It's what neighbours do, right?'

'Depends on the neighbour,' he said.

The postman set off back down the path. His hand was already in his red bag sorting the mail for the next house.

Charlie had considered setting up a PO Box for correspondence. She didn't want anyone questioning why the name on her letters didn't match the one on her lips. Were the Royal Mail bound by confidentiality? Would the postman recognise the name? Would he tell someone? So far, her face hadn't sparked any recognition. She'd been nervous that everyone would know who she was but, out of context, without a police escort, she hoped they wouldn't be able to place her.

Piece by piece she was erasing Steffi. It still remained for her to change her name by deed poll and then Steffi Finn would be a name of the past. So far, she'd had all the utility accounts set up in her new name. And no one seemed surprised, or perhaps no one cared, when she said that the direct debit would be coming out of Miss S. Finn's account.

Oh God, that reminded her. She still hadn't given the bank her change of address. Lee had insisted on paper statements so he could file them and show her how she could manage her finances better. And it worked. She always thought twice before buying anything she didn't really need because she knew that Lee would see what she'd bought and ask her why.

Charlie shook her head. She should have seen his controlling nature sooner. The signs had been clear enough.

She was still standing on the doorstep with the parcel in her hand when two women with dogs began walking up the path.

'Oh God,' she said through ventriloquist's teeth. She put her free hand on her stomach to settle the resident butterflies.

The older of the two women smiled in Charlie's direction. They were coming straight for her, their eyes brimming with curiosity and expectation.

'Hello and welcome,' the woman said. 'You've moved in, then? Must say we've been wondering who was taking on this place. Welcome. Welcome.' She had a nest of grey hair pinned to the top of her head though her face was younger than her hair colour suggested.

She swapped the dog lead over into her left hand and then offered Charlie her right. She had an ebullient handshake – too much energy and force – the kind you felt right up to your shoulder. Charlie didn't know whether to be alarmed or charmed by the woman's vigour.

'This is Penny and I'm Decca. And these scamps are Coco and Baldrick.'

She had an old-money look about her: slightly unkempt yet well bred, with ruddy cheeks and protruding teeth. Above the fusty smell of her wax jacket Charlie could detect the scent of her perfume. She assumed Decca lived at one of the expensive houses with the perfect lawns.

'Hello,' Charlie said. 'Nice to meet you.'

The younger woman was perched on giraffe-like legs. She offered a narrow hand and squeezed hard, holding tightly as she looked into Charlie's eyes and said, 'Great to meet you,' as if she really meant it. She was wearing a yellow rain mac that didn't look like it could survive a sudden shower, never mind the full force of the Cornish weather system. She wore bright red lipstick that was harsh against her pale skin and straw-coloured hair. She crouched down to pet the dogs and pull at their ears. She was obviously more of a dog person than a people person. Charlie could respect that.

'I don't believe I caught your name,' Decca said.

A moment of silence hung between them. She knew, as well as Charlie did, that no name had been offered.

'Sorry, yes, I'm Charlie Miller. I just moved in on Friday. Still surrounded by boxes,' she said for the second time in five minutes, sticking to the script.

'You're not actually living here while you renovate, are you?' Decca said. 'I'd have thought it was uninhabitable. No one's lived here in donkey's. For a start you've got no kitchen window. The house was sold a while back and they began ripping out some of the old fittings and put in central heating, thank God, but it all ground to a halt. Ran out of money or something. Never saw the couple who owned it, only ever the contractors. Still, it's a hell of a lot of work to take on. Who's doing it for you? You got local builders or is your husband handy about the house?'

Remember to smile, Charlie thought. It was natural for people to be curious about the single woman who had taken on a wreck of a house in the middle of nowhere. She knew she had to give them just enough information so they wouldn't dig any further.

'No husband for me, and no builders either. Actually, I'm going to do most of the work myself, though any rewiring will need to be done by the professionals.'

Decca's eyes widened and she placed a hand on Charlie's upper arm. 'Of course you're doing it yourself. Unforgiveable of me to assume otherwise.'

They both laughed, though Decca's laugh was louder and more believable than Charlie's.

The smaller of the two dogs, a Border collie apparently named Coco, banged into Charlie's legs, sniffing at her. She liked dogs, but knew they weren't as easily fooled as humans. Could they smell prison on her? Could they sniff out her lies? Coco leaned against Charlie's shins and slid down to sit on her foot.

'What brings you to Penderrion?' Decca asked.

The two women were looking at her expectantly. Penny stood up and the black Labrador she had on a lead proceeded to make a maypole of her legs as he circled her.

'Well,' Charlie took a deep breath, 'I've always loved this part of the country. It's been a dream of mine to live by the coast.'

Lies, lies, lies.

'I've spent the last few months taking courses in different aspects of building work,' she continued. 'I'm lucky that I've been able to find a house that I can put my stamp on. Still, I've never done anything on this scale before, so I might need a builder yet.'

'But not a husband?' Decca ventured with a laugh.

'Oh, most definitely not. No. God, no.'

She looked away as a vision of Lee came into her mind. Lee had always said that he didn't need a ring to show the world how committed he was to her. They'd talked about starting a family but she could see now that it was just another way to manipulate her.

'Good for you,' said Decca. 'I used to have one of those and he was worse than useless. But then, who am I to talk? I'm not much better. Penny's great at that kind of thing, though. Good with furnishings, decorating and whatnot, aren't you, Penny?'

Charlie looked at Penny, who didn't seem to have blinked since they'd been introduced. Penny shrugged and looked away, though the compliment obviously pleased her.

'Well, I do try,' she said.

'I live just over the road,' Decca said, pointing in a direction Charlie didn't bother looking in, knowing already where the houses with the perfect lawns were. 'And Penny's up opposite the church. It's a lovely place, really it is. Isn't it, Pen? And everyone's so friendly.'

Penny nodded. 'So friendly.' She pressed her lips together like she was blotting her lipstick and said, 'How're you settling in?'

'Yeah, good, thanks. I've not finished unpacking yet, because I don't have anywhere to put anything, and there's a lot of work to do but, yeah, I think it's going to be okay.'

As she said it, she thought that, maybe, it was true. Why not make the best of the situation? This was a new start; a chance to put all that was bad behind her. Why shouldn't it be okay?

'I remember when I first moved down here,' said Penny. 'I thought I'd never settle but now I can hardly remember living anywhere else.'

'You should watch that,' Decca said to her. 'That could be early onset dementia.'

Penny frowned and ignored her friend. 'You'll see me around a fair bit. I look after the holiday cottages just across from you. I do the cleaning and get them ready for guests. So if you ever need a cleaner . . .'

'Thanks.'

'Where have you moved from?' Penny asked.

Charlie had practised this, but she still felt the panic tighten her chest. She pretended to cough, cleared her throat.

'Before moving to Penderrion, I worked abroad,' she said, remembering her lines. 'Telecoms. I moved around with my company and decided that what I really wanted was to try my hand at renovating a beautiful old house. My parents died and left me a little money so I decided it was time to put down some roots.'

'Sorry about your folks,' said Decca. 'Recent, was it?'

Charlie blinked hard. Was it usual for people to ask so many personal questions? The truth, though difficult, was necessary where possible. There were only so many lies she could remember. And so it was with complete honesty she said, 'My mum died four months ago from cancer. Dad died two weeks after that. It was his heart.'

Even though she'd been furious with him, her world had shattered when she was told that he'd died in his sleep shortly after her mum's funeral. She kept telling herself it didn't matter. That they didn't like each other anyway. There'd been no love there, just duty.

In the end she'd cried anyway, but it was for the dad she wished she'd had, not the one that she'd been saddled with. She hadn't gone to her mum's funeral. Dad said he wouldn't have her making a sombre occasion into a circus even if she could have got permission to leave the prison. When Dad's funeral came around two weeks later Conor attended in her place. He ordered a wreath on her behalf and sang the same hymns that he'd sung at her mum's funeral. He told her she wasn't mentioned in either eulogy, though everyone at the church must have known where she was and what she'd done.

'Oh goodness, that's rotten. A new start is just what you need then,' Decca said. 'We're a close-knit community so anything you need . . . In fact, next Tuesday, and no,' she held up her hand as if Charlie was going to say something, 'I'm not taking "no" for an answer. We've recently started a book and pudding club. You have to like at least one of those things, right? We're doing *Wuthering Heights* this month because Jenn will only read the classics. Yawn. Lovely woman, always trying to better herself, but goodness me her choice in books is conservative at best. Now, don't worry if you've not read it. I read it forty-odd years ago and I'm not putting myself through that all over again. What do you say?'

Charlie wanted to say no, she wanted to curl up and hide away, but this was the best opportunity she was going to get to meet her new neighbours.

'Oh, yes, you just have to,' said Penny.

Charlie took a deep breath. 'Thank you. I'd love to.'

Penny's dog strained at his lead and barked suddenly, setting the other dog off too.

'Baldrick!' Penny said. 'Stop it!' The other dog joined and backed him up by standing and growling.

Charlie put her hand to her chest and laughed. The dogs had made her jump. She was already on edge, and their volley of barks suggested alarm and danger, though it could just as easily signify a squirrel or the postman.

Charlie followed the direction of the pointed noses and bared teeth. A lone walker, in a black coat and a hat pulled low over his ears, was making his way down the path on the other side of the road under the trees. Charlie stepped to the side to see him better. He had a rucksack on his back and he carried a stick, which he was stabbing at the ground. She didn't think it was the same person she'd seen walking by the house on the day she'd arrived. This one looked shorter, slower and fatter, but she couldn't be sure.

'Do you know who that is?' Charlie asked, her voice a fraction high and betraying the unease she felt. She wrapped her arms around herself, squeezing the parcel to her chest, as if she could protect her heart from the fear that was pumping through it.

'Where?' asked Decca. 'Oh, him? We get a lot of walkers around here. There's a path running behind yours that leads down to the beach. He won't get very far because the steps have eroded. This storm has destroyed them so if you want to get to the beach you'll need to go down the path by The Rectory.'

She pointed behind herself. 'It's a longer walk, though, half a mile or so. I sometimes take the dogs down there when the tide's out. It's a beautiful route following the stream. You'll find when the tide's in, it's *really* in. It covers the entire beach; you'll have to check tidal times before you go down there.'

Charlie was watching the spot where the man in black had disappeared, fixing him in her mind, considering his height and build, running him through her mental database, wondering if she knew him from anywhere, whether she might have seen him in court.

'Swimming,' said Decca.

'Sorry?' asked Charlie, turning back to face her.

'I said, I like to do a spot of swimming, in the sea, so if you ever fancy it . . . Of course, at this time of the year if you spend any more than half an hour in the water, you're likely to get hypothermia.'

Penny turned to Decca as if she was seeing the woman for the first time. 'Decca, you don't swim in the sea?'

'Not when the weather's atrocious but, yes, give me a fine morning and I'll be getting my bathers on before you've had your morning coffee, my love. Besides, it's no crazier than you going for a run in this weather. Anyway . . .' Decca turned her attention back to Charlie.

'Madness,' Penny muttered under her breath. 'Utter madness.'

'We'll see you next week, then? Seven o'clock at The Rectory. You can't miss it, it's the grand old house next to the church,' Decca said. 'No need to bring anything, just yourself.'

'Yes,' said Charlie. 'Thank you. I'm really looking forward to it.'

'And we're looking forward to finding out every last thing about you,' said Decca.

CHAPTER NINE

Ben Jarvis

Tuesday, 9 October 2018

'And through here you'll find the generous kitchen-diner,' the estate agent said without any intonation. 'As you can see, we have French doors leading out to a large and mature garden.'

Ben wondered how many times the young man had shown people around. Were the others genuinely interested in buying the house or, like him, did they have other reasons for being there?

'And how long's it been on the market?' Ben asked.

He already knew the answer. He knew it all.

'Ten months, which is great news for you. As you can see, it's a vacant property, no chain, and it's been priced for quick sale. You get a lot of house for your money with this one so, if you're interested, I'd act quickly.'

Slowly nodding and pursing his lips, Ben tried to look like he was seriously considering the house. He'd polished his shoes and ironed his blue striped shirt in the hope that he gave the impression he could afford something like this. In truth, it was his only shirt and his only pair of shoes apart from his tatty old trainers.

He'd had to borrow Amanda's iron. Ben told her it was for a job interview and she'd been so pleased for him, she'd ironed the shirt herself. Anything to get him off her doorstep and off her conscience. She was a good woman. It wasn't her fault that their marriage had disintegrated.

He also borrowed two hundred pounds off her with a promise that he'd pay her back from his first pay-cheque if he got the job. He didn't feel comfortable lying to her but they'd been married for over twenty-five years, it wasn't like it was the first time.

'All the white goods and carpets are included in the sale. It was recently redecorated to a very high standard,' the estate agent was saying.

Every wall was painted magnolia. The door frames and skirting boards were a high-gloss white. The carpets were beige, slightly mottled, so they didn't show the dirt as easily. Ben was disappointed. He'd hoped to see more of *their* style, learn a little bit more about Lee Fisher and Steffi Finn.

The estate agent was right about one thing: the asking price was remarkably low for this type of house. Pinchdale was a desirable area near a high-performing school with good transport links into Sheffield. Houses around here usually sold before the FOR SALE sign could be erected. The lack of interest in the house only served as a reminder of how much the owners were despised.

'And what's through there?' Ben pointed to a closed door off the kitchen.

'The utility room.' The estate agent took two strides to the door and pulled it open. A phone buzzed in the pocket of his suit jacket. Both men ignored it.

'Plumbing for the washing machine. Separate sink. Plenty of storage.'

'Right,' said Ben. 'That's handy. Is it okay if I . . . ?' He pointed towards the ceiling.

'Go upstairs?' the estate agent asked. 'No problem, mate. Be my guest. Shout out if you have any questions at all.' He slid his hand into his inside pocket, itching to answer the phone.

'Cheers.'

Ben walked towards the foot of the stairs, wiping his clammy palms on his trousers. The house wasn't what he'd been expecting. It was light, airy, clean. Well maintained. It felt like an empty house, though, and there was an echoing in the rooms. Given who owned it, he'd expected an air of darkness to hang over it.

He was going to put in an offer on the house just to take it off the market for a short while. He wouldn't go through with the sale, of course. How could he? As soon as they looked into his finances, they'd see how futile that was. It was petty, really, but he wanted to get Finn's hopes up at the same time as deterring potential buyers. And then he would let her down because she didn't deserve life to go her way, not after she'd destroyed so many others.

On the third stair was a large pile of mail. There were brown envelopes, white envelopes and gaudy flyers to catch the eye. It confirmed what Ben already suspected, that Finn hadn't been home since she'd been released from prison. There was nothing for her here. No photos on the wall, no cupboards full of mismatched mugs. She was off enjoying her freedom somewhere else. He picked up the letters and mounted the stairs two at a time.

He pictured her with cocktail in hand, smile on her face, and involuntarily began to crush the letters in his hand. He went straight for the master bedroom that overlooked the garden. It was overgrown and at odds with the neat squares of green on either side.

Ben dropped the flyers on to the window ledge by the dead flies. Chinese, Indian, Italian takeaways. Cards for taxis, for cleaners, for a man to clean your gutters. His hands were shaking as he flicked through the letters but it was eagerness, not fear, that made his big hands clumsy.

He discarded a brown envelope addressed to The Occupier, a catalogue for an expensive clothes company, a circular from the water board, but stopped when he saw a letter from the bank addressed to Ms Stephanie Finn. He couldn't believe his luck. He thought most people had digital statements nowadays. He put it to one side and searched through the others. Something from the council. A letter from her dentist. One from a pension company. He wasn't sure what he'd hoped for when he'd requested a viewing, but he knew he was right to have come.

'Always trust your instincts,' he muttered.

Ben folded up the letters that were addressed to Finn and slipped them into his pocket. He grabbed the useless mail and headed back downstairs.

'All right, mate. I'll call you later.' The estate agent was in the hallway as Ben reached the bottom of the stairs. 'Sorry about that,' he said, gesturing to the phone. 'I had to take it.'

'No problem at all.'

Ben saw the younger man's eyes slip to the bundle of crumpled mail in his hand.

'I picked these up,' said Ben. 'They really should get their mail redirected.'

'Yeah, the redirection stops after a while. They must have forgotten to renew it. I'll have the office contact the vendor.'

'Where's the vendor moved to? Anywhere nice?'

'No idea,' he said.

Ben wondered how desperately he wanted this sale. He probably earned commission.

'Look,' said Ben, taking a step towards the estate agent, 'what did you say your name was again?'

'Ryan.'

'Look, Ryan, I'm going to be honest with you. I'm interested. But, when I arrived here this morning, one of the neighbours was hanging around out front. He told me that the people who used to live here were criminals. He says they're,' Ben lowered his voice to little more than a whisper, 'in prison.'

Ryan tapped the bundle of mail against the palm of his hand. 'Ah. I see. Well, by law we're not required to tell you if something like—'

'But, you see, it's got me worried that they might want to come back here when they get out. Or someone's going to turn up here in the middle of the night looking for them? Surely, you can understand why I've got my concerns, Ryan.'

'Absolutely. Absolutely,' Ryan said. 'And that's perfectly understandable, Ben. Let me put your mind at rest by telling you that you've nothing to worry about. The couple in question, well, the guy has been put away for life.'

'Life?' Ben reared back as if he was in shock. 'What for?'

'Well, you didn't hear it from me, but he murdered someone.'

Ben shook his head. 'No. Seriously? Not . . .' He pointed at the floor. 'Not here? In this house?'

'No. Nothing like that.'

Ben let out a low whistle and managed not to correct Ryan by pointing out that Lee Fisher had killed more than one person. Perhaps even more than the two he'd been convicted of.

'Well, I wasn't expecting that,' Ben said. 'And his missis? Was she put away for murder too?'

'Not murder, no, but she covered for him. She's already out of prison but she's not stayed around long. This is her house, actually, not his.'

'Really?'

'As you can imagine, she's desperate to sell up and put this whole business behind her. I probably shouldn't tell you this, but I think she'd accept any offer that came close to the asking price.'

Ben shook his head. 'Wow. I don't suppose you know where she is now, do you? I'd be happier if I knew I wasn't going to find her in my flower bed one morning.'

Ryan grimaced. 'We don't deal with her direct. Everything's going through her solicitors.'

'Which solicitor is she using?'

'Hunt, Fellows and Bartlett.'

Ben knew of them. They were the firm who had represented her at court, too. If he remembered correctly – and he knew he did, because Steffi Finn was his specialist subject – her ex-boyfriend, Conor Fletcher, worked there. She'd managed to keep it quiet that they were handling her house sale as well.

'I'd appreciate it if you could find out for me, Ryan. Will you let me know if you hear anything?'

'Of course, but really, you've got nothing to worry about,' continued Ryan. 'There's no chance of her coming back. People round here have long memories.'

Ben pushed his hands into his pockets, touching the letters with Steffi Finn's name on them.

Yes, he thought.

He had the longest memory of all.

'Go on, then,' Ben said. 'I'd like to put in an offer. But on the understanding that you take it off the market straight away. I don't want anyone else trying to out-bid me.'

'I can ask,' said Ryan with a shrug.

'You do that. I'm quite single-minded when I decide I want something, Ryan. I haven't always got my own way, but I reckon that's about to change.'

CHAPTER TEN

Charlie Miller

Tuesday, 9 October 2018

Charlie left the house in a head-down hurry against the steady drizzle. The insistent wind had shooed the fine morning away, replacing it with a heavy grey afternoon.

Coal smoke tickled her nostrils, reminding her of a time long past when she'd eaten bread fresh from the oven and pulled her socks over her knees.

The gate at her next-door neighbour's garden creaked loudly as it swung open like an early-warning system for intruders. Charlie knocked loudly and watched through the glass panel of the door as an old gentleman made his slow progress towards her with a walking stick. Just as the postman had told her, there was a note taped to the glass.

Leave post at Buttery.

She held up his parcel, so he could see why she'd come knocking on his door, yet he still opened the door at a leisurely pace.

'Hello. Mr Hollingsworth?' Charlie said.

The old man narrowed his eyes as if he had trouble seeing her. Or maybe he just didn't like what he saw.

'Who're you?'

'My name's Charlie Miller. I live up at The Buttery.' She pointed at the house unnecessarily. 'I moved in on Friday.'

He sneered at her.

'The postman gave me your parcel?' She said it as if it was a question, an upturned lilt at the end of the sentence. She didn't speak like that or, at least, didn't used to, but her footing in this new world was uncertain and she found herself double-checking every word that came out of her mouth.

'You've got a note,' she said. 'On your door. It says to leave your parcel with me?'

'I know what it says. I bleddy wrote it, didn't I?'

The old man stepped back for her to come into the house.

'No, you're okay,' she said quickly. 'I don't want to come in. I was just delivering this.'

'Quick now,' the man said. 'You're letting all the heat out.'

He extended an arm into the kitchen.

'Well, maybe for a minute. But I really can't stay.'

The kitchen had light blue walls and a blue linoleum floor. A spider plant in a macramé planter hung from the ceiling above the cluttered dinner table. Cups and plates were stacked in the sink.

Charlie attempted to pass the parcel to him. 'Here you are, then.'

'Through there,' he said, pointing down the hallway.

He had to be approaching the far end of eighty and, if it hadn't been for a back so curved that he was almost bent double, he would have been a tall man. He had a thick white beard that was flecked with russet and was in stark contrast with his brown, creased skin.

The living room was cluttered with old newspapers piled high on a threadbare armchair, a sideboard, the floor. The furniture was beige, the curtains were beige and the carpet was beige. The room was cold even though a small gas fire glowed beside the old man's chair.

Charlie gravitated towards the weak heat that was struggling out of the inadequate fire.

'Took yer time,' Mr Hollingsworth said.

'I'm sorry?'

'I saw Peter taking that up to yours hours ago.'

Peter. *That* was his name.

'Sorry. I got talking to some of the neighbours.'

'What?' He tilted his ear towards her, and she spoke louder.

'I said, I was talking to the neighbours.'

'I saw you,' he said gruffly. 'You'd do well to stay away from them. Pair of busybodies they are. Especially the old one. Always, "How are you?" and, "What you got there, then?" and, "Should you be doing that?" Nosy parkers.'

Charlie pushed some old newspapers to one side and placed the parcel on a sideboard that was littered with circles from hot mugs like the Olympic rings.

'I suppose you find it difficult to get to the door,' Charlie said.

'I do not,' said Mr Hollingsworth, affronted. 'I'm just a bit slow, that's all.'

'But . . .' Charlie frowned at him. 'You asked the postman to leave your parcel with me.'

'You didn't come an' introduce yourself. Had to take matters into me own hands, otherwise you wouldn't've come over. I like to know who I'm living next door to. Can't abide strangers. What were you waiting for? The formal invite or the red carpet?'

'Oh. Right. I see. Well, I only arrived on Friday and I've been busy cleaning up the house and unpacking,' she said. 'I promise you I'd have got around to introducing myself eventually. So, tell me,' she went on, 'what's in the parcel?'

'My sister's kid sends me one of them listening books month in, month out, whether I like it or not. Says me eyes aren't good enough for reading no more but how she'd know is anyone's guess. Haven't seen her in years. Not saying it's a bad idea, mind. Only problem is, the silly mare never thought to send me a CD player, did she? Suppose they'll be handy come spring when I dangle them from poles over my seeds to keep the birds away from me allotment. Anyway, the kettle's through there,' Mr Hollingsworth said. 'White. Three sugars. I'll take one cup for now and one in the flask for later.'

He grunted his way over to a sturdy chair and lowered himself into it gently. Charlie looked him up and down. He didn't seem infirm, just stiff and tired. There was something in his manner that, rather than being pushy, seemed to assume that an agreement had already been made between them and making him a cup of tea or coffee was the right thing to do. It felt like she was being interviewed for the position of helpful neighbour.

For a moment Charlie neither moved nor spoke. 'Is there a reason . . . ?' She brushed her hair out of her eyes. 'Sorry, but why can't you make your own drink?'

'I'm an old man,' he croaked.

'Well, yes, but it looks like you're doing okay for yourself.'

'Looks can be deceiving,' he replied.

Charlie smiled. She was the last person who needed to be told that.

'Do you have a gardener?' she asked him.

A momentary look of surprise at the change of topic was replaced with an insulted frown. He looked at her as though she'd slapped him.

'I bleddy well do not. Who says I do? No one round here knows as much about gardens as me. Couldn't grow mould on a slice of bread, this lot.'

'You've an impressive garden. You obviously put a lot of work into it.'

He nodded. He took it as a fact not a compliment.

'So,' she continued, 'if you're able to maintain those impeccable borders yourself, you're capable of making a cup of tea.'

He raised a bushy eyebrow in her direction. He'd expected her to be far more compliant.

'I *am* old,' he said.

Charlie inclined her head. 'True.'

'In my day, you used to respect your elders.'

'Ah,' said Charlie. 'The old *in my day* argument. The only thing your age tells me is that you've managed to stay alive for, what? Eight decades? That's luck, not skill.'

'I don't agree. A lot of skill has gone into making this fine specimen you see before you.' He patted his stomach. 'If you're not putting the kettle on there's no point you just standing there. Sit down, sit down. You're making the place look untidy.'

Even though the old man was gruff, rude even, there was something about him that Charlie liked. A hint of her grandfather, perhaps.

She perched on the edge of a rocking chair, which tipped forward under her weight. Her grandfather used to have one just like it. The arms were smooth and the varnish thinned to nothing at the curves.

'Now then,' he said, 'what's your story?'

'Sorry?' Charlie snapped her head back to look at him.

'Why are you here in the arse-end of beyond?'

'Difficult to know where to start,' Charlie said, shifting in her seat.

'What did you say your name was?'

'Charlie Miller.' She said it with as much conviction as she could muster.

'What are you hiding from, Charlie Miller?'

Charlie stiffened and looked out of the window rather than risk him reading her face.

'What makes you think I'm hiding?'

'If God was a sympathetic man, he'd have picked me for his choir a long time since. With age as great as mine, you get a certain amount of wisdom for dodging death so long. I like it here. People mostly keep 'emselves to 'emselves, 'cept when they don't. What I don't know is why anyone would come here, on their own, to a place where they don't know a soul unless they're hiding from something. I've seen it a lot over the years and they usually leave again when they realise that they can't run from their problems. So what is it?'

'Oh, it's nothing exciting. I wouldn't want to bore you with my woes,' she said, turning to look at him.

'Your what?' He turned his head again so that his right ear was facing her.

'My woes.' She spoke louder this time. 'My troubles.'

'Where you from? I can't get an accent from you.'

'North,' Charlie said vaguely with a wave of the hand.

'How far north?'

'Sheffield. What about you?' she asked, changing the subject back to him. 'Is that a Cornish accent I hear?'

'Plymouth. Used to come to Cornwall as a kid. Visited my uncle every summer but then my uncle died, as uncles do, and there were no need to visit no more. Came here with my wife when I retired.'

'That's nice,' Charlie said.

'Not really. She died.'

'Sorry.'

'Was that an apology or a question?' he asked.

'Apology. I'm sorry your wife died.'

'Hmm.'

Charlie glanced towards the door. Thinking she'd only be a moment delivering the parcel, she hadn't locked the door of The Buttery, but she couldn't walk out on a lonely man who had just told her his wife had died. Besides, she was enjoying the company.

'Does your niece live close by?' she asked.

She was struggling for conversation. Suddenly small talk had become a big deal and she was having difficulty remembering how it went.

'How d'you know about my niece?' the old man asked.

'You said she sent you audio books.'

Satisfied, he nodded.

'No. She's in Suffolk. Or is it Norfolk? Married to a complete waste of space. Thinks he's God's bleddy gift, he does. Can't stand him and I reckon he feels the same.'

'Right.'

'Don't think I don't hear you avoiding my questions. What you come all the way down here for?'

Charlie had rehearsed this, knew her lines off by heart, but they felt thin. He would see straight through them.

She shrugged.

'Not a lot gets past me,' he said. 'I've seen it all. Still got eyes in my head, even if they're not working as well as they should, mind. But I got all the marbles I were born with and that's the truth.'

He smacked his lips together and pulled a handkerchief from the arm of his cardigan.

'I'm not a betting man but if I was, I'd place it all on red. A broken heart.'

He pointed a crooked finger in the direction of Charlie's chest. She smiled and sighed at the same time.

'You got me,' she said. 'There's certainly been a bit of heartache.'

And it wasn't even a lie. Her heart wasn't just broken, it was crushed.

Charlie stood up quickly and the chair rocked behind her.

'Okay then, I'll make you this drink. Tea or coffee, Mr Hollingsworth?'

He wiped the end of his nose.

'Tea,' he said. 'And call me Aubrey.'

CHAPTER ELEVEN

Steffi Finn

Monday, 11 July 2016

'Please,' she said. 'Call me Steffi.'

Steffi pointed towards the kettle and a couple of mugs upended on the draining board. 'Can I get you a drink, Detective Harper?'

'No, you're all right, thanks.'

Tina told Steffi to take the detective into the staff room. It was the right thing to do, but Steffi could tell that Tina was desperate to know what he was after. She wouldn't have called him fat, but he was tall enough and wide enough that high-street clothes wouldn't fit him.

It was late morning. Steffi had typed up Dr Maguire's letters. Collected three coffees from that new place on the corner, actioned the requests for repeat prescriptions and yet she was still as crisp as she'd been when she walked through the automatic doors at eight a.m. on the dot. The detective, however, looked like it had already been a long shift. Stubble-dusted cheeks, the faint vestige of dried-on sweat and a shirt that looked slept in.

'So, how can I help you?' she asked.

They sat down and Steffi clasped her hands in her lap. Unease bubbled in her stomach and she was sure that the large man had noticed that nervous tic she had of fiddling with her earring. She hadn't done anything wrong – not that she knew of – but she felt herself going red. It was the same if she saw a police car behind her in traffic: she forgot how to drive when they were watching, constantly checked her speed.

'We're carrying out some routine inquiries about a missing woman.'

'Oh. Is it someone I know?' She reached for her earring again.

'Her name is Katy Foster. Does that ring any bells?'

Steffi narrowed her eyes as she thought about it. She was terrible with names; she had to deal with so many people on a day-to-day basis that they all became a blur.

'No. No, I don't think so. Is she one of our patients?'

'No, she isn't. Katy went missing after a night out with friends in a town-centre bar.'

'Oh, in that case, I don't see how I can . . .'

She recalled hearing something on the local radio. An appeal for a missing woman. Steffi hadn't paid much attention at the time but she remembered the news reporter saying the young woman had been drinking in a pub in town – several of them, in fact – and had called her sister saying she'd lost her friends. CCTV footage showed her smoking outside a pub with an unidentified and unrecognisable man. Police said he was *a person of interest*.

The implication was that she'd brought it on herself. Drunk and talking to men she didn't know. Was it any wonder?

'Lee Fisher,' said the detective. 'He's your boyfriend, I believe?'

She looked at the detective and tried to smile. She didn't like where this was heading.

'Lee? Yes, he's my partner.'

'Do you know where Mr Fisher was on Friday the first of July?'

'Goodness. The first? Well, I don't know off the top of my head. I would have to check the calendar, but I don't recall him going anywhere. I'm assuming he would've been at work during the day. He's a pharmaceutical rep, you see, and he travels all over the country, but he hasn't had any trips for the last few weeks so yes, I'm sure he would've been in the office. And then . . .' Steffi looked out the window trying to catch hold of anything she could remember about that Friday. 'Yes, in the evening we'd have been home, I suppose.'

'You suppose?' Harper asked.

'Yes. I mean, no. We were definitely at home. We don't usually go out at night unless it's to the cinema or theatre.'

Steffi was starting to feel queasy. She was glad she hadn't had any breakfast otherwise it might have ended up on the detective's shoes. She wondered whether other people felt guilty in the presence of the police or whether they led such blameless lives that they never had to.

'We've already spoken to him, and that's what he said too.'

'Oh, good.' She smiled as if she'd passed a test and was pleased with herself, but then she swapped her smile for a frown. 'You've spoken to Lee? Why?'

'We're just trying to piece together Katy's movements on that night.'

'But you're not suggesting that Lee knows anything about this . . . this . . . missing woman?'

The detective smiled; it was a sweet smile for such a big man. There were dimples in his cheeks and his chin. 'Her name is Katy,' he said.

'Yes, so you said. Look I . . . goodness, the last thing I want to be is rude, but we've never heard of her. Well, I certainly haven't and Lee has never mentioned her to me. And even if we had heard of her, why would you think that we'd know anything about what happened that night?'

Steffi pushed her lips together. She wouldn't be sick. She couldn't. She must be misunderstanding the situation because they couldn't think Lee had anything to do with a missing woman. The idea was preposterous. Unless . . .

Lee had warned her this might happen one day. Years ago, before they met, he'd been arrested. The charges were never brought against him because they were dropped due to lack of evidence – in other words the woman had completely made the whole thing up. He'd tried to get her home safely. She was alone, unable to look after herself, and, when he tried to assist her, she started screaming. She was lucky that he hadn't had her charged with assault.

'On the night she disappeared, a man who fits Mr Fisher's description was seen at the same bar where Katy was last seen by her friends.'

'Lee, in a bar?' Steffi almost laughed with relief. 'You wouldn't catch Lee dead in a bar. He can't stand them. He absolutely hates drunk people.' As soon as she said the word 'hates' she tried to backtrack. 'What I mean is, it's never nice being surrounded by drunk people when you're sober, is it? Why would he go to a bar when there's nothing to interest him there? He doesn't drink, and neither do I.'

Though, she thought, there was that time, a couple of weeks back, at Suki's leaving party. She'd had a few drinks and they'd gone straight to her head. Steffi hadn't eaten all day. Lee had told her that she was getting a bit chunky so she was trying to lose a few pounds by skipping lunch.

'Sorry, when did you say this was again?' she asked the detective.

'Friday the first of July.'

She couldn't be sure of the date of Suki's party, it could have been the first, but then again, it probably wasn't.

Steffi searched the detective's face to see if he really thought that Lee could have anything to do with this woman's disappearance or if he was lazily clutching at straws and questioning every man in Sheffield who'd ever been accused of assault.

'Was there anything different about that Friday? Anything you can remember, no matter how small?' he asked.

DC Harper took a pen and notebook out of his inside suit pocket. He was sensing that Steffi had something to tell him, but she had nothing to add. In fact, if anything, she found herself not wanting to help at all. He might say he wasn't accusing Lee of anything but the very fact he was here asking questions suggested otherwise. Lee was right when he told her that the police would always have their suspicions about him.

'If I could help you, I would. But no, sorry. We don't go out much. There's nothing we like more than an evening in with a film and a takeaway. I really think that you must be mistaken if you think that Lee was at a pub that night.'

She shook her head vigorously. No. She knew Lee. And she knew, without a shadow of a doubt, that he would never go in to a pub.

'How would you describe your relationship with Mr Fisher?'

'Good, really good. We've been together for two years and, yeah, everything's going really well.'

What she and Lee had was special. They were happy together. He'd been under a lot of stress at work lately, but that didn't mean that there was anything wrong with their relationship. Besides, why was it relevant?

That argument they'd had the other week was an anomaly. After Suki's party Steffi had been a little late home and Lee had been annoyed with her because he could smell alcohol on her breath. She'd been a little unsteady on her feet and had knocked over a vase of flowers.

'So, you and Mr Fisher spent the entire evening together on the Friday in question?' Harper asked.

'Yes.'

Was it just her or was it getting hot in here? She stood up to check the display on the air con. 'Do you mind if I . . .?' She poked at the button until the temperature was two degrees lower.

Steffi and Lee rarely argued; it had upset her when he'd got so angry. One moment she was stumbling over her own feet, giggling, and the next she was crying as he told her that she had ruined everything.

Steffi understood why he'd been so furious. He had every right to be angry. His mother had been an abusive alcoholic. At times she'd been so drunk that Lee couldn't go to school because he was scared that, if he did, his mother would choke on her own vomit or burn down the house. Steffi had once asked him why he hadn't got help from social services. He said that, as difficult as his mother was, she was still his mother and if he was taken into care who would look after her? Steffi had thought this was the sweetest, yet the saddest, thing she had ever heard. Even as a child, his first thought had been for the safety of his mother, not himself.

Steffi regretted drinking at Suki's party. She'd set her limit at two gin and slimline tonics, but the second drink had taken the safety catch off and two or three more were set in her path. She should have known how much it would hurt Lee. It was selfish of her to act in such a heartless manner.

'And neither of you left the house at all?' said Harper.

Steffi sat down again. 'No. Not that I recall.'

'Not that you recall?'

The detective must have been able to hear the uncertainty in her voice. He must have noted the shift in her demeanour. She twisted her earring and pushed the back on as tight as it would go.

The evening of Suki's party, Lee had sent her to bed like a naughty child. He'd told her to sleep it off. Looking at the anger in his face, she had never felt so sober. She had pulled the pillow over her eyes to eclipse the sun, to block out self-pity. Lee had driven around for an hour or two and when he got home Steffi had cried herself to sleep. He'd slept in the guest room so he didn't wake her but left a glass of water by her bed because he was good at the little things. He was considerate like that.

When Steffi got out of bed the next morning, he'd cooked her breakfast and, for the first time since they'd lived together, put a load of washing in the machine. They'd hugged and she'd apologised to him, swearing that she hadn't meant to drink so much and promising that she wouldn't do it again.

Detective Harper wrote something in his notebook. It was just two words, but she couldn't see what they were.

'Do you need anything else, Detective? Because I really do have other things I should be getting on with. Sorry, only I've got so much to do, we're a staff member down since Suki left and work builds up so quickly around here.'

She was desperate to call Lee, to express her dismay at the police questioning him over this, but she couldn't do it in an office where gossip was currency. There would already be whispers lying in in-trays, pinned to bulletin boards and slipped between the teabags in the kitchen. Words, like germs, spreading and multiplying, taking on a life of their own.

'Just to recap, then,' said Harper, 'you're saying you were with Mr Fisher all of that Friday evening. That he didn't leave you for the duration of said evening and that you have no reason to suspect that he was planning to meet someone else.'

'Yes, I was with him and no, he wasn't meeting anyone else.'

'Right, and am I correct in thinking that Mr Fisher is insured to drive your car? A red Toyota RAV4? And that no one else except you and Mr Fisher have access to that vehicle?'

'Yes, that's right.'

'And did he have access to that vehicle on Friday the first?'

'Yes, I suppose so. He doesn't own a car, prefers to catch the bus, and his work have a fleet of cars for him to choose from for meetings. If he needs to pop to the shops he some- times uses the Toyota.'

'Okay. And one more question: does Mr Fisher smoke?'

'Smoke?' Steffi shook her head and began to relax a little. The man they were after smoked and drank. Lee did neither of those things. He hadn't smoked for two years and, as far as she knew, had never ever drunk alcohol. He was too trauma- tised by his mother's alcoholism to ever turn to drink.

'No, Lee doesn't smoke,' she said.

'Okay. Well, thank you for your time. I'll be in touch if I have any more questions, but in the meantime, if you remember anything, no matter how small, please give me a call.'

'I will, thank you.'

Harper stood and waited for Steffi to do the same. At the door the detective turned to her and said, 'Let me leave you my card.'

Steffi took it but couldn't focus on the letters and numbers.

'Thank you,' she said. 'I hope you find Katy soon.'

'Me too,' he said.

But the slight shake of his head as he spoke betrayed his thoughts that there was little chance of finding her alive.

CHAPTER TWELVE

Truth comes naturally for the majority of us. From the colour of the shoes we're wearing to how we take our coffee. But a believable lie takes crafting. Perhaps it occurred to you only a split second ago, or maybe it's been years in the shaping, but a lie is a deliberate act.

To lie is a verb; a doing word. When we lie, we do it with purpose. We plant it, we grow it, we slip it among the truest of statements and hope no one notices the cuckoo in the nest.

There are good lies, bad lies and sweet little white lies, which we deploy in the name of kindness. 'You look great!', 'Oh, I adore this gift!' and, 'Of course I love you, darling.' There are lies that spare feelings and brush aside conflict. There are lies of concealment, cover-ups, camouflage, and lies where the truth has gone missing.

Lies alter our course, they define us. They are the grains of sand in an oyster and there are times that we make believe that good will come of it, though that's just the lie we tell to make ourselves feel better.

How do you live with the lies you've told, Steffi? You can try to ignore the deceit, but the unease, like an abscess, is growing. You can cover it up, but it can't stay hidden for ever because to lie is a verb; a doing word. It can't sit still. It runs, it creates chaos, it sneaks in the shadows.

You knew exactly what you were doing when you told your lies. But here's something you've overlooked: you're not the only one who knows how to lie, Steffi.

Shall I tell you the difference between our untruths? Yours destroyed lives, mine rebuilds them. I will bring justice for all who deserve it.

You will get what's coming to you.

CHAPTER THIRTEEN

Charlie Miller

Tuesday, 16 October 2018

The Rectory was as grand as its name suggested. Charlie thought it was a shame that so few of them were owned by churches nowadays. Though for Jenn, whose house it was, it was no bad thing.

The hallway was a vast echoing chamber. White lilies in a trumpet-shaped vase sat on a tall marble table and a patterned rug over the black-and-white tiles muffled Charlie's steps as she shook out her umbrella. She couldn't remember a time when she'd set foot in such an impressive house. Even before she'd been sent to prison, the company she kept didn't live like this. The closest she'd ever got to a building on this scale was a spa that Lee took her to for their first anniversary. She'd felt out of place there, too.

A whisper above her had Charlie looking up the stairs and spying two small girls peering over the banister. They scattered with a shriek when she spotted them.

'You should be in bed!' Jenn shouted after the children.

'Don't mind them,' she said to Charlie. 'Relatively harmless. They'll not settle until my husband gets home.' She glanced at the clock on the wall. 'He's been away for five days on business, but he'll be home tonight. Come through, come through.'

Charlie stared through open doorways as they passed them. One room housed a grand piano and overstuffed bookshelves. An open violin case was on the floor and sheets of music were scattered about it.

'You'll have to excuse the mess,' Jenn said, reaching in and turning off the light.

Charlie had never seen anything so elegant. Everything from the paintings to the rugs was luxurious. Fringed lamps cast a warm glow in corners.

Jenn's heels clackety-clacked against the parquet flooring as they walked towards the back of the house. Charlie felt clumsy in her practical boots and her second-hand parka. She smoothed her hair behind her ears and hitched up her jeans. She was wearing an old cashmere jumper, the nicest item she owned, but it still looked like she hadn't made an effort whereas Jenn struck her as the kind of woman who would look stylish in a sack.

They walked into a large kitchen at the back of the house. A small dining table, large enough for intimate breakfasts, not dinner parties, was covered with bottles and snacks in Royal Stafford bowls. Charlie recognised the patterns, wanted to reach out and touch them. She'd never been able to afford beautiful pottery like this.

'Here she is!' cried Decca.

Decca and Penny were sitting on brightly coloured sofas with a woman Charlie hadn't yet met. The third woman had her sleeves rolled up showing arms and hands covered in tattoos.

'Hi.'

Decca pulled Charlie into a hug as if they were old friends. 'Charlie, come and meet Bo.'

Bo waved in her direction but didn't get up. 'Hiya. Decca's been so excited for you to join us. She hopes you'll be able to convince Jenn to read something other than classics. Tell us you're not a classics bore too? I don't think I could stand it.'

Charlie smiled. 'Well, I read anything really,' she said.

'Oh no,' said Bo in mock horror. 'We have ourselves a fence sitter!'

The others laughed and Decca slumped back down on to the sofa and patted the seat next to her indicating for Charlie to sit.

'Bo lives at the farmhouse just by the turning for the village. It's not much of a farm, but she'll sell you a dozen eggs at an exorbitant price.'

'Hey!' said Bo.

'But don't rely on her for them because she's never there. Always travelling about the country doing art exhibitions. And you remember Penny, of course?' said Decca.

'Yes. Nice to see you again,' said Charlie.

'You too. How's the house coming on?' Penny asked.

Charlie shook her head; she didn't know where to start.

'Good. Really good, thanks.'

'But?' prompted Bo.

'But it's cold, it's damp and it still looks a bit like a squat. I'll get there eventually. My priority is to get that broken window replaced. If I'd known about it, I'd have got it repaired before I moved in but the estate agent didn't mention anything.'

'You didn't look at the house before you bought it?' asked Bo.

'It was all a bit of a rush. I was away when it came up at auction and I took a gamble on it. A friend of mine came to look at it but he failed to tell me how much work needed doing. Still, I suppose that was reflected in the price.'

Hovering at the edge of the conversation, Jenn said, 'Charlie, what can I get you to drink? We have an array of wines and gins, but these old lushes are drinking fizz.'

'Could I trouble you for a cup of tea?' asked Charlie.

'Tea?' said Bo. 'You're not driving, are you? Go on, have a proper drink. What's the point in living within staggering distance of each other if you don't drink enough to stagger?'

'Leave her alone, Bo. Some people don't need alcohol to relax,' said Jenn. 'Cup of tea coming right up.'

'Thanks.'

Decca took a gulp of her Prosecco. 'Listen. Why don't I send Jack by your place? He'll sort that window out in no time. You can't live with the window boarded up like that. You must be freezing.'

'If you don't mind? That'd be great,' said Charlie. 'Is Jack your . . .' She tried to remember what Decca had said about her husband. She seemed to think she'd mentioned a divorce and so finished with, '. . . partner?'

Apparently, she'd said something hilarious and the others all laughed, even Penny, who had to cover her mouth to stop from spitting out her drink.

'Lordy, no!' Decca wiped her eyes. 'Not if he was the last man on earth, my love. So, tell us about you. You're not working at the moment, then? And you used to live up north?'

'And you've got no family, is that right?' said Bo.

They already knew a fair bit about her so Charlie wasn't required to say much except 'that's right' and the occasional 'not exactly'. She looked at Penny, who was staring off into space, her eyes vacant for a moment. As if she felt Charlie's gaze on her, Penny turned and smiled.

'You don't mind all the questions, do you, Charlie?' Bo asked. 'You don't have to answer anything you don't want to. But you should know that if you choose not to answer our questions then we shall fill in the gaps ourselves. Be warned, we have the most active imaginations, don't we, Decca?'

Decca leaned across and clinked glasses with her.

'I don't mind at all,' said Charlie, though her red cheeks indicated otherwise.

'Sugar in your tea?' called Jenn from the kitchen.

'No thank you. Just milk.'

'And,' continued Decca, 'you can ask us anything you like. We're not shy.'

'How are you finding that old fart who lives next door to you?' Bo asked.

'Awful man,' said Decca. 'Just awful.'

'Terrible,' agreed Penny.

'I've only met him once, but he seemed nice enough,' Charlie said.

'Your tea,' said Jenn, handing her a cup.

'Thanks.'

'Well, I don't know what your last neighbours were like but if you think that Aubrey Hollingsworth seems nice enough ...' said Decca.

'He's a little grumpy, I suppose, but he's losing his hearing and can't get around very well. I think I'd be a bit short with people too.'

'Short with people?' asked Bo. 'He's a nuisance. He used to chase walkers away from his house with a stick. No matter how many times we've told him it's a public right of way through the fields. Gives Penderrion a bad name. I'd steer well clear if I were you. He's a lost cause.'

'Oh no, I'd like to think there's no such thing,' Charlie said. 'He's harmless enough and he's still grieving for his wife.'

Charlie had no reason to be loyal to Aubrey, not really, but it was in her own best interests to believe that no one was a lost cause.

'Shall we begin?' Jenn said, sitting down. 'And can I remind everyone that it's book first and then dessert.' This comment was obviously intended for Bo, who pretended to go limp with hunger.

'Why do you always do this to us?' asked Bo. 'You know I only come for the pudding.'

'I do. Which is why I save it until the end, otherwise you'd leave halfway through the evening.'

They were a friendly bunch of women who found every-thing hilarious. Charlie was able to contribute occasionally to the book discussion having read *Wuthering Heights* at school, but it was far too long ago for her to remember much. For too many years she'd rarely read, and then she'd found her-self in prison, and books became her only escape. The library was the first place she had visited. She sought comfort and freedom between the pages of a book. They spirited her away from her cell and allowed her to wander freely across times and continents.

There were no books at The Buttery. She hadn't owned any in a very long time and they were a luxury she couldn't afford. Even before prison she borrowed books from the library though that was mainly due to the fact that Lee didn't like the look of bookcases, nor did he see the point of read-ing. Now she looked back on that period of her life, she realised that she should never have trusted a man who took pride in not reading a book since school.

Light-hearted arguments ensued when Bo disagreed, most vehemently, with Jenn about *Wuthering Heights* being a romantic story but they were good natured about it. Charlie couldn't remember a time she'd ever seen a person get so much enjoyment from arguing as Decca did. Her arms made windmills in the air as she tried to get her point across. Penny and Charlie sat back and watched with amusement. Neither of them felt up to the task of disagreeing with Decca. Bo and Jenn had no such reservations, though.

Charlie marvelled at the ease she felt in their company, in this house, even though she had never met anyone quite like these women. She said little, still scared in case she gave too much away, but time passed quickly and easily.

'For the love of God, Jenn, only that pavlova can save us now. Do something, unless you want me to take the cake knife to Decca's throat,' said Bo.

They all moved to the table while Decca got some plates out.

Without asking, Jenn topped up everybody's glasses and looked at Charlie with questioning eyes and an almost empty bottle in her hand. Charlie shook her head. 'No thanks.'

If she wanted to drink there was nothing Lee, or anyone, could do to stop her. However, there was too much for her to lose and she was still getting used to Charlie Miller. If she let her guard down, Steffi Finn could slip back in and ruin everything for her.

Decca started cutting through the meringue with a large serving spoon. 'Pass me your plate, Bo.'

The plate slipped into the air between Bo and Decca's hands. Even though she knew the smash was coming Charlie jumped to her feet, knocking over the chair as the plate scattered shards of porcelain at her feet.

'Shit,' said Bo. 'Sorry, Jenn. Tell me it's not a family heirloom.'

'Not to worry. You've not cut yourself, have you? Charlie? Did it get you?'

'No. I'm fine. Sorry.' Charlie put her hand to her chest. 'It just made me jump, that's all. I don't know what I was thinking.'

Penny picked up Charlie's overturned chair and set it down. 'You okay?' she asked.

'Yeah. Loud noises, that's all. I just . . .' Charlie was flustered and didn't know what she was saying. The others were looking at her like she was fragile.

Jenn began clearing up the sharp triangular pieces of plate while Charlie sat back down and attempted to start another conversation to stop them looking at her any more.

'So, this is, what, a monthly thing?' Charlie asked. Her face was burning as it always did when she was embarrassed in public.

'Yes. Usually the second Tuesday of the month, but it can be a bit of a moveable feast sometimes,' said Decca. 'Pass another plate would you, Penny?'

They heard the slam of the front door and the thunder of small feet overhead. Charlie flinched again at the noise.

'That'll be Marcus,' said Jenn, standing up. 'Do excuse me for a moment.'

'Daddy,' came a cry of young voices from the hallway.

Decca took Charlie's plate and slid a generous wedge of cream, meringue and strawberries on to it.

'Marcus is some kind of hot-shot lawyer. Rarely home, but that suits Jenn perfectly. He makes obscene amounts of money, which pays for all of this.' Decca waved the serving spoon around the room. 'I used to give her a rotten time for not working, but then I met her children. Trust me, staying home with those two is not the easy option.'

Jenn came back into the kitchen followed by a tall man in a crumpled suit, who had a child under each arm.

'Hello, ladies,' he said.

'Hello,' they chimed.

'Darling,' said Jenn, 'I'd like you to meet Charlie; she's new to the village. She's taken on the old Buttery. You were just asking whether anyone had moved in yet, weren't you?'

Charlie turned to face Jenn's husband. He was impeccably groomed with the face of a man who used to be handsome, and the air of a man who believed he still was.

'Hello,' he said. 'A very warm welcome to Penderrion.'

'Thank you,' said Charlie.

He placed the children on the floor and leaned in to kiss Jenn on the cheek. She blushed.

'Right then, you two,' he said, addressing the blonde-haired children who Charlie guessed to be somewhere between five and ten. 'Off to bed and pick out one story each. One!' The girls ran off, laughing, and Marcus turned his focus back to Charlie.

She shifted in her chair, crossed her legs and uncrossed them. Everyone seemed to be sitting a little straighter, talking a little quieter since Marcus joined them. Or was that just her? She seemed unable to act naturally in his presence.

To fill the silence, she said, 'You have a lovely home.'

'Thank you. I can take very little credit for it; Jenn is the brains and the beauty around here.'

'It's about time you realised that,' said Decca with a smile. 'How was America?'

'Good,' he said, taking off his jacket and walking towards them. 'Great, in fact.'

He stepped behind Charlie's chair and hung his jacket over the back of it. She instinctively sat forward, uncomfortable. She turned in her seat to look at him and caught his frown. She reached for her ear before she remembered she didn't wear earrings any more. Though she could have worn simple jewellery in prison she'd chosen not to. The skin had grown over the holes now, leaving just a hint of what used to be.

'I have to ask,' Marcus said, tilting his head to one side as if looking at her with a new perspective, 'do I know you from somewhere? There's something familiar about you.'

CHAPTER FOURTEEN

Steffi Finn

Monday, 7 May 2018

Day 167 of sentence

This. This was the real punishment.

Not that the man she loved had been unmasked as a murderer, nor the humiliation of everyone knowing her business. Not the removal of her home comforts, her liberty and her self-respect. Not even the guilt of whether she could have done more to prevent the last murder.

This.

The news that her mum was days away from death and she couldn't be with her.

Her legal team had been busy. They'd managed to get Steffi permission to visit the hospice. She didn't know how many strings her solicitor had had to pull to get them to agree to it, but now there'd been a delay and those strings had been cut. They said there was a problem with staff numbers and their priority was prisoner and staff safety, not whether a convicted criminal got to visit her dying mother.

She was scared to ask someone about it, or complain, in case they used it as a reason to revoke the permission entirely.

Like everything in here, it was a balancing act and she couldn't look down. All she could do was wait.

Steffi had practised her apologies, her declarations of love, her sorrow at not being there when Mum needed her, but they were useless if she couldn't get to her in time. Her mum was that one constant in her life that she'd taken for granted. Mum never complained or shouted. The closest Steffi ever got to her mother's disapproval was a tiny shake of the head or a sigh. If Mum was the calm, then Dad was the storm.

The truth was that Steffi had grown distant from her mum in the last few years. The difficulties with her dad had meant she didn't go home as often as she could have done. Lee had helped her see that she didn't need to be around her dad when all he did was belittle her. Unfortunately, she'd swapped one controlling man for another.

Lee had moved into Steffi's house within weeks of them meeting. Those who said it was too quick, and that they didn't think Lee was right for her, were cut from Steffi's life. Looking at it now, she could see the warning signs were all there, but at the time she thought Lee was all she needed. She'd never been so happy, or so loved. Theirs had been a passionate relationship, never wanting to be apart from each other, always wanting more. She should have known that it was too good to be true.

Steffi could hear shouting from the other cells. They weren't usually locked in at this time of the day. Something was wrong and the other women were making their disapproval known. There wasn't much they could rely on in prison, but they always had their routine. Their classes and their library visits and the jobs that they did in the laundry room and the kitchen were all they had to keep them sane.

She heard footsteps outside and as her door clicked open, Steffi jumped to her feet.

'What is it?' she asked. 'What's wrong? Has something happened?'

Callaghan stepped into the room and took Steffi by the arm.

'Your carriage awaits, Stephanie.'

Relief rushed over her so quickly that she forgot to hide it from the prison officers.

'Thank you,' she said.

They were strong-looking women. Steffi wondered whether they'd volunteered for the job of babysitting her that day. Callaghan and Petrenko were her least favourite of the prison officers. The others seemed like they were just doing their job, while these two seemed to enjoy her discomfort a little too much.

'Come on, then. Let's be having you,' Petrenko said in her heavily accented voice. 'Chop, chop.'

Steffi kept her eyes on the toes of her shoes as she walked past the other cells. She wished they would move a little faster. There were too many doors, buzzers, locks and paperwork that were keeping her from her mum's final moments.

'When you get back, you'll not be so popular,' Petrenko said. 'My ladies don't like being locked in cells all the day.'

Steffi kept her eyes on her shoes. She couldn't think about that now.

'Already we have not enough prison officers and now we have to take you on nice day trip. So, the ladies, they have to be in cell. All so you can have jolly holiday. Did you want for us to bring picnic?' She laughed. 'Scotch eggs, yes?'

'She thinks she's something special,' said Callaghan. 'Doesn't belong with the rest of them. That's what you think, isn't it, Stephanie?'

Steffi bit back all of the things she wanted to say. She knew this would change her standing with the other prisoners. She'd reached a point where the other inmates were indifferent to her but this would make them take notice again. It was worth it for the chance to say goodbye to her mum, though. She'd thought she would get the chance to make amends when she got out. She was going to be the perfect daughter. But then the cancer spread, and the time had passed. She wouldn't get the opportunity to make things right; her sentence would last beyond the day of her release.

The journey to the hospice was slow and uncomfortable. Steffi inwardly cursed the traffic, the traffic lights, the speed limit. The van smelled of disinfectant. She didn't want to think about why it had needed to be bleached clean. She couldn't see where they were but imagined each sway and turn taking her closer to her mum.

When the van came to a halt, she thought they were at another set of lights until she heard the slam of a door, and the opening of another. She looked up at the light spilling in to the van.

'You've got half an hour,' Callaghan said. 'So let's not hang about, eh?'

At the hospice they barrelled through the swing doors. A soft-faced nurse led them to a side room as if she showed prisoners through the corridors on a daily basis.

Steffi was suddenly embarrassed about her clothes, her hair. She wished she'd made an effort. The room was stuffy and smelled sickly sweet. Yellow and purple freesias were in a narrow vase by the bed.

At first, Steffi didn't recognise her mother. She was close to calling over her shoulder, 'Wait! This is the wrong room.' But then she saw her name – Maggie Finn – on a whiteboard above the bed. And there was Dad in the high-backed chair, holding her weak and unresponsive hand. He looked at Steffi with tired eyes and then frowned.

'Is this really necessary?' he asked, nodding towards the restraints.

Steffi was staring at the imposter in the bed. She was unconscious and breathing noisily through an open mouth and hollowed-out cheeks. There was nothing left of her under that blanket. She looked so much older than her fifty-two years.

Steffi felt her cuffs being unlocked and her hands fell to her side.

'Mum?' she whispered.

'She's not . . .' Dad cleared his throat. 'They think she's not got long.'

'Does she know I'm here?' asked Steffi.

'I don't know. I really don't know.'

Her hair was in soft tufts like a new-born. The chemotherapy had taken her hair, and her smile, yet it hadn't even held death at bay.

'Oh, Mum.'

Steffi stepped closer and picked up her mum's hand. So warm, like she should be squeezing her back and telling her 'not to worry'. Her fingernails were too long and thick, more like talons.

'Mum, can you hear me? It's Steffi.'

Her face was smooth and her cheeks had a rosy tinge. She was a mannequin waiting to be dressed. A wig, some casual trousers and a blouse, and she'd be ready for the window at M&S. This was her mother stripped back to the basics, before hair, before speech, before personality, before life.

Steffi didn't cry. Part of her was in shock, but it seemed unnatural to cry over this stranger, these bones that once provided scaffolding to support her mother's soul. Steffi sank down on to the edge of the bed.

'You shouldn't sit on the bed,' said Dad.

Steffi ignored him. If her mum didn't want her sitting there she was going to have to open her eyes and say it herself. But her mum was no longer here. She wasn't in that husk. Steffi pictured Mum sitting on the edge of the bed next to her, looking at her own broken body with affectionate pity.

The words that Steffi had so carefully considered were useless now. All she could do was hope that, in the end, her mum knew how much she'd always loved her. The times she should have called, should have visited, they didn't mean that she didn't care.

She sat in silence. They all did. Watching. Staring. It seemed wrong to make small talk over Mum's lifeless body and it was too exposing for Steffi to speak out loud. Her dad kept clearing his throat. Over and over again. She wanted to snap at him to drink some water. Something. Anything. But when she looked at him, she realised that the throat-clearing was directed at her. It was time for her to go. He wanted to be left alone with his wife. He wouldn't let his wife take her final breath with prison officers and her disappointment-of-a-daughter in the room.

Steffi knew she would never forget the sound of Mum's breath catching in her chest and would never get over the knowledge that she was already too late. She put her hand on top of her mum's. It was all she could manage as a good-bye. She nodded to the prison officers. There would never be a good time to leave, so they might as well get it over with.

It was the last time she would ever see her mum. She wished she had enough faith in an afterlife that she could console herself with the thought that her mum would be waiting for her there. But she was too numb for hope to take hold.

She felt the weight of every minute of pain she'd caused her mother. Felt she would split from the inside out from the loss of her.

'I'll see you out,' Dad said.

He walked slightly ahead of Steffi. Callaghan by her side, by virtue of the cuffs linking them. They bumped shoulders as they walked in silence. The hospice was a hush-hush build-ing where laughter had no place and tears fell softly.

They paused by the front desk. Dad had something he wanted to say but was unsure how to say it in front of stran-gers. She wanted to give him a hug – to be hugged *by* him – but, with the cuffs on, she didn't know how.

'You'll be out soon,' Dad said in little more than a whisper.

The 'soon' that he spoke of was still months away. Months of being told what to eat, when to eat. Months of loneliness, of not showing a single emotion in case they used it against her.

Better to be a cold bitch than a soft target.

'And I won't be here when you get out,' he said.

'What is it?' Steffi asked. 'Are you sick?'

He shook his head. 'No. I, when this is . . . when your mum . . . I'll need some time to get over everything. This year, it's been . . .'

He pushed his hands into his pockets. He was fighting back the tears. Steffi had only seen him cry a handful of times over the years, and always because she'd done something terrible that had broken his heart. Those tears had been used to manipulate her whereas these tears came straight from the heart.

'What I'm saying is, good luck with everything. I wish you well but, I can't be part of . . . don't want to have anything to do with . . . That is, we're done.'

He scratched his neck and the loose skin under his chin juddered.

'I don't understand,' Steffi said.

They kept their voices lower than Dad's opinion of Steffi.

'Good luck with,' he cleared his throat, 'whatever you intend to do with your life.'

His eyes didn't meet Steffi's. He looked at the clock above the desk and the nurse bustling by.

'What are you saying? That you're . . . what? Disowning me?' Steffi asked.

'The strain this has put on your mum . . .'

'She has cancer.'

'It only came back when you were arrested. That's all I'm saying.'

'Is it?'

'Is it what?' he asked. He looked her in the eye for the first time since she'd arrived in the hospital.

'Is that *all* you're saying, Dad? Because it sounds to me like you're implying that I gave her cancer.'

He looked back at the clock again. It wasn't ticking fast enough for him. He wanted Steffi gone. He wanted to get back to his wife.

'So, to be clear then,' Steffi continued, 'because I don't want us to walk away from today with any confusion, you are turning your back on me. You want nothing to do with me ever again? Am I hearing you right? You are going to walk away from me today and never see me again. This is how you want this to end?'

She hadn't forgotten they were in death's waiting room, but still she spat the words in his face with such venom that he took a step back. Callaghan put a strong hand on her arm as if to restrain her.

Steffi saw her dad give the prison officers an embarrassed look and shrug his shoulders in a, 'kids, eh?' gesture. She wanted to slap him but, luckily, the handcuffs limited her movements. Instead, all she could do was glare and shake her head.

Steffi was steered away from the hospice towards the waiting van and she let herself be guided. She was shaking all over. Her skin was burning with rage. God, she wanted to scream, to lash out.

Mum wasn't choosing to leave her. Cancer was dragging her away. But the fact that Dad took the decision to desert her crushed her heart more than she thought possible. Parents loved their children no matter what they did, didn't they? But the fact that he was able to stand in front of her on the worst day of her life and tell her that he didn't want anything to do with her any more was almost too much to bear. She was furious with him. Not for deserting her, but for making today about him instead of about Mum.

Steffi's whole life had been about him. No one was happy if he wasn't happy. Don't upset your dad, don't tell your dad, don't wake your dad. No wonder she'd grown up fearful of upsetting the men in her life. Shame it had taken her until today to realise how toxic that relationship really was. She dried her face on her sleeve and Callaghan passed her a tissue.

'None of my business, like,' Callaghan said as she motioned her towards the idling van, 'but your old man's a bit of a twat, isn't he?'

The words took Steffi by surprise and a smile hijacked her face at the unexpected support.

She was done crying over not living up to the expectations of the men in her life.

Steffi lost two parents that day.

And she lost part of herself, too.

That's when she decided she needed a new name. As far as she was concerned Steffi Finn was dead.

CHAPTER FIFTEEN

Charlie Miller

Friday, 19 October 2018

Charlie stood at the window to watch the sun come up. Her hands were wrapped around a cup of tea for warmth. That first cup of the day was always something to be savoured. It was so cold that she could see the wisps of steam rising from the hot liquid.

'I am thankful for the chance to lead a normal life. I'm thankful the central heating in this place works. I'm thankful for the opportunity to meet new people . . .'

She was trying to practise gratitude, like her counsellor had taught her, but it wasn't coming easily this morning. The words were hollow.

She'd enjoyed spending time with Penny, Decca, Jenn and Bo but the evening had soured once Marcus turned up. When he said he thought he recognised her from somewhere a jolt had gone through her body. She knew that Penny had seen it, noticed the colour drain from her face, and the sheen of sweat across her forehead.

Charlie said that she was often mistaken for other people. She told Marcus, and it was true, that she would have remembered if she'd met him before. He was the kind of man who demanded attention. There was no way of knowing how many people had seen her picture in the papers. She'd been blonder, curvier then, and altogether softer, but perhaps he could see through it all. As a lawyer, how closely did he follow other cases?

Penny declared that Charlie must have *one of those faces*, and went on to tell a funny story about how she'd been in a restaurant in Manchester once where she'd been mistaken for a soap actress and got a bottle of champagne on the house. They all laughed but Charlie had noticed the way that Penny had artfully manoeuvred the conversation away from her and was grateful for the gesture.

Once Marcus had gone upstairs to read stories to the children and grab a shower, Charlie made her excuses and left. Long day, terribly tired, up since the crack of dawn. None of the reasons were lies but they didn't tell the whole truth either.

That night, the one after, and the one after that, she hadn't been able to sleep. No, that wasn't true. She hadn't been able to *stay* asleep. She kept waking up in the night, convinced there was someone in the house, convinced she could hear noises outside, convinced that half the village were sitting around Jenn's kitchen table saying, 'I knew I recognised her from somewhere. Look!' And they'd point to a computer screen where a news article would be detailing how she'd protected a murderer.

At the time of the trial she wished that she'd got the chance to tell her side of the story but she'd been advised to stay quiet and refuse all interviews. Her life had been unremarkable, but comfortable, until DC Harper had walked into her workplace and started sowing seeds of doubt. After he'd left, the minutes had ticked slowly by. She'd sat at her computer typing, deleting and retyping the same sentences. An hour had gone by, two, three, while she waited for Lee to return her call.

Her head had started to pound. Tina said she looked terrible and sent her home early. Charlie – or Steffi, as she was back then – never took sick days, never cut corners, never broke the rules, and she certainly would never lie to the police. But had she lied? Really? She didn't know for certain that it was *that* Friday, not without checking. But then she had looked in her diary and saw in capital letters over Friday, 1 July: SUKI'S LAST DAY.

On her way home, she had stopped to get a pre-made Greek salad and a crusty, still-warm baguette. She didn't think she could eat; she certainly wouldn't be able to cook. She was halfway to the exit before she realised she hadn't paid. She flushed red and ran back to the checkout mumbling, 'Forget my head if it wasn't screwed on,' and 'Don't know what's wrong with me today.'

Something about the day hadn't felt right. Why hadn't Lee returned her calls? Why had the detective been so sure that she would know something about this woman? It had been nearly three years since that incident with the woman accusing Lee of trying to attack her; would the police really make such a giant leap to link him to a woman he'd never met?

Charlie followed her feet but didn't notice anything about the journey home. She was surprised to see Lee's shoes in the hallway when she opened the front door. He wasn't due home for another hour.

'Lee?' she called.

She could smell onions and garlic cooking in butter. As she walked through the house she could hear the hiss of frying, and the sound of jazz music playing gently in the background.

She peered cautiously around the door, unsure what mood he'd be in.

'Hey!' he said. 'You're back early.' He flicked the tea towel on to his shoulder and shook the pan. He was relaxed and smiling, unaware of the torment she was suffering.

'I wasn't expecting you home yet,' she said from the doorway. She didn't want to move towards him in case it broke the spell.

'Tough day. Thought I'd cook us a nice meal.'

He looked at the reusable shopping bag in her hand, the top of the baguette sticking out.

'Ah, perfect. You read my mind.'

She edged into the kitchen and put the bag on the side. If only she *could* read his mind, or his face. Lee had already changed from his work clothes into shorts and a T-shirt. The fair hairs on his legs were lost against his golden skin.

'The police came to see me at work today,' she said.

He frowned. 'Yes. They came to see me, too. Sorry, darling, I did listen to your message on my mobile but it's been a crazy afternoon. I've half a mind to complain about that detective. They shouldn't have upset you like that. Still, I suppose they've got a job to do, and they don't have an easy time of it. What did he say?'

She was relieved by how calm he was. It couldn't be a problem if he wasn't concerned.

'They said a woman called Katy was missing and the last place she'd been seen was a bar. They said that you were there too.'

Lee looked at her and raised an eyebrow.

'I know! It's too ridiculous for words. I said that you didn't drink and that there was no way you could've been there and that you were with me all evening.'

Lee turned the heat down under the pan. The blue flames dipped suddenly.

'Bless you,' he said. He took her in his arms and kissed the top of her head. 'Don't you remember, though? I *did* go out that night.'

'Did you?' She rested her head on his chest, didn't want to look into his eyes. 'Oh, yeah, it was *that* evening, wasn't it? But you just went for a drive, right? I mean, you weren't where they said you were.'

'Actually,' said Lee, 'I wasn't going to say anything, but I did drive to a pub that evening. The car was picked up on ANPR.'

'AN . . . ?'

'Automatic number plate recognition. The police have to check these things out and rule people out of their investigations, and because of that nasty business . . . Well, I don't like it, but I can see why they questioned me, I suppose.'

Steffi tried to keep her voice light when she said, 'But you hate pubs.'

'God, yes; and I hated that one too. I wanted to clear my mind. We'd . . . Now, I'm not saying it's your fault . . .' He let go of her and turned to reach for two plates from the cupboard. 'But you came home drunk, remember?'

She nodded and lowered her eyes. She felt shame whenever he brought up that evening.

'I went into a pub to . . . well, to see if I could understand what the appeal was. I wondered whether I was being harsh on you, asking you not to drink but . . . If you could have seen the sights in that pub. The women were the worst, falling over themselves, showing too much flesh. I felt sorry for them. It was horrible. I came straight home and found you sleeping like a baby.'

Steffi poured herself a glass of water and asked, as casually as she dared, 'But this woman . . . Katy. Did you . . . did you speak to her?'

'I don't think so. She might have been there, but the place was packed. The police showed me a photograph but I didn't recognise her. I wasn't really there long enough. I was back here by nine.'

'Were you?'

'Yes, don't you remember? I spoke to you when I brought you a drink.'

'Did you? I don't . . .'

'You were very sleepy. You'd been drinking on an empty stomach, hadn't you?'

'Yes, but . . .'

'Look, let's not dwell on it, eh? And I don't want you to blame yourself for all of this, either. You hear me?' He smiled sadly. 'I know what you're like. You'll beat yourself up, because I wouldn't have got dragged into this mess if you hadn't come home drunk in the first place. But this is absolutely not your fault. Okay?'

'Okay.' Her voice was unsure. She'd not looked at it like that, but now he mentioned it . . . 'But I told the police you were with me all night. Will I get into trouble for lying?'

'You didn't lie. You made a mistake. I've already told them what really happened so all you need to do is call the police tomorrow and tell them you've remembered that I did pop out that night but I was back here by nine o'clock. Make sure to tell him that you spoke to me when I came home. The last thing they need is to be sent on a wild-goose chase checking out alibis just because you got drunk. They need to find this girl, though I doubt there's much chance of finding her alive now, poor thing.'

Charlie excused herself to go to the bathroom where she sat on the edge of the bath with her head in her hands. She knew Lee wasn't capable of hurting anyone, but her mind was spinning. He'd kept it from her that he'd been at that pub. If he could keep that from her, what else could he be concealing? She patted cold water on her face and pinched the bridge of her nose.

'Pull yourself together,' she ordered the woman in the mirror.

If she stopped to think about it, Lee had only kept it from her because he was trying to protect her. He hadn't wanted her to feel bad that her selfish behaviour had made him go to a pub.

When would she realise that she was lucky to have a man like Lee in her life?

CHAPTER SIXTEEN

Charlie Miller

Monday, 22 October 2018

Jack hitched up his paint-splattered trousers and adjusted his cap.

He told Charlie his full name was Jack-of-all-trades-master-of-none. It had the well-worn edges of a joke often told, yet he still found it funny.

'Decca told me I'd better make this job my priority,' he said. 'Couldn't tell you why, but that woman has my balls in a vice. You're lucky that this is a standard window. You don't usually find that in cottages this old. I've got three other jobs that should've taken priority over this one, but here I am. Do you think Decca has that effect on everyone?'

Before Charlie could open her mouth, Jack chuckled and said, 'Nope. Just me, then. Now, you'll have to get the upstairs windows replaced at some point too but I'll have to order those. Tell me when you're ready and I'll get on to it. I'll do what I can to fill in any gaps I see in the frames but you'd be best to get new ones. They're rotten, they are. Crumbling apart.'

Jack was the handyman for most of the villagers and, more importantly, he charged well below the going rate and would only work for cash in hand.

Charlie had no way of earning money yet and it was playing on her mind. She was nervous about applying for jobs where references would be sought. She had no experience or history except the one she was desperate to erase. She knew there were employers who offered jobs to people with criminal records, but she was nervous about being honest with them and exposing her true identity.

'I've been doing some work for Jenn up at The Rectory,' Jack said. 'Have you met her yet? Lovely lady. Don't think I'll be invited back, though. I had words with her other half. I won't be looked down upon. He was on my shoulder the whole time questioning what I was doing, asking how long it took for a man to drink a cup of tea. Anyway, there's plenty of other work to do, especially since this last storm, eh? More than wheelie bins blown over this time and the church roof can't take another gale. They're fundraising to get the tower fixed, you know. You'll have noticed that the bell's not been ringing? That bothers me more than I thought it would. Never know when to have me tea break without that bell. You'll get dragged in to help with the fundraising before long. You bake?'

Charlie shook her head. 'No, it's not really my . . . thing.' She'd not noticed that the church bell had been silent. It wasn't a sound she'd been expecting and so its absence wasn't noted.

'Dear me,' Jack said. 'You don't bake? What, no cakes or pies or biscuits or anything?'

She gave an apologetic shrug, as if to acknowledge her shortcomings; she'd never seen herself as the home-cook type. Cake baking was for people with families and she had no one to bake for. Life was too short to make puff pastry.

'Well I never. I suppose it won't be a problem,' he said, though his tone didn't match his words. 'There's plenty round here that do and there'll be no shortage of cakes at the church. In that case they'll have you making tea and coffee. You know, bar work and the like. You can make tea, can't you?'

'I can just about manage that,' she said.

'In that case, I won't say no to one sugar and a dash of milk.'

Jack had brought someone with him to help fit the new windows. It was hard to know whether to call him a man or a boy. He was somewhere on the cusp and it looked like it was uncomfortable for him. He was only introduced as 'The Lad'. He had spots on his chin and long, thin limbs waiting for him to grow into them. The Lad was given the same amount of attention as any other tool alongside the screwdriver and the hammer.

The Lad stared at Charlie but never spoke. He would blink rapidly when she caught him looking at her but, invariably, it was Charlie who looked away first. Did he recognise her too? He looked at her the way Marcus had, like he couldn't quite place her. Perhaps she'd been unwise to let people into her house. She didn't like having them here.

If she could've put the windows in herself, she would have done, but no amount of YouTube videos would help her there. It wasn't just the cost. Even if her old house sold and she had the money to pay builders to do up the house for her, she wouldn't. This was entirely hers. Hers. She wanted to plaster her own walls, choose the colours, hang the shelves. She was going to sand the doors, replace the skirting boards and install a shower. She wanted to sit back at the end of the day and say, 'I did that.'

The house she'd shared with Lee had been hers on paper, but she never had the freedom to experiment with it. She'd put down the deposit with money her grandfather had left her but Conor had bought the furniture when her budget was stretched as far as it could go. When Conor moved out so did his sofa, his television and his rugs. Lee had old-fashioned tastes. Bowls of potpourri, a three-piece suite, a nest of tables like his mum used to have as if he was trying to recreate his childhood home – before his mother drank herself to death.

Charlie had tried her best to understand Lee's complicated emotions relating to his mum. He'd never known his dad so he and his mum had relied heavily upon each other. He loved her, of course he did, but Lee was angry with her for not giving up drinking when he pleaded with her. If she loved him as much as he loved her then why wouldn't she do that for him? With the help of counselling Lee had learned to separate his mum from her addiction. He hadn't kept many of her things, the pain had been too much for him at first, but he still had her jewellery box. There wasn't much in it because his mum had sold the valuable items to pay for booze, but there was comfort in knowing these things had touched her skin and in knowing she wore them when she was happy and well.

Charlie still had a little money left, but until her house in Pinchdale sold, there would be no soft furnishings, no television, no AGA. The money she'd received from her parents' estate had paid for the house at auction and left her enough to do the basic refurbishments but there was no way it could stretch to a new roof.

She was racing against the weather, had to make what she could of the house before the harsh winter set in. Partly she was desperate to have someplace where she could feel safe and call home. If she'd learned anything from prison it was that there was nothing better than waking up in your own bed, in your own home, with no one to answer to. For her, that was the true meaning of freedom. The other reason for renovating the house as quickly as possible was because she might need to move on and get it sold if she was discovered by those who wished to harm her.

She left Jack to his work and went outside to look up at the ivy-covered bathroom window. It was a dry, quiet day and she was sick of being indoors and even sicker of being watched by The Lad. The few clouds that hung in the sky were in no rush to pass on by and she wouldn't find better conditions to climb a ladder before the end of the year.

A couple in sturdy walking boots walked up the lane, saying, 'Morning,' before heading on up the track through the trees under the arrow of the Coastal Path sign. Charlie would have to get used to the fact that strangers walked through here from time to time, seeking out exercise, or to be at one with nature, or maybe a bit of both. She'd assumed a village as remote as this would be cut off from civilisation through autumn and winter, but the summer was most certainly over and yet the walkers still came.

She peered over the fence as she heard the sound of a car engine, but it was only Peter pulling to a halt in the Royal Mail van. There were very few vehicles that came by here, especially in comparison to where she used to live, and they stuck out due to their rarity value. Peter got out of the van and waved. Charlie waved back. Unless Aubrey was expecting any more parcels today there was no reason for Peter to walk up her path.

Charlie went back to the house and looked up at the bathroom window. From its impossible-to-close window, its strange crucifixes to its unfeasibly-large resident spider, the bathroom was her least favourite room of the house. It would need an entirely new suite, but she couldn't work in there without allowing some natural light in. Had she been this obsessed with natural light before going to prison?

In one of the outbuildings she found a battered metal ladder. She dragged it out, brushing off cobwebs and spiders, and leaned it against the back wall of the house. She slid the extension into place and wedged it under the bathroom window. It didn't quite reach, and she would have to stretch to get at the ivy, but it was stable enough. She checked that the safety catch was firmly fastened and then went back for bucket and secateurs.

The previous owners had left a lot of equipment in the buildings but there was nothing of value. There were old paint pots and brushes, cobwebs without spiders, and a wheelbarrow with no wheel that she supposed was just a barrow, then.

She put on her gloves and moved a wooden crate to get a good look at the furniture that had been pushed into the back corner. What she'd originally taken to be a table turned out to be a potter's wheel. She used to spend every spare teenage moment at a wheel. It was funny to see one here, as if her past had been in storage all these years in a dark corner of Cornwall. Pottery used to be her passion. She loved to shape and create and to give gifts that she'd crafted herself.

Strange what people left behind.

Apart from the items that her parents had decided were necessary, Charlie had left everything else in Sheffield. She hadn't expected to be sent to prison that day. Conor was right, she *was* naïve.

Charlie went back to the ladder before she could get distracted and placed one foot on the lowest rung. The legs of the ladder dug into the mud and seemed secure enough. She didn't like heights but refused to call it a phobia. Any sane person should be fearful of being twenty feet off the ground without a safety harness.

She put the secateurs into the bucket over the crook of her arm and began to climb the ladder. Already she was sweating, and it wasn't because of the heat of the day, because there wasn't any. And it wasn't because of exertion, because she hadn't yet exerted herself.

'Don't look down,' she muttered. 'Don't.'

With each step up, she began to see why ladders didn't feature in her life. Every bend of the knee connected with a metal rung, and she was having to turn her legs outwards as she climbed. Though Charlie was enjoying the sensation of *getting things done*, she wasn't so keen on actually doing them. Her once smooth hands were already rough and her nails were broken and thin. She used to be proud of her long elegant hands but now they were wrinkled and dry.

Charlie pushed herself closer to the window. She hadn't got far, hadn't yet reached the top of the ladder, when she heard the crunch of feet on the path behind her. She glanced, taking care not to turn her whole body, but the sound stopped abruptly and she couldn't see anyone. She turned back to the wall and waited for the steps to start again but all she could hear were the sounds of Jack and The Lad coming from inside the house. They had the radio on, playing a song from Charlie's previous life.

She breathed deeply through her nose and thought she caught the smell of something feral on the wind. A fox, perhaps. The hairs on the back of her neck stood up as if there was someone watching her. She imagined their eyes on her back and animosity as strong as if they were spitting in her face.

She turned a little, letting her shoulders twist this time.

Maybe she was imagining things, or maybe the sound was coming from a rabbit or bird. She couldn't help but think of the man in black walking past her house that first day, or the feeling that someone was in the house with her. And then there was the way that Marcus had looked at her. She thought back to the shouts of Anna Atkins' family as they told her that they'd find her and make her pay. She pictured the letters of hate she used to get in prison. Some of them were laughable, some physically impossible, but all of them scared her. They wrote with so much conviction that it was impossible to ignore them.

There were times when she'd wanted to respond to them and to tell them that, yes, they were right, she had done something terrible in covering for Lee and if she knew how to make it right, she would. But in the end, she stopped reading them. She didn't need anyone else to tell her how many lives she had destroyed. Both her waking and her sleeping hours were coloured by this knowledge.

There was a part of her that expected the worst. That's why she was assuming the noises were manmade instead of the usual sounds of nature. She would have to learn to relax if she was going to survive out here.

Charlie stayed immobile as one minute ticked to the next but there were no more sounds and no one spoke. The song on the radio had finished and a falsely melodic voice was encouraging people to order their new sofas now in time for

Christmas delivery. She leaned her forehead briefly against her hand that was gripping the ladder so tightly her knuckles were white.

Perhaps today wasn't the day to be at the top of a ladder. She didn't feel safe, neither up high nor on the ground. She took two steps down the ladder and the cuff of her jumper caught on the sharp metal edge. She tugged it gently, but it wouldn't come away. She pulled harder and the grey material began to tear. She was about to step back up the ladder to loosen it when she thought she heard a cough. She spun around, quicker this time, hoping to catch them out in a childish game of *What's the time, Mr Wolf?*

The ladder jolted and the steps seemed to disappear behind her feet. She saw the ground rushing towards her, noted the flattened grass where she'd walked, the green paint on the ladder. It banged against the wall and Charlie's foot slipped from the rung. She hung in mid-air, petrified, still hoping that the ladder would right itself. But optimism was no match for gravity, and the ladder banked to the side, like an aircraft coming in to land.

CHAPTER SEVENTEEN

Charlie Miller

Monday, 22 October 2018

Charlie opened her eyes.

The light was too bright so she put her hand above her face and squinted. There were figures crouched over her. She could see that one of them was Jack but the others were in silhouette and Charlie couldn't see them clearly.

Jack said, 'Reckon she's banged her head.'

The woman's voice was familiar when she asked, 'Charlie, can you hear me?'

'Someone was here,' Charlie said.

'I've seen it before,' Jack continued as if she hadn't spoken. 'Had a fella that worked for me who banged his head and started talking with a Welsh accent. We need to get her to Treliske sharpish.'

'For goodness' sake, Jack, do shut up.' It was a different woman this time.

'Give her a minute.' The first woman's voice was soft. 'Hospitals aren't the answer, Jack.'

'What? And your lavender oil's going to mend her, is it, Penny? Shall I bring you some vinegar and brown paper while I'm at it?'

Penny, thought Charlie, finally able to place the voice. 'I was trying to clear the, um, the . . .' She struggled to find the word she was looking for. It was skipping ahead of her just out of reach. 'Ivy. Yes, the ivy from the window. I thought I heard someone behind me but I don't know what happened. I think I was trying to get down but my sleeve got caught and the ladder just . . . I don't know, it seemed to collapse. I fell.'

'It's okay. Don't worry about that now. Is anything broken? Can you move your legs?' Penny asked.

Charlie winced. 'My wrist hurts. And my shoulder. But I'm fine.'

'Thank God.' It was the other female voice this time. 'Looks like you've escaped without any broken bones. Do you think you can walk? Let's get you inside, shall we?'

'Decca?' Charlie asked.

'That's right, my love. If she has no problem remembering me, I think we can rule out concussion,' said Decca.

'You've got a way of sticking in people's heads. And not always for the right reasons,' said Jack with a wink.

'Slowly now,' said Penny as Charlie started to get to her feet.

Charlie could see another set of feet behind Penny and Jack. Large scuffed black boots. But, whoever it was, they weren't speaking. She glanced down at the hole in the cuff of her jumper where the wool had pulled out of shape. She looked back to the boots. Was that the person who'd coughed? She sucked in her breath sharply through clenched teeth. She was in one piece and, apart from the throbbing in her shoulder, wrist and hip, she was relatively unscathed.

'I thought I heard someone behind me,' Charlie said, trying to peer around Penny who stood a couple of inches taller than she did.

Charlie put her hand on Penny's arm and pushed her gently to the side so she could see who was standing there. She let out a relieved sigh. It was only The Lad. There was no one to fear. Penny took hold of Charlie's shoulders to steer her towards the house.

'We should definitely get her checked over,' said Jack.

Charlie thought about going to a hospital. She imagined lying in crisp white sheets while nurses brought painkillers and food. There was a lot to be said for lying in bed all day, encouraged to do nothing, but then she thought about the questions they would ask. Name, date of birth, GP's surgery. The answers were the ends of pieces of string that, once pulled, would lead to her unravelling. Just like her jumper. She only needed to be caught out once.

Charlie said, 'I'm fine, really. Just a bit sore.'

'Let's put the kettle on,' said Decca. 'Get your feet up.' She stood on the opposite side of Charlie and took her arm.

Charlie tried to pull her arm away but, now she had hold of it, Decca held firm with strong fingers. Jack pushed open the back door and ushered her in to her own house. She was slow and tentative while she worked out which bit hurt the most. She sat on one of the wooden dining chairs and cried out. She'd found where she was going to have a bruise tomorrow.

Jack put his hands on his hips.

'You're lucky you've not broken anything,' he said. 'When I came round the corner and saw you lying there . . . well, I was just glad to see you breathing.'

'I thought someone was behind me. I turned to see them but I got my sleeve caught and . . .'

'I reckon you didn't put the safety catch on,' Jack said.

'I did. I know I did. I remember doing it. Do you think someone could have undone it when I went to get the bucket?'

Jack tilted his head and asked her, 'Why would someone do something like that? Did you see anyone?'

Charlie looked from Jack's frown to Penny's sympathetic gaze and wished one of them would believe her.

'There was a couple. Walkers. They went by just before I went up the ladder,' said Charlie. 'Peter was there too. He might have seen something.'

'I'll ask him,' said Jack. 'But I didn't see anyone when I came out.'

'I didn't see anyone either,' Penny said. 'I was cleaning the windows over at Chi an Mor when I heard Jack shout. I'd have seen if there'd been anyone else on the lane. I've only been here a few months but I'm not aware of us having had any problems with walkers in the village before. Have we, Decca?' Penny asked as the older woman walked into the room.

'None that I know of, my love,' said Decca.

'Hold on,' said Jack. 'What about the time someone set fire to the church?'

'Hardly the same thing,' said Decca with a roll of her eyes as she went back to the kitchen.

'It's an old ladder,' Penny said. 'The catch probably broke. Please don't go up it again, Charlie. It needs throwing away. Perhaps Jack could clear that ivy for you? What do you say, Jack?'

'Aye, why not? I've got a ladder on the van and I can take a proper look at that window when I'm up there. I'll take a look around while I'm at it; see if I can spot anyone hanging around who shouldn't be here.'

'Thanks, Jack. I appreciate it,' said Charlie.

'I'm putting sugar in your tea. For the shock,' called Decca from the kitchen over the sound of the kettle rumbling to boiling point.

Charlie wanted to cry. It was silly really; she wasn't even that badly injured. But she wouldn't let herself fall apart in front of people she barely knew. She'd learned that from prison. Tears were private and best reserved for the dark where they could fall freely without judgement. Charlie knew they were only a kind comment away, but she wouldn't break. She tried to busy her mind, to give it something to do before she let it consider all the things she was scared of. She couldn't let her mind go down that path. It might get lost and never come back again.

'Do you have any ice for your injuries?' asked Penny, gesturing towards the kitchen where she assumed the freezer resided.

'I don't even have a fridge,' replied Charlie. 'You'll find the milk in a box outside the back door.'

A new fridge was high on her list. She had planned to go into the nearest big town this weekend but, judging by the ache in her hip, she wouldn't be driving anywhere for the next few days. At least, with the weather likely to get a whole lot colder before it got any warmer, she didn't have to worry about things going off.

'Oh,' said Penny.

It was just a small word but she lengthened it and let it cover an octave from high to low before it was done with. *Oh* conveyed that she felt that it was unacceptable to be without a fridge. *Oh* suggested that people who kept perishable food in boxes outside of back doors were asking for trouble, and *Oh* indicated that she didn't want Charlie to know that she was thinking any of those things.

'I'll just help Decca with the tea. Let her know where you keep the,' she frowned as if she still couldn't quite believe it herself, 'milk.'

Charlie could hear Jack and The Lad at the upstairs window. There was the rasping sound like a plaster being pulled off taut skin again and again as they tore down the ivy. Occasionally there would be the rumble of small stones scuttling down the walls as the mortar came away with the long, thin fingers that stuck fast to the wall.

Penny carried two cups of strong, orange tea into the room. She was wearing fine frown-lines on her forehead.

'I was just thinking,' she said. 'I've got an old fridge you can have if you want? I was going to get the council to take it, but . . . What d'you think?' She held her mug in both hands and it obscured the bottom half of her face. Charlie remembered that mug, it was one of a pair that her parents had bought her when she first moved out. The other one was long gone, just like her parents.

'Thanks, but I couldn't accept that. It's far too generous of you.'

'Generous?' Decca came into the room and looked around for somewhere to sit. In the end she leaned against the window ledge, and said, 'You'd be doing her a favour. Saves paying for an advert in the Parish magazine. And, do you know, the council charges an arm and a leg to get these things taken away?'

'And there's nothing wrong with the fridge either,' Penny said. 'I wanted a bigger freezer, that's all.'

Charlie hesitated. She needed a fridge and Penny was giving one away. It should have been a straightforward decision. The only problem was, she couldn't help but think she was manoeuvring herself into Penny's debt. She was conflicted. Charlie wanted to keep people at arm's length so that they didn't find out too much about her, and she didn't let her guard down. Of course, she hadn't planned on falling from a ladder or on having such lovely people offer to help her.

Penny sipped at her cup of tea, leaving a stain of red lipstick on its rim. Charlie knew she'd made her feel uncomfortable by refusing the offer but how could she explain to Penny that she wasn't used to such generosity without expecting to give something in return? How could she make her see that she had nothing left to give?

'Actually,' Charlie said, making up her mind, 'if you're sure that's okay, I'd love to take you up on your offer.'

Penny nodded. 'Fabulous! I don't think I can shift it on my own. I wonder if I can borrow one of those trolley things?' She looked up at Decca but the other woman just shrugged.

'Jenn might have one. Or Jack,' Decca said.

'You're in no great rush, are you?' Penny asked Charlie. 'It might take me a while to get it shifted, but I'll get it to you as soon as I can.'

Charlie shook her head. 'No rush.'

'Now,' said Decca, 'what can I do for you before I get back? Can I get you some lunch? Soup? A sandwich?'

'No, really, I'm fine. Thanks.'

'No one is fine after falling off a ladder, Charlie. So stop being stubborn and take help where it's offered.' Decca wagged a finger at her and Charlie smiled.

No, she wasn't fine. She was bruised and embarrassed but it could have been so much worse. Her over-active imagination was likely to get her killed before anyone found out who she really was. She couldn't jump at every unexplained noise.

Jack and The Lad loaded up their van but not before Jack tutted and sighed and told her she'd need a new roof before long. Decca and Penny made Charlie another cup of tea and threw half the contents of her make-do cupboard into something resembling a casserole, which would last her a few days at least. They disappeared after the narrowing light with promises to check on her later in the week.

Charlie could see the kitchen floor from where she was sitting, and the light streaming in through the new window. The floor was now a deep blood red where, before, it had been the brown of dark chocolate. She marvelled at the difference the late-afternoon light had made. Hidden in the shadows, the floor had been dismal and dirty but the exposure to natural light had given it new life. It wasn't recognisable as the same floor as before. Perhaps the same could be said for her. If she kept to the shadows she was going to be tarnished, but if she stepped forward into the light, made more of an effort to join in, then she wouldn't look like someone who was hiding.

She would feel a lot safer now she'd had the window repaired. Perhaps she could unpack the rest of her things and get a sofa so it could start to feel a bit more like home.

Home.

It was a long time since she'd felt able to call a place that.

CHAPTER EIGHTEEN

You looked different to how I remembered you. For a moment I thought I'd made a terrible mistake but, when you spoke, my uncertainty vanished. I'd know that voice anywhere, though I see that the tremor you faked in court has disappeared.

You're smaller. Diminished, somehow. Prison has taken away your curves and replaced them with the angles of an adolescent boy.

Your attempts at camouflage are good, but not quite good enough. You're trying to blend into the background, but I can still see you because my eyes have grown accustomed to the illusion. You were never what you seemed.

Do you ever think about the lives you destroyed? It worries me, this thought that you don't have a conscience. The world is full of people like you who think they can walk all over everyone else without consequence. I was so insignificant to you that, even now, you don't see me.

But I see you.

And now I'm here, watching you. You must want me to look at you or you wouldn't sit in the cottage with the light on and no curtains at the window. You can't bear to be invisible, can you?

If no one is watching you, do you even exist?

You looked out of the window then, and I almost ducked behind a tree, but all you see is your own reflection. You are the leading lady in your own play. A one-woman monologue about how life has done you wrong.

What would the papers say if they could see you now? Imagine the outrage as they tell the world how you now live a peaceful life in an idyllic cottage by the coast. What would your neighbours say if they knew exactly who they were inviting into their homes? I won't tell them if you won't.

Your secret is safe with me.

For now.

CHAPTER NINETEEN

Charlie Miller

Thursday, 25 October 2018

Charlie lay in bed and listened to the rain. She felt safer now the new window was in but it hadn't resulted in more restful sleep.

Jack had removed the ivy from the outside wall, and the bathroom window now closed properly for the first time since she'd moved in. It was quieter and warmer with latches latched and locks locked, but still she couldn't persuade her muscles to soften or her mind to quieten.

Noises in the countryside were alien to her. She wasn't used to the constant sounds, the rustling in the trees, the distant hush of the sea, the call of the gulls. But she'd been living with the whispering in her head, the constant fear that someone was going to hurt her, for two years.

No matter how much Charlie thought about it, she couldn't make sense of what had happened. Breezes in the trees didn't clear their throats. Rabbits in the undergrowth didn't crunch gravel under their paws. Charlie's imagination didn't undo safety catches on ladders. And yet there had been no one else there and everything pointed to the safety catch having not been on in the first place.

Even without the accident giving her mind something to mull over, the aching in her hip would have kept her awake. The outside of Charlie's head ached from where she'd smacked it off the ground and the inside of it throbbed from lack of sleep and an over-active imagination.

She wished she had painkillers in the house but she didn't even have a first-aid kit. It would be a miracle if she didn't pick up a few cuts and scrapes while she was renovating the house and she didn't have so much as a plaster. Charlie's mum had thrown out every aspirin and paracetamol in the house as soon as Lee was arrested. She feared that Charlie would take them all in the middle of the night. Anything to get away from the pain. Charlie told her there was no need but her mum had said, 'Better to be safe than sorry.'

It was a mantra she should have taken to heart a lot sooner. Now she was living in a remote part of the country with no friends, no family and no sense of what the future held for her. She wasn't safe, but, my God, she was sorry.

The truth was, Charlie was desperate. She'd been hurting and wished she drank or did drugs so that she could leave her own sorry existence behind for a while. But she would never have taken her own life.

Giving up on the futile battle for sleep, Charlie pulled a sweatshirt on over her pyjamas and hobbled to the window. The rain was steady enough that the edges of the church spire had blurred and the far side of the valley was only a pale grey outline. On another, pre-prison day her mood would have mirrored the weather. But now she marvelled at its power.

The rain fell from a cloud-filled sky into a makeshift stream running freely down the path towards the lane. Constant and rhythmic, it blended into the background as Charlie hobbled from room to room. She'd planned on going to the nearest city or big town to buy some furniture but, even if her stiff hip and leg hadn't precluded it, she didn't fancy trying to navigate narrow Cornish lanes in this rain.

Too sore to work on the house and too stiff to drive anywhere, Charlie picked up her phone and held it in the air. If she could find the elixir of full mobile coverage she would do some online research. She wanted to see if the papers were still writing about her and, if possible, find out whether Marcus had any reason to recognise her. She found the signal to be strongest in the room with the stained floorboards. She hovered on the threshold. She tried not to study the suspicious brown spot at the centre of the room, but her imagination was in overdrive. Everything from ritual sacrifices to gruesome murder played across her mind.

She searched for any articles and photos associated with her case, with Lee's case. She looked for pictures of the families who'd been in court watching her and Lee's every move. Any one of them could turn up in Penderrion if they found out where she was. Strangers from across the country could book the holiday cottages on the other side of the lane and recognise her face.

Anna Atkins had a vocal and angry brother, a quiet but broken uncle and an ex-husband who believed it would have been only a matter of time until they reconciled. Charlie remembered his letters to her in prison. He had a particularly wide-ranging and colourful vocabulary.

She had wanted to reach out to him and tell him that she would have given anything for Anna to have her life back but, when she sat down in prison to reply to him, her words weren't enough and so she screwed her efforts up and threw them in the bin. If she'd been better at expressing herself, she would have tried to comfort those that wrote to her in pain, reasoned with those who wrote to her in anger, and defended herself against those who attacked her.

If anyone wanted to do her harm it was probably one of these three. But why would they sneak around outside her house taking catches off ladders? Besides, they couldn't have found out where she was so quickly, unless someone had told them. The only person who could have done that was Conor and she was as sure as she could be that he would never betray her.

No one knew where she was hiding except Conor and her solicitor, Hal. They had no reason to come after her, or to let anyone know where she was. She knew she had to work hard to fit in and make sure everyone knew her recently crafted backstory. If Marcus thought she looked familiar she would just have to shrug it off and make him believe that it was a coincidence. He couldn't prove that Charlie Miller and Steffi Finn were one and the same.

Unless, of course, Lee turned up. He wouldn't mistake her for anyone else. Though he had an appeal pending there was no chance he would get out. The evidence against him had been overwhelming.

She imagined finding Lee looking in at the window, but, even if he'd scaled the wall and escaped from prison, she was miles away from anywhere he'd look. If there was any justice, they'd never let him out, but fairness was a fairy tale that only the naïve and the young believed in.

Charlie tapped the corner of the phone on her lips. There was a chance that Lee could have paid somebody to work on his behalf to track her down. He'd always been persuasive and he was angry enough with her for going to the police in the first place. There'd been a group of women outside the courtroom, hoping for a glimpse of him, proclaiming his innocence. It was as if he'd hired a PR team when he hired a solicitor. He gave an interview saying he wept for the murdered women and that he feared that others were in danger because the police had wrongly charged him with the crimes. The real murderer was still out there, he said. Most people saw straight through him, but the small group who believed his every word were louder than all the rest. Charlie had been one of those gullible fools once. She almost wished for that blissful ignorance again.

Since she'd been in Penderrion the only two people who looked like they might have recognised her were Marcus and The Lad. Jack's sidekick was the wrong age to have anything to do with the victims: too old to be Anna's son, too young to be her brother. She was being paranoid. Marcus, though, was a different matter. Decca said he was a lawyer. Had he been involved somehow? Had he followed the case? She wanted to find out more about him but she didn't know any of her neighbours' surnames.

A loud knock at the back door made Charlie jump. She was wondering whether she should answer it or pretend she wasn't in when she heard the door open. She clutched her mobile and tiptoed on to the landing, listening to the door scrape over the kitchen tiles.

A woman's voice called up the stairs.

'Hello? Charlie? Are you in?'

Charlie bowed her head. Just Penny.

'Coming,' she replied.

Charlie cleared the search history on her phone and switched it off before slowly and clumsily going down the stairs. She paused, out of sight, to watch Penny hang her yellow rain mac on the back of the door and divest herself of layer after layer of waterproofs and warmth. Becoming smaller with each unwrapping, like a Russian doll.

Charlie smiled as she walked into the kitchen but suddenly froze.

'Marcus,' she said. 'I didn't know you were—'

'Ta-daa!' Penny said grandly. 'The fridge was a lot heavier than I expected. I asked Marcus to help me lift it into the car and he gallantly stepped in and offered to drive it over himself.'

Marcus's leather jacket was glistening with the rain and his hair was wet.

'Oh,' Charlie said, 'that's very kind of you.'

Marcus smiled and said, 'I couldn't resist the opportunity to come over. I was curious to have a look inside the cottage. You don't mind, do you?'

Charlie smiled, shook her head. 'Of course not; be my guest. Though I should warn you it's a bit of a mess.'

She wrapped her arms around her body, suddenly very conscious of the fact she wasn't wearing any underwear and hadn't brushed her hair.

'How are the aches this morning?' Penny asked.

'Not too bad. I seem to have stiffened up, but the swelling in my wrist has gone down.'

'God, yes, I heard about the fall. Nasty business,' said Marcus, walking past her and peering into the living room. She saw the curl of his top lip and the furrow between his brows. 'Jenn wanted to rush over as soon as she heard but I told her that the last thing you needed was her flapping about.'

She watched as he disappeared upstairs and felt self-conscious about her unmade bed and her unpacked boxes. Not that she wanted to agree with Marcus, but Charlie was glad that no one else had come by to see her. Knowing that Jenn had expressed an interest in wanting to come was enough. Charlie hadn't yet got the measure of her. She was polite, welcoming, but gave away very little about herself. Charlie could hardly complain, it wasn't like she'd given away much of herself either. With Decca, Bo and Penny she was able to relax a little, and the same could be said for Aubrey. They were the kind of people who made you smile just to be around them and they all had a quirkiness about them that made them outsiders too. Penny was relatively new to the village, so she knew what it was like to try to fit into a community as close knit as this one.

Charlie would get used to her other neighbours eventually; perhaps she'd even stop assuming they were out to get her. But that would take time, and she was reaching the limit of coherent small talk with people she barely knew. It was all moving a little fast for her, even though her best chance of flying below the radar was to embrace her new community.

Charlie went over to the small white fridge and crouched down. She immediately wished she hadn't, as a sharp pain shot up her back.

'You were throwing this out?' she asked Penny. 'But it's perfect.'

It had a small freezer compartment barely big enough for ice and a box of fish-fingers. It was more than she needed. Penny took the milk, the chocolate, the butter and the cheese from the cool box that had been outside the back door and placed them in the fridge.

'There,' she said. 'And there's already plenty of ice in the freezer section in case of any more swellings.'

Charlie was suddenly, and awkwardly, aware that she had little to put in the fridge. Her life didn't work that way any more. With difficulty she stood back up and saw that Marcus had come back downstairs and was staring at her.

'That bathroom is going to need a lot of work, isn't it? I've got the number of a good plumber if you want it. You know, I was tempted to buy this place myself when it came up at auction. I wanted to turn it into three holiday lets but I couldn't get the planning permission. I'd forgotten what a state it was.'

'Yes,' said Charlie, 'it's quite the project, which is why I bought it. I wanted something that I could do myself.'

'Really? I imagine it put a fair few people off. The sale went through months ago, though. Why has it taken you so long to move down here?'

'I had to . . . work out my notice.'

'Still, you could've got someone in to start the work,' he said.

'As I said, I wanted to do it myself.'

Marcus raised an eyebrow, though Charlie couldn't tell if it was because he doubted what she said or just thought she was crazy.

'Anyway, much as I'd love to stay and chat . . .' He pushed past her and patted his pocket for car keys.

'I've got a conference call at ten so I'd better be off,' he said to Penny.

'Thanks for helping with the fridge,' she said.

'No problem.'

Before he disappeared into the rain, Marcus turned and said, 'Oh, and Charlie? Try to be more careful climbing ladders. Next time you might not be so lucky.'

CHAPTER TWENTY

Ben Jarvis

Thursday, 25 October 2018

Ben was so close. The estate agent said they'd still not managed to get hold of the vendor but thanked him for his patience. It appeared that Steffi hadn't given her solicitor her new phone number so they'd have to do it the old-fashioned way and write to her. Miss Finn was playing it clever. No phone line, not even a mobile number for her dear friend and solicitor Conor Fletcher. She was playing hard to get.

Patience was one of the many things Ben was running out of – along with food and money. The same could not be said for Finn, though. The bank statement he'd taken from her house in Pinchdale told him that she wasn't having to live on her overdraft like he was. She might not be rolling in money but she had more of everything than he did. More cash, more freedom, more future.

She'd set up a few direct debits and a standing order as if she deserved to build a new life. The most recent transactions were three weeks old now but they almost made him smile.

There was a large transaction at a service station in Bristol. He judged it the approximate price of a full tank of diesel. Where had she been and where was she going? And then the following day she spent £64.53 on groceries in Asda, and the day after, had taken £250 cash out of a bank. Both the bank and the supermarket were in St Austell, Cornwall.

She'd fled down south. Now all he had to do was pinpoint where. She was probably still in Cornwall. That much shopping for one person would last her for longer than a long weekend at the beach. He was almost certain she was living there for the time being but he needed to act quickly before she moved on.

He paced the floor, with his hands stuffed deep into his pockets. He had a lead. Of course, she might just have been passing through Cornwall, it didn't mean she was definitely still there. What if she'd only gone there for a holiday after getting out of prison? No. He couldn't let himself think like that.

No.

He had to trust his instincts. They'd never let him down yet.

But what now?

He took out his phone and googled the words *Finn, St Austell*. But nothing much came up. There was no trace of Finn yet but she probably wasn't using her real name. It might take two months or two years but he would get his show-down with Steffi Finn. Perhaps he should just go down there? He was being kicked out of the bedsit anyway.

If only he could be sure she was in Cornwall.

He brought up another number that he'd saved into his contacts and pressed the call symbol. And then he waited to be put through to the conveyancing department at Hunt, Fellows & Bartlett.

'Hello?' A man's voice, young but professional. Ben could almost hear the crisp white collar and the skinny suit.

'Hi, yeah, it's Ryan here, from Moyes and Co estate agents,' said Ben into the telephone, mimicking Ryan's easy style. 'Who's that?'

'It's Christopher.'

'All right, mate? Look, I've been at the Finn house, yeah. You're dealing with the house sale, right?'

'Well, not me personally but—'

'No, but it's your department, yeah? Conor said you were the man to talk to.'

He knew he was taking a big risk but Conor would likely be shut away in his own corner office rather than sitting with the more junior members of staff.

'Two things,' said Ben before Christopher could doubt him. 'First, this fella who's put an offer in on the house. I reckon he's getting cold feet, mate. I don't suppose you've heard back from the vendor, have you?'

'Sorry, not yet.'

'Could you chase her, yeah? It's been a slow one, this. I don't want to lose this offer. Second, there's a pile of mail here for her. Conor had said to post anything straight on to her. Problem is, I've got it all in an envelope on my desk and can't find what I've done with Miss Finn's address. Can you let me have it again and I'll get this in the post to her?'

'I don't know whether we . . . I've not had much to do with this. Let me just get the file.'

Ben waited while Christopher looked for the information. He tapped his pen on his leg impatiently and looked around the room at what was left of his life. All his belongings would fit into two rucksacks and a bin liner. It wasn't much to show for having been on this earth for nearly five decades.

'Hello, Ryan?'

Ben blinked. For a moment he'd forgotten who he was pretending to be. 'Yeah, mate. I'm here.'

'I'm not sure I'm allowed to give out information about—'

'Mate, let me tell you something, you absolutely cannot give that information out to just anyone who phones up. You, me and Conor are the only people who should have that address. Okay? It's important that Steffi is given the confidentiality she deserves. Am I right?'

'Absolutely. It's just Conor didn't say anything to me about . . .'

Ben was going to have to take a risk if he was going to convince Christopher that he should share the information with him.

'Let me confirm this with you, Chris. She's in Cornwall, isn't she? How would I know that if Conor hadn't told me already? Eh? Now just give me the address again and I'll get these in the post to her. It's St Austell, right?'

'Yeah, it is. Okay, have you got a pen?'

Ben let out a deep breath. He was right. She was in Cornwall and he was getting closer. 'Yes, mate. Go ahead.'

'Okay. It's The B— Oh, Conor's just walked in. Do you want to talk to him?'

'No, don't disturb him. You go ahead and give me the address.'

He heard a man's voice in the background and clenched his teeth as Christopher covered the mouthpiece. There was a moment's silence and then a different man's voice came on the phone.

'Hello? Who is this?'

Ben put the phone down quickly, as if stung, and stared at it.

So close.

She was definitely in St Austell.

CHAPTER TWENTY-ONE

Charlie Miller

Friday, 26 October 2018

Charlie pulled her brand-new recycling bin to the side of the road like she'd seen the others do. The council had delivered it the day before and it was already full of cardboard from the moving boxes and the packaging from her kettle and toaster. She felt oddly excited by this normal, boring and practical act of a person who was free and living in their own home. Recycling was such a grown-up, responsible thing to do. She found herself feeling a little smug.

She looked over the valley, away from the sea. How did they get the bin lorries down the Cornish lanes? She wasn't confident squeezing her little car between the hedgerows. There must be a trick to driving on these roads.

Aubrey hadn't put his bin out yet and Charlie thought she could hear the rumble of a bin lorry in the distance. She hesitated. It was the neighbourly thing to do, right? If she put his recycling out for him, it would be seen as a good thing. It was what people did for their elderly neighbours.

On the other hand, in the spirit of keeping herself to herself, why was it anything to do with her if he put his bin out or not? Surely it wasn't her problem if it wasn't collected this week. How was she even to know whether her neighbour recycled anything? Judging by the piles of newspapers around the bungalow, it was safe to assume he didn't.

First, she knocked on his door to check he was okay and to remind him it was Friday. It was easy to forget which day it was even if you weren't an octogenarian. Charlie did it all the time. It couldn't do any harm to put his bin out. Not even her grumpy old neighbour could object to that.

She took the brick off the bin lid that was weighing it down against wind and wild animals and dragged his bin along the path and out to the road. She lined it up next to hers. Satisfied.

She headed back towards the cottage, and she was certain she could hear the bin lorries now. Could Aubrey hear them too? He definitely put his bin out last week; Charlie had heard it being dragged down the path. It was odd that he hadn't answered the door when she knocked. His hearing wasn't great, though, she'd noticed that.

Did he ever go out? He didn't have a car and she would have noticed if anyone had come by to pick him up. Of course, he could have been in the bathroom when she knocked. Perhaps she should try again. Just to make sure.

She tried to ignore the negative thoughts scampering across her mind. What if he's hurt? What if he needs help? What if, what if, what if . . . ?

She could feel the tremble of panic in her chest. To put her own mind at rest she had to knock again.

'Aubrey?' she shouted as she knocked as loud as she could on the door. She pressed her ear against the glass but couldn't hear anything.

She walked around the house, peering through windows. In the kitchen there were fat, pink sausages on the side. The fridge door was slightly open, casting a wedge of light on the floor. Charlie looked about her, but there was no one to ask for advice. She could have ignored the fact that Aubrey had not put his bin out, could have forgiven him for not answering the door, but it wasn't normal to leave your fridge door open. Something didn't feel right, and, now she was aware of it, she couldn't walk away.

Charlie tried the handle on the back door and found it unlocked. She snatched her hand back as the door slowly inched its way open. Still she didn't step into the house. With one hand on the door frame she leaned into the kitchen.

'Aubrey?'

Silence.

'Aubrey, it's Charlie from next door. Are you okay?'

There was no sound of movement, no radio, no television, no sound of a shower running. She sniffed the air. There was the faint smell of something starting to decay.

'Aubrey, I'm coming in. Is that okay?'

She threw another look over her shoulder, wondered about running to get help but she didn't even know what help she needed or who she could ask.

She stepped into the kitchen and instinctively closed the fridge. She hoped that the bad smell was coming from there. In the living room there was a half-drunk cup of tea on the sideboard. When she touched it, it was cold and a thick film had formed on the top of the liquid. She went through the only other door. It went into another corridor with two rooms off it. The first was an empty bathroom, the second was a bedroom. Piles of newspapers were on the floor and the curtains were still closed. Charlie was turning to go when she noticed something move.

'Shit!'

Aubrey was coiled on the floor between the wall and the bed.

'Aubrey!'

She threw herself down next to him. His eyes opened, blinked rapidly and closed again.

'Aubrey, thank God! Are you okay?'

'Do I look okay?' he croaked.

She leaned over him and closed her eyes with relief. At least he was conscious.

'I'm going to call an ambulance,' she said.

She placed her open palm on his cheek. He was cold to the touch.

'No!' Aubrey started coughing. 'No. No ambulance.'

She dragged the quilt off his bed and covered him with it, slipped a pillow under his head.

'But Aubrey, you're hurt. I have to get help.'

'I'm not hurt. An old injury, that's all. My knee. Don't call an ambulance. They'll never let me out again,' he wheezed.

'Don't be ridiculous, Aubrey, I have to—'

Aubrey grabbed Charlie's wrist. His grasp was stronger than she'd expected. He lifted his head off the pillow. 'Please. I'm begging you. Don't call them. Don't let them take me away.'

She helped him sit up. He wasn't as heavy as he should have been for a man of his height.

'Bathroom,' he murmured. 'I've . . .'

Charlie could smell it. 'It's okay. Let me get behind you and I'll lift you up.'

He couldn't put any weight on his knee but, with his walking stick on one side and Charlie on the other, he managed to get to the bathroom to get cleaned up.

It was embarrassing to them both, but necessary. The humiliation in the old man's eyes made Charlie cover her own emotions with a smile and the gentlest of words. She averted her eyes and passed him clean towels, fresh pyjamas and a soft cardigan that hung loosely off him as she half carried him back to bed.

'Are you eating properly?' she asked.

'What's that?' he asked, straining to hear her.

Charlie kept forgetting to speak loudly to him. His hearing was poor and her words had lost some of their confidence. It wasn't a good combination.

She told him that she could feel his angular bones through his shirt, that he wasn't difficult to lift up. Naturally she assumed that he must have lost some weight.

'I'll be sure to leave a pack of Jammie Dodgers under the bed for next time,' he said with a roll of his eyes.

Charlie settled him under the duvet and brought him a cup of tea that she held out of his reach until he drank a glass of orange juice.

'You're dehydrated,' she said.

Aubrey grumbled but drank the juice quickly and put his hand out for the tea.

'I was stupid,' he said. 'I'd been looking for a box of photos on the top of the wardrobe. Wanted to see some more pictures of Mary-Jane but I fell off the step. Got the photo I'd been looking for, though. I won't be doing that again, will I? Just because I fell doesn't mean I can't look after myself.'

Aubrey's plea for her not to call an ambulance had touched Charlie's heart, but she wasn't making any promises. If hospital was the best place for him, he'd have to go.

'No one said anything about you not being able to look after yourself. I'm not a doctor. For all I know that leg could be broken. If I promise to bring you back again, will you let me drive you to the hospital?'

'Stop your fussing, woman. I'm fine.'

'How long had you been lying there?' she asked him.

'An hour or two, that's all.'

'I don't believe you. You've been there for at least a day. Probably two.'

Aubrey tried to straighten his leg and Charlie watched him scowl at the pain. He was elderly but he wasn't fragile. The advancing years had taken the sharpness from his hearing and his eyesight but not his mind. He was fully aware that his body was beginning to let him down. There was grief in his eyes, mourning the loss of his strength and vitality.

If he was assessed by the hospital as being unfit to live alone, he'd be placed in a facility where he could get the support he needed. He had no family, except a niece he wasn't close to. Charlie understood why he didn't want other people making decisions for him and cooking his meals. She'd experienced that first hand in prison and she doubted it got any easier with age. He'd earned his right to live in his own home. She knew what it felt like to leave a home you loved and know that you would never see it again, but unless she could make living here easier for him, he'd have no choice.

'Right,' she said, 'I'm going to put grab rails in your bathroom and by your doors, okay? We are going to have to get rid of these old newspapers and the rest of the clutter, too. It's a fire hazard and you could trip over any number of things. If you break a hip you're going to hospital and there's not much

I can do for you. If you don't help me to help you, then I'm going to have to call someone to come in here and look after you. Is that clear?'

He scowled. 'Haven't you got enough to do without making me a pet project?' he asked.

'Yes, I have, but my kitchen units aren't as important as making sure you can carry on living in your own home, are they? Besides, I'm having to take it easy. Still a bit stiff myself from when I fell.'

'What did you say?'

'I said, I fell off a ladder. I was trying to clear ivy off the back of the cottage but I used an old ladder and I guess it broke.' If she said it enough, perhaps Charlie could convince herself that's all there was to it.

'You know,' Charlie went on, 'I think you're probably entitled to some money from the local authority to make the house safer for you. I can look into it for you, if you like?'

'And what if they decide that they can't make the house safe enough? Then you'll have to put a target on my back.'

'What have you got against care homes anyway? My grandfather loved his. He ran a gambling racket out of it. The staff thought the residents were having nice sedate games of dominoes while Gramps was taking bets.'

'Sounds like a good man.'

'He was. I think you two would've got on a bit too well.'

Aubrey sighed and pulled a tissue out of his sleeve. He dabbed it at the end of his nose and then put it away again. Time enough for him to make sense of those thoughts in his head.

'It's not because I'm old,' he said. 'People trip up every day. D'ya hear me?' He wasn't shouting, but his voice was louder.

'You took a tumble off that ladder,' he continued, 'but is anyone saying you're not okay to look after yourself? Anyone calling you old?'

'No one's said anything about your age, Aubrey. And, for the record, I question whether I'm all right to look after myself sometimes. It's got nothing to do with how old you are. Some things are beyond you. Beyond all of us. If you're lucky you can push on and deal with it yourself, surprise yourself with what you can do. All I'm saying is let me make life easier for you. It doesn't have to be a constant battle.'

'But no hospitals,' he said.

'Unless they have a cure for stubbornness, they wouldn't be much use to you right now anyway,' Charlie said. 'But if you fall and break something, I'm calling an ambulance. If you don't want to fall and break something, stop climbing up on top of wardrobes. Deal?'

'Women,' he said, shaking his head sadly. 'Are you always like this? Because maybe this is why you don't have a husband.'

'Men,' she countered. 'Are *you* always like this? Because perhaps that's why I don't *want* one.'

Aubrey's eyes creased at the corners and he let out a small laugh. Charlie put another blanket on his bed and straightened the duvet. He was still cold and the heating hadn't yet reached throughout the room. She picked up a photo from the side of his bed. It was a wedding photo, stiff and formal, a huge bouquet of flowers at the centre.

'Is this your wife?' she asked.

'No,' Aubrey said. 'I make a habit of having wedding photos of strangers all about my house.'

Charlie tutted. 'She was quite a looker. In fact,' she brought the picture closer to her face, 'you both were. Look at your hair!'

Aubrey's hair was in an Elvis-like quiff and he was wearing thick-soled shoes that made him tower over his equally big-haired bride.

The old man smiled. 'And I haven't changed one little bit.'

Charlie placed the picture back carefully. 'If you believe that, we need to get you to an optician's.'

The old man laughed. It was a comforting sound.

Aubrey patted his cardigan like he was searching for something. He slipped his hand into his pocket and it closed around the black-and-white photo Charlie had seen him put there. His face softened, his eyes misty.

'There's no one left who understands,' he said. 'There's more past than future about me and there has been for far too long. I've not given much thought to it until lately. Sort of snuck up on me, it did. I was needed back then, useful. No matter how many dark days I had, I always had faith that better days were to come. I can't say that any more, can I? Now the only thing I can hope for is that I die peacefully in my sleep. You have no idea how that feels.'

CHAPTER TWENTY-TWO

Steffi Finn

Sunday, 24 July 2016

Sunday morning and Steffi was up early, cleaning the car. She found it relaxing, satisfying even. The soapy water trickled down the driveway and into the gutter.

Lee had been telling her all week that he'd noticed a strange smell in the car. She hadn't noticed anything except Lee's wrinkled-up nose and the fact he refused to drive it any more. You see, he said, they couldn't really think about selling it if it had *a funny smell*.

'Sell it?' she asked. She liked her car and had no reason to consider getting rid of it. It was only four years old and had less than thirty thousand miles on the clock.

'It's been a good year at work,' he said. 'I'm expecting a pretty big bonus and I was thinking that it might be a good time to get an upgrade.'

'An upgrade?' Steffi wasn't a fan of flash cars.

'When I say upgrade,' he grinned, 'I was thinking more of a spacious family car.'

Steffi's heart had fluttered and she'd felt giddy. Hopeful. It was enough to make her get the Vax machine out and shampoo the interior, boot and all. Things had been strained between her and Lee lately. They'd skirted around each other ever since the police had been sniffing about. Steffi had the impression that she had failed Lee somehow. Perhaps he'd seen the doubt in her eyes.

Now, though, they could put all that behind them and start planning for their future. The fact that Lee was talking about buying a family car – the kind of car that had room for a buggy in the boot – meant that he'd forgiven her for whatever she was meant to have done. They'd discussed having kids. It was a 'one day' topic. Like marriage. It was as if they both knew it was something that would happen to them in the future but she didn't want to tempt fate by mentioning it. She was a traditional girl at heart and she would have loved a white wedding and three kids, no, four. In fact, why stop there? She wanted to fill a house with children.

Steffi was surprised by exactly how excited she was. Her relationship with her own parents was difficult. Growing up as an only child was fine but it was never part of the plan. She'd had a younger brother who'd died when he was a baby and, though she was too young to remember him, she felt his loss. He never took his first steps nor threw his food around the room, and yet he took up more space than she did. The grief had made her parents crumble. They couldn't go through that again, they said. No more children.

Once, when her dad had been furious with her for failing her maths GCSE, he told her that the wrong child had died. He tried to take it back; even by his pretty low standards that was poor. But some things, once said, can never be taken back. Steffi didn't cry. At least now she knew what she'd always suspected. Even as an only child she wasn't her dad's favourite.

She'd never be able to live up to the vision of what Thomas could have been. Knowing that took some of the pressure off her. She stopped trying to impress her dad after that.

Steffi was just finishing up cleaning the car by polishing the hub caps when she heard the front door open. She looked up to see Lee come outside, holding his phone in his hand.

'Are you okay?' she asked.

Lee shook his head. 'They've found her body.'

She knew who he was talking about but still she had to ask. 'Whose body?'

'Katy Foster. I've been reading the news on my phone. A dog walker found her body this morning.'

'Oh, God. She's dead then?'

Lee nodded. 'Christ. I never even met her but I can't stop looking at the articles, the pictures of her. Perhaps if I'd seen her at that pub, spoken to her . . . Instead of sitting there judging them all for drinking too much, what if I'd struck up a conversation with her? Imagine how different it could have been.'

He rubbed his hand over his clean-shaven face. Even at a weekend he spent twenty minutes in the bathroom shaving and moisturising.

'Are you okay?' Steffi asked gently, going to him and putting her arms around his waist.

'I don't know. I'm not sure how to feel. I don't think I ever thought she'd turn up alive after all this time but, still, I hoped. Her poor parents. They must be devastated.'

'Let's go inside.'

They sat on the sofa, Steffi with her head on Lee's shoulder. She kissed his hand, stroked the hair from his face. It showed how big his heart was that he could be so affected by the death of a woman he had never met. He was going to make a great father.

The news came on the television and Katy's family filled the screen. They were distraught, her brother was angry. He had the same fine features, but his hair was darker, ash-blond. The murderer was sick, he said, twisted, he spat, and he would get what was coming to him. Someone must know something, and if anyone was hiding him, they were to come forward immediately. The police were offering a reward for information that would lead to an arrest, but, essentially, they were no closer to finding who was responsible.

'What kind of a person would need money to come forward?' Steffi asked. 'The only reason for ever keeping quiet about it would be because they were protecting someone they loved, I guess? I don't know. And surely no amount of money would be enough to turn in someone you love.'

The police were still looking for witnesses, and some of Katy's jewellery was missing. A post-mortem would be required to find out exactly how she'd died. Speculation at this time was unhelpful. Katy had been unlucky in love, the news reader said. She always picked the wrong sort. A number of dating sites carried her profile and the police were looking into this as a line of inquiry.

Steffi shook her head. She was so lucky that she didn't have to go on dates any more. Not only was there the trepidation of going on a date with someone you barely knew, but there was the added fear that they could turn out to be dangerous.

She was so lucky to have found Lee.

CHAPTER TWENTY-THREE

Charlie Miller

Saturday, 3 November 2018

Insomnia had Charlie out of bed and on her second cup of coffee while the morning was still a glint in the horizon's eye.

She opened one of her boxes and grabbed a jumper from the top of the pile. Her mother's handwriting was bold and black on the cardboard. *Winter clothes*. Charlie pushed her face into the folds of the fabric, breathing deeply and wanting so desperately for it to smell of home, but it only reminded her of dusty attics and long, damp winters.

She dressed quickly, before self-pity could take hold, grabbed her charity-shop coat and hat and stepped into the dawn. The cold morning air felt sharp in her lungs and the birdsong keener. For that moment the world seemed amplified and she wanted to believe she was the only person in it; that there was no one who could hurt her; that no one sleeping under this sky hated her enough to come looking for her.

In the first two weeks after being released from HMP Hillstone she used her mobile phone to search for the name Steffi Finn, to make sure no one was talking about her release, and that there weren't any rumours that she planned to move down south. But since being in Penderrion she'd stopped relentlessly checking for news. And it wasn't just because of the sketchy 4G coverage in the village.

She'd been a free woman for six weeks now. It simultaneously felt like a lifetime and the blink of an eye. Nothing in her life was the same as it had been and, in that regard, felt like a previous life. And yet, she was still growing into Charlie Miller with all the grace of a new-born foal. She was covering her tracks by paying for most things in cash and by not contacting anyone from her old life, but that didn't stop her old life from contacting her.

A letter from Conor, the day before, had unsettled her. He'd addressed it to Charlie Miller, even though she was a stranger to him. She'd felt sick when she'd seen the letter on the mat and almost threw it in the bin but she recognised the thick cream paper and elaborate script as being from Hunt, Fellows & Bartlett. It was perfectly professional and stuck to the facts. An offer on the house. Was she happy to proceed? Could they have a phone number for their files?

She didn't know whether she was relieved or upset by the impersonal nature of the letter, but it gave her a renewed impetus to anchor herself in Penderrion and make more of her life here. She wouldn't be sucked back into her old existence.

She'd spent the night trying to imagine what her future would look like and found it almost impossible because she was scared to envisage it, terrified that it could be taken from her at any moment, but she couldn't keep living in fear, because that wasn't living at all.

It occurred to her that she still hadn't embraced the fact that she was lucky enough to live by the sea. She hadn't walked along the beach or found inspiration in the sun rising over the waves. She'd checked the tidal times online and knew that, in ten minutes, it would be low tide and the creamy beach would be exposed, leaving behind rock pools and driftwood.

She walked down the lane, watching gulls soar overhead and taking lungfuls of sea-salted air. It was a clear dawn and the birds were singing just for her. There were no signs of anyone stirring in the neat houses as she passed them. Charlie pictured her neighbours sleeping soundly in their beds. Jealousy flickered within her for a moment but she wouldn't have swapped this feeling of being out in the dawn – not even for a solid eight hours of sleep.

Decca had offered to take her round door to door to introduce her to people in the village but Charlie had politely declined. She'd meet them all in time. Charlie hoped to nestle into the village without causing a fuss. The last thing she wanted was to bring attention to herself.

She heard the sound of a door slam and glanced over her shoulder. Annoyance creased her brow. One of the perks of being up so early was that she wouldn't bump into anyone else on her walk.

She saw Penny coming out of Decca's house with Coco and Baldrick pulling her towards the lane. It looked like she was the one on the leash, not the dogs. Penny was speaking quietly to them and checking her pockets for something. She hadn't spotted Charlie yet. Even at such an early hour Penny was wearing her signature red lipstick and looked remarkably well put together.

Charlie could quicken her pace, pretend that she hadn't noticed the other woman, but that could ruin a friendship that had barely begun. And, God knows, she could do with a friend or two.

She raised a tentative hand as Penny looked up. She looked surprised, but happy, to see her and let the dogs drag her in Charlie's direction as she leaned backwards to anchor herself against toppling over with the force of their enthusiasm.

'Hey! What are you doing up so early?' she asked. 'Coco, down!'

Charlie bent over to meet the dogs' excitement halfway and got headbutted in the chin by Baldrick who was muscling in for some attention.

'Couldn't sleep,' Charlie said. 'Thought I'd head down to the beach.'

'Do you mind some company?' asked Penny.

'Not at all.'

And she didn't. After her initial disappointment that someone else was awake and about to break the silence, she had been pleased to see that it was Penny.

'Decca's sister isn't well,' said Penny. 'She's gone to see her in hospital up in Bath so I said I'd keep an eye on the dogs. I'd have them at my house but they'd trash the place. One wag of Baldrick's tail is enough to knock cups clean off the tables. I feel terrible that they've been on their own overnight.'

'Sorry to hear that. About Decca's sister, I mean. Is she okay?'

'She's had a stroke. They don't really know how bad it is yet. I think she got medical attention quite quickly, so . . .'

She handed Coco's lead to Charlie. 'You may as well have her. She seems to have decided that you're her human for the day.'

They walked quietly through the village; there was only the sound of Baldrick straining against his collar and panting. As they came upon The Rectory, Charlie could see lights on and Jenn standing at an upstairs window. She was wearing a white dressing gown, her hair pulled back in a high ponytail.

'She's terrible in the mornings,' said Penny with a smile. 'That perfect woman you saw the other evening doesn't take shape before lunch. Right about now she'll be yelling at the kids to get dressed and then she'll pull on her gym clothes. I don't know if she goes to the gym or just uses it as an excuse for not doing her hair before the school run.'

They veered off the lane and on to a pathway that went down the side of The Rectory. Charlie waited while Penny unlatched the gate. She looked at the window where Jenn still stood. Marcus stepped behind her; he was bare chested and had a towel tied around his waist. Jenn laid her head back on to his shoulder while Marcus bent and kissed her neck. Charlie turned away and let herself be pulled by Coco through the gate.

'We can let them off now,' said Penny, crouching to unclip Baldrick's lead. 'Here, let me do Coco too.'

The dogs sped off and Charlie pushed the lead into her pocket.

'Are you okay?' asked Penny. 'You look a bit pale.'

'I'm fine. I'm just not sleeping great. For one thing, I don't have a proper bed yet; I'm still sleeping on a camp bed, which isn't doing my back any good. And every time I turn over the sound of the sleeping bag rustling wakes me up.'

'No bed? That'd be my priority. I love my bed. Seriously, I'm in bed by nine with a hot chocolate every night and I've more pyjamas than I have actual clothes. I probably spend more time in my bedroom than any other room in the house. Why are you working on the downstairs before the upstairs?'

Charlie was about to say that a kitchen was essential, that the broken window had been the one thing that couldn't wait and so it had made sense for her to start in that room, but Penny's question made her examine her logic. Why had she started downstairs and prioritised kitchen cabinets over beds and duvets? Why did the ivy on the outside of the house need sorting before she had a functioning shower?

'I don't know,' she said after a minute.

But maybe she did.

She'd had counselling after Lee was arrested. It continued when she was in prison, too. She believed that 'how it looked' was more important than 'how it was'. And that wasn't just her own hang-up either; it was the way of the world. Growing up she'd noticed that her dad pretended to the outside world that they were a close family when in reality he didn't speak to her for weeks at a time. Arguments between her parents were conducted in whispers so that the neighbours didn't hear them and think they were one of *those* couples.

With The Buttery it mattered that, from the outside, it looked respectable, loved. And if anyone glanced in the windows, they would see a neat, tidy house, where a normal person lived. She had no intention of ever letting another person into her bedroom so she didn't have to worry how it might be perceived by others.

Besides, did it matter that she was uncomfortable? Who cared that her bedroom didn't have curtains at the window and rugs on the floor? It was a damn sight better than the cell she'd been living in for the past ten months. Next on her list was the bathroom, but only because she feared that someone would ask to use it and she would be embarrassed by the dated suite and the grotesque crosses on the walls.

Image was everything. The trial and the newspaper coverage had confirmed that appearances were the only thing that mattered. Lee had the look of an innocent man, not a murderer. If she hadn't been able to see it, why would anyone else?

At first, she hadn't been able to believe that the man she loved could be capable of the things they were suggesting. But then it turned out that the man she loved didn't really exist.

Even after he was arrested, he continued to charm and to woo. But this time it wasn't Charlie he was seducing, it was the whole word, and his supporters were smitten. Yes, he had supporters. Strange that a murderer could be admired, but his magnetism and his good looks made it difficult for anyone to believe the worst in him. Those bright blue eyes and those long dark eyelashes under a blond floppy fringe, that little-boy smile. How could he be a killer?

Murderers were ugly monsters with shark eyes. Murderers were loners. Social misfits. Outsiders. Lee was none of those things. At least, that's what she told herself when she lay awake at night wondering whether she should have known what he was like.

'Another thing that'd help you sleep,' said Penny, jolting Charlie back to the present day, 'is to give up sugar and caffeine completely. You'd have much more energy. Studies have shown that too much caffeine can lead to adrenal exhaustion.'

Charlie put an arm around Penny's shoulder and said, 'I'm going to let you get away with that kind of crazy talk just the once. But if you ever try to get between me and my coffee again . . .'

They laughed as they walked. Penny linked arms with Charlie as they followed the stream and crossed over the wooden bridge. It had been a long time since Charlie had felt comfortable enough around another person to let them touch her without flinching.

Penny pointed out where foxes had made paths through the hedges and showed her the marks made by badger claws. The ferns grew high here, and the trees were thick. Every five minutes Penny would whistle for the dogs and they would come pelting back to be rewarded with treats.

Charlie could hear the rumble of the sea now, smell it in the air.

'Not far,' said Penny, stepping over a stile.

Thankfully it was lighter now, because Charlie had to watch her step. They walked in single file as the ground fell away steeply to their right. Charlie could see the stream they'd been following and a small, sandy cove littered with drift-wood and plastic bottles. There were dark caves behind large limpet-covered rocks. The sun was still low over the horizon, making the sea a sheet of gold.

It took Charlie's breath away.

'It's easier to get to the beach from the other path,' Penny said. 'But that's completely closed off for now. The good news is you don't get many tourists in Penderrion, so it's always quiet and peaceful. I can count the number of times I've bumped into other people down here on one hand.' She raised her hand and wriggled her fingers. 'One hand.'

She slipped between a gap in the rocks and jumped down on to the sand. Charlie followed. The dogs were chasing each other across the beach now. The wind blew in from the sea and caressed Charlie's face. She closed her eyes and let it. Perhaps, given time, she could learn to love the sea.

She was a nervous swimmer: a snorkelling incident on a childhood holiday had put her off swimming for life. She'd swum over the shimmering, shifting sands until a dark chasm opened beneath her. Technically it was no different from before, her position hadn't changed, yet she had felt the drop in the water's temperature, felt the spike in adrenalin. She'd gasped, panicked and choked on the seawater. A Frenchman, a stranger, had dragged her to the side of a boat and safety. Her dad had called her pathetic, an embarrassment for making that poor man rescue her. The sea hadn't been above her knees since.

'They'll be arriving at Chi an Mor today,' said Penny.

'Sorry, who will?' Charlie opened her eyes and turned back to the cliffs.

Penny pointed to the two cottages above them with windows that shone like mirrors in the early-morning sun.

'Those are Marcus's holiday cottages that I told you about. I clean them and change the sheets. I do those welcome baskets of Cornish produce for them. You know, fudge, Cornish Yarg, Tregothnan tea . . .'

'Cornwall grows its own tea?' Charlie asked.

'The Cornish do their own *everything*. Jenn said they've not got any bookings for Gwel an Mor, which is odd. Might be because of the bad weather we've had. They're expensive to rent, but they've got views of the sea and hot tubs, so what do you expect?'

'Do the house names mean anything?' asked Charlie, picking up a stick and throwing it for Coco.

'You'll regret doing that,' said Penny, nodding after the dog. 'She'll never let you stop now. Yeah, so the names are Cornish. *Chi an Mor* means house by the sea and *Gwel an Mor* means sea view.'

'So, *mor* means sea?'

Penny nodded. 'A mermaid is a morvoren. Literally a maid of the sea.'

Coco was dashing back, stick in mouth. 'Do you know much Cornish?'

They started walking together up the beach. Coco dropped the stick at Charlie's feet and she paused to pick it up and throw it again.

'God, no. No one really speaks it any more but I guess the locals don't want it to die out completely so it's on some of the street signs and house names. And I'm genuinely interested in the language and the culture. When I first moved to Cornwall, I was determined that I wouldn't be one of those people who come to Cornwall for the nice views and only stay in it for three weeks a year. I want to really integrate myself into the community, you know?'

'How's that working out?' asked Charlie.

'Well, they let me walk their dogs and clean their houses so . . . not so good.' Penny laughed. 'No, I'm kidding. They're all lovely. I've been lucky that I can set myself up as a kind of housekeeper. I'm a glorified cleaner really but I also help with childcare, ironing, shopping and dog walking. You know, the things that can be outsourced when you're desperate to get some extra hours in the day. I had a friend who paid for childcare while she was at work, had a cleaner, sent her ironing out once a week. It was only an offhand comment, but she said to me, "What I need is a housekeeper." But of course, she couldn't really afford one and didn't need one all the time. Still, it got me thinking.'

Coco was back with the stick. Charlie threw it again.

'It's a great idea. If anyone you're working for needs any odd jobs doing, would you bear me in mind? I can't do the big jobs like Jack can, but if anyone needs a room painting or any flat-pack furniture putting up . . . I'm doing some work for Aubrey at the moment. I'm not charging him for it but I'm sure he can give me a reference if you need one.'

'Of course. Ow! Bloody dog,' said Penny as Coco banged into her shins with the piece of wood she was carrying. 'Do you think that, maybe, you're being a bit soft on Aubrey? He's probably got loads of money stashed under his mattress and it's not like it's your responsibility to look after him.'

'He's got no one else.'

'He's driven them all away, I bet. You are going to regret getting involved there. He's so rude to everyone.'

'I think he's the way he is because he's been living on his own for too long and he's too proud to ask for help. He feels like he's the same man he was when he was twenty and forty years old, and he's angry with his body for letting him down. It must be horrendous to go from being strong and vibrant to being patronised and sidelined.'

Charlie looked out at the sea. Aubrey might not get down to the beach any more but she could understand why he didn't want to leave it. She could see why he didn't want to be told when to eat and what to eat.

And, God, she knew why he didn't want to live by someone else's rules.

CHAPTER TWENTY-FOUR

Charlie Miller

Monday, 5 November 2018

Her newly installed landline was ringing.

Charlie stood and stared at it.

It was a strange sound. Not really a ringing at all, more a bleat. The biggest problem with a ringing phone was that it meant someone wanted to talk to her. And without answering it, she had no idea who it was.

The phone continued to ring. There seemed to be no end to how long it could carry on chiming. Surely it would cut off eventually? Charlie had bought the most basic of all phones. There was no answerphone about to cut in, no caller display. When she'd bought it, she'd only wanted it to be capable of calling out, seeing as her mobile rarely had any coverage. She had never expected anyone to call in. She realised now that her desire to screen callers was more important than the need to make phone calls.

She placed her hand on the handset and snatched it up. 'Hello.'

The phone continued to bleat in her ear.

'Bloody hell.'

She looked at the handset and pressed the button with the green phone symbol on it and the noise suddenly stopped.

'Hello,' Charlie said again.

She could hear someone fumbling with the phone. Clumsy fingers, muffled sounds.

She looked out of the window. Was someone outside watching her? She stepped to the side so that she was concealed by the wall.

'Hello?' she said again, louder this time.

'Oh,' said a woman voice. 'Is that you, Charlie?'

Not a wrong number, then, and not a cold caller.

'Yes. Who's that?'

'It's Jenn. Sorry to bother you, but Penny gave me your number. I need to ask a favour.'

Charlie let her tense shoulders relax.

'Of course. How can I help?'

'There's a problem at one of the holiday cottages. Penny usually handles any issues but she says you've offered to do odd jobs, and Marcus isn't keen on us using Jack any more. Long story. Anyway, can you do it?'

'Yes, well, it depends. What exactly needs doing?'

'Apparently the oven door's fallen off,' said Jenn.

'Fallen off?'

'So they say. Obviously, I'll pay you. Any chance you could go over there now? They've made some almighty fuss about how they have to go out for lunch now and it's an expense they could've done without. If it could be fixed by the time they get back . . .'

'No problem. I'll head there now. Oh, wait. What about a key?'

'There's a box on the wall by the front door with a combination lock. There's always a spare key in there. Let me give you the code. It changes with each new guest.'

Ten minutes later Charlie was heading over to Chi an Mor. She felt uneasy. It was the first time she'd done any DIY for anyone other than herself and she was struck with the certainty that she'd oversold her ability to be able to fix things.

Even stranger, though, was the combination code for the security box.

The chances of those four digits meaning anything significant were slim, but Charlie had difficulty believing in coincidences. There were ten thousand possibilities for that code, yet the one she'd been given was Lee's birthday.

Charlie stopped outside the front door.

She didn't think that anyone knew who she was. Even if they had their suspicions, why would they use Lee's birthday? To let her know they were on to her? If that was the case, it was better to not react.

She'd been so careful. Surely no one could recognise her? She barely recognised herself any more. Plenty of people looked like other people. Even if someone said to her face, 'You look like Steffi Finn', she could laugh it off. Say, 'Really? I can't see it myself.'

All around the country famous people, *infamous* people, were managing to go about their day-to-day lives without being recognised. Just to be on the safe side, though, Charlie was going to need a different date of birth to go with her different name. It looked like she was going to get her wish for a summer birthday after all.

The code was right and the slim key was in the silver box as promised. The door swung open on oiled hinges. Chi an Mor was immaculately decorated. Charlie could sense Jenn's style, but here it was sleek and streamlined rather than bold and opulent like The Rectory. There was a long corridor down the centre of the house. Bedrooms were either side of the front doorway, one with a double bed and en suite, and one with two singles. Another door was closed, and opposite that was a family bathroom with a stand-alone claw-footed bath in the middle of a powder-grey slate floor. It was the bathroom of Charlie's dreams.

She walked into a wide-open space with a kitchen-diner and sofas. The entire room was painted the soft white of chalk, not the bright white of snow. There were white wooden shutters at the windows, which overlooked the beach, and a double door of floor-to-ceiling glass through which she could see a small terrace with a covered hot tub. She couldn't believe that people holidayed like this. Hot tubs and sea views didn't come cheaply.

'Oh, God,' she groaned. It was almost painfully beautiful.

She opened the shutters and stared. The sea was throwing itself against the cliffs that jutted out on either side of the bay like crab claws. It was wild and unceasing. Mesmerising. Charlie couldn't hear the sea through the double glazing, or maybe she'd grown used to it now, but she felt the pounding of its heart as it dashed itself against the rocks. She could see the small inlet beyond the edge of the bay. The rough waves were jumping into the sky from there.

There was a brass telescope on a tripod by one of the windows, angled towards the floor, waiting to be tipped back and pointed to the horizon so it could watch for ships to come in. Artwork fashioned from driftwood leaned in the corner; blue-green glass panels were stuck to the wall like framed paintings, but they changed colour as she moved, and would do so again when the sun shone upon them.

The bookcase was the hull of a rowing boat standing on end with the bottom chopped off. It was painted white and blue and only books with blue or white spines lined the shelves. She reached out a hand to touch them but stopped short. She recognised some of them from the prison library.

She took a deep breath and could smell the dried flowers in the vase in the corner as though she were in an upmarket florist. She'd never been in such a peaceful and inviting room. It didn't feel like she was trespassing, it felt like she had come home. Charlie knew that she wanted to feel this kind of peace when she locked the door at night over at The Buttery. This was what she was missing. A sanctuary for her soul. A safe house.

She was almost frantic to touch something that felt like home. Something was tugging at her heart, craving a connection, impatient to put down roots. She still hadn't unpacked all her boxes, and was continuing to sleep on the camp bed, but this time tomorrow there would be new carpets in the hallway, living room, stairs, landing and bedrooms. It was starting to come together and, for the first time in a very long time, she was feeling proud of something she'd done.

She'd always thought of herself as creative rather than practical but she was enjoying the work she was doing around the house. Taking courses while she'd been in prison had partly been a way to pass the time and to keep her separate from the other inmates, but she'd surprised herself by enjoying making and fixing, and realised that she could use those skills to pay her way when she was released.

She'd been a creative child. As a birthday treat every year her mother would take her to art galleries and museums. Tate Modern. The Ashmolean Museum. The last trip they'd taken together was to The Hepworth Wakefield when her mother had urged her to take up art again, but Charlie said she didn't have time. 'Maybe when I'm old and retired,' she'd told her. Her mum had replied that not everyone had that luxury.

Charlie liked to sculpt and chisel from wood and clay; she had considered going to art college until Dad pointed out that there was no way he was going to fund her to sit around and 'colour in' all day. And she'd started to doubt whether she was any good at it anyway so it made sense to concentrate on more conventional studies.

It was a foreign and long-forgotten feeling that stirred within her as Charlie ran her fingers over the driftwood fla-mingo standing on one wooden leg in the corner. It had bottle corks for feathers, pitted wood for a head, and foraged sea-glass for an eye. She could smell her childhood bedroom, which used to reek of pastels before perfume. She looked down at her hands. Before she discovered nail varnish, paint and clay would become embedded under her nails and only an hour-long soak in the bathtub would shift it.

She surprised herself by missing *that* girl more than she realised. She'd been given the opportunity to take art classes in prison but it was too close to something she might enjoy and she'd locked that part of herself away a long time ago.

She was drawn back to the view as if the sea was beckon-ing her with curling white fingers. The tide was out, and she could see the smooth sands of the beach. A golden crescent. A line of seaweed showed where the water's edge used to be.

Charlie was so transfixed by the view that, at first, she didn't hear the footsteps of someone creeping up behind her.

CHAPTER TWENTY-FIVE

Charlie Miller

Monday, 5 November 2018

'What d'you do that for?' the young woman shrieked at Charlie.

She was lying on the floor with her arms out in front of her, in case Charlie lashed out again. Her red baseball cap lay on the floor where it had landed when Charlie had slammed her shoulder into the girl's chest.

'Oh, God. Sorry. You made me jump.' Charlie crouched down with her head in her hands waiting for the shaking to stop.

'You hit me, you crazy bitch!'

'You crept up on me. It was instinctive, I . . .' Charlie was panicking.

'I crept up on you? On *you*?' the woman was saying. 'You broke into the house while I was sleeping.'

'I came to fix the oven. I didn't think there was anyone here.'

'Yeah, well, we keep the oven in the kitchen not out the fucking window.'

Charlie pulled the sleeve of her sweatshirt past her hands to wipe her face.

'Are you okay?' she asked. 'I mean, did I hurt you? I didn't mean to . . . I'm on edge. What would you have done if you heard someone creeping up behind you?'

Now she was looking at her closely, Charlie could see that she was no more than a girl. A teenager.

'I could call the police, y'know. This is assault.'

'Christ.'

Assault. What if the girl called the police? Charlie would have to tell them who she really was and they would never believe this was an accident. She stood up and offered her hand to the girl who ignored it and pushed herself to her feet. Picking up her red hat, she threaded her blonde ponytail through the gap at the back.

'To be fair, you've got wicked reflexes.' She smiled for the first time.

'What?'

'That was kinda cool the way you spun round and pinned me to the floor.'

'It wasn't quite like—'

'I'm Maris.'

'Hi. I'm Charlie.'

'D'you need a drink or something? For the shock. There's some wine somewhere. Mum doesn't go anywhere without wine. She needs it for stress, celebrating, commiserating. She needs it to calm her down, wind her up. She thinks I haven't noticed what a fucking lush she is.'

'No thanks, I don't drink.'

'Me neither. You have an alcoholic mother too, eh?'

Charlie shook her head. *No*, she thought, *not her*.

'Look, I'm not one to tell you your job but shouldn't you get on with fixing the door before Mum and Steve get back? They were really pissed off about the oven. They say that this place has gone downhill in the last couple of years. They say it's not as clean as it could be either.'

'Right. God, are you sure you want me to . . . ?'

'I play netball, I've had worse falls than that; just I wasn't expecting it from someone as small as you. No, go on. I mean, that's what you came for, right?'

The oven door was lying on top of the hob. The hinge had come away and would be a simple fix as long as Charlie could locate the missing screw. She got down on her knees and searched for it.

'I thought you'd be a guy,' Maris said.

Charlie jumped and smacked her hand on the corner of the oven. 'If you could stop creeping up on me, that'd be great,' she said.

'Sorry. You don't usually get girls doing this kinda thing, though, do you? At home we have this old retired bloke do all the fixing. I think it's cool that you're a girl.'

Charlie's fingers alighted on the screw and she held it up in triumph.

'Have you always done this type of work? I mean, like, is this your actual job?' Maris leaned on the kitchen side.

'No. I used to do all sorts really, I did some office work. Reception. But I needed a change so I moved down here and bought a house that's a bit of a project, so I've been learning how to do the work myself.'

'Why the job change?'

Charlie shrugged. 'My parents died, left me some money. My life was a mess and it was time to start again.'

'Cool. I fixed my mum's hairdryer once. I changed the fuse and it worked again. She still threw it out and bought a new one, though.'

Charlie got to her feet and looked again at the oven door. 'You want to give me a hand?'

The girl nodded.

Charlie indicated to Maris to support the weight of the door while she got the screws lined up.

'So how come you're not at lunch with your family?'

'Argument,' she said.

'Oh.'

'Steve doesn't like me having a mind of my own and Mum doesn't like me upsetting Steve. They don't really want me here. I could've stayed back home. I'm old enough. We're going to have *fun*, apparently, but there's not even any Wi-Fi here. I've deferred uni for a year and I should be travelling around Indonesia now but it all fell through because the friend I was meant to be going with fell in love.' She rolled her eyes. 'And now she won't leave him, like, for even a month. Can you imagine putting your whole life on hold for a boy? I mean, like, she's so going to regret that. I'm going after Christmas, though. I'll be fine on my own, I've never had problems meeting people, you know? Just saving up money and planning my routes and stuff and then I'm off.'

'Sounds good. You're far more confident in your abilities than I was at your age.' Charlie didn't add that her confidence levels had only lessened over the years.

Charlie swung the door open and closed; it seemed secure enough.

'Right. If there are any other problems I'm just over the road at the house on the corner, The Buttery.'

'Is that it? Are you done?'

Charlie nodded. 'Look, I'm sorry about, you know, knocking you to the floor.'

'S'okay. You were right. I shouldn't have crept up on you. If I'd been really scared I would have run screaming out of the house. I knew you weren't here to hurt me.'

Charlie rushed out of there as quickly as she could. The sun was slipping from the day and she wanted to get home. Home. She was starting to feel like The Buttery was home.

The thought made her smile. She had just completed her first paid job since getting out of prison and, despite assaulting the person who was staying there, it had gone pretty well. Perhaps she really could make a go of it.

Until she looked at the key in her hand, she'd almost forgotten that the code on the lock box was the same as Lee's birthday. It could be just a coincidence.

Could be.

Or Marcus was sending her a warning. The cottage belonged to him and this could be his way of telling her he knew who she was, in a way that he could easily deny if confronted. After all, they were just numbers. She tightened her hand around the key until it cut into her hand. Just numbers.

She put the key back where she'd found it and headed for The Buttery, her good mood dwindling. She'd served her sentence and she'd helped the police as much as she could. Now she deserved to put down roots. Unless Marcus showed his hand she was going to keep away from him and carry on with her life. If he confronted her with what he knew, and left her with no way to deny it, she would simply have to show him that she wasn't the woman they said she was.

She would prove to them all that she deserved a second chance.

She was deep in thought as she stopped to look up at her home: the sagging roof, the chipped paint . . . and the man with his back to her, who was staring in through her window.

CHAPTER TWENTY-SIX

Charlie Miller

Monday, 5 November 2018

Charlie stood in the road and watched as the man pushed at the window that she'd just had replaced.

He was wearing a deer-stalker hat and a thick scarf wound around his neck, which obscured his face. He was there in broad daylight, not hiding from view. Whoever he was, he had no fear of being caught. Did he know she was over at Chi an Mor?

She placed her toolbox on the ground and quietly opened it. A hammer was on the top of the tray. She took it out and weighed it in her hand. She straightened up and crept towards the man. She didn't recognise him. He was short, a little too big around the middle. His shoulders were hunched and his grey hair was touching his collar. He stepped backwards and looked up at the upper-floor windows. There was something about the way he moved that seemed familiar. Could he be the man she had seen by the house the day she'd moved in or one of the walkers on the day she'd fallen off the ladder?

Charlie was close enough to be heard without shouting.

'What are you doing?' she said.

He began to turn around, moving slowly, not at all surprised that she was there. She'd expected him to run – either at her or away – but he stood there as if he had every right to be looking into her house.

He put his hand over his mouth and stifled a cough. 'Just checking your windows,' he said.

'Jack!' Charlie exclaimed. 'Bloody hell, you scared the life out of me.'

'Came to check the windows,' he said. 'We went off pretty sharpish after you'd had that fall. I like to make sure that I've done a decent job. Don't want Decca breathing down my neck.'

'The windows. Right.'

'What did you think I was doing?' he asked with a chuckle.

Charlie shrugged.

'I saw you creeping up on me,' he said. 'In the reflection. Should've seen your face.'

Charlie let her head drop. Finding that the code to the holiday house was the same as Lee's birthday had affected her more than she'd realised. First she'd attacked a teenage girl who walked up behind her and then she'd almost hit Jack with a hammer. She couldn't carry on like this; she was going to have to learn to relax a little.

'Shit,' said Jack suddenly. His face had gone white and he was looking past Charlie to the lane.

Charlie looked over her shoulder to see Decca strolling towards her with the two dogs by her side.

'Came to check on your handiwork, Jack,' she shouted.

'I bet you have,' he muttered.

'Charlie, my love, how are you?' Decca asked, leaning in to kiss Charlie's cheek.

'Good, thanks. Jack gave me a fright by loitering outside my house and looking through my windows.' She pulled the hammer out of her sleeve. 'I was about to scare him off with this.'

Decca threw her head back and laughed. 'Marvellous!'

'Right, I'd best be off then,' said Jack. 'Let me know when you're thinking about getting those upstairs windows replaced.'

'I'm not sure when I'll be able to afford it,' said Charlie. 'Still waiting on my old house to sell.'

'Well, when you're ready,' said Decca, 'Jack'll give you a very good price. Won't you, Jack?'

He scratched his head. 'Suppose I don't have much choice, do I?'

Charlie went back to collect her toolbox from where she'd left it in the middle of the lane. She put her hammer away and joined Decca. Jack had already disappeared. Coco seemed pleased to see her and Charlie dropped to her knees and let the dog lick her nose.

'How's your sister?' she asked.

'As good as can be expected. She's going to need physiotherapy to get her mobile again and her speech is . . . well, let's just say I can finally get a word in edgeways.' Decca smiled sadly. 'I don't see her as much as I should. I really must change that. Now, the reason I popped by was to tell you there's been a change of plan for next week's book club. We're going to meet during the day while Jenn's brood are at school. Is that okay? We thought we could head into Mevagissey and go to a lovely new café there.'

'I've not read the book yet,' said Charlie.

She'd downloaded it on her phone but she found it frustrating to read on such a small screen. *Little Women* was one of many books she was embarrassed to say she'd never read.

'I envy you, my love. I envy you. Come and drink coffee and eat cake. Really we just want to see you and have a good old natter. Don't worry about the book. By the way, I'm putting my foot down and demanding a modern book next time. Something with a bit of oomph. And sex. Yes, something steamy. I expect you to back me up. Shall I pick you up about ten-ish?'

'Actually, do you mind if I make my own way there? I've been meaning to have a look around and choose some furniture.'

'Of course not.'

Charlie fussed over the dogs. She had a soft spot for Coco. As a child she'd always wanted a Border collie. Baldrick looked at her with his sad brown eyes and she rubbed his silky ears. Perhaps she should get a puppy. It would be good company and extra security too.

Aubrey's door opened behind them and he came outside waving his stick in their direction.

'Shoo. Go on. Get away with you. You're trespassing,' he called.

Decca sighed and frowned. 'That man is an absolute menace. I wonder whether there's someone we should call. If we got a doctor out to assess him we'd probably find he's got dementia or something.'

'No,' said Charlie, 'I don't think it's that. His eyesight is poor, he just doesn't recognise us. That's all.'

'He belongs in a home,' said Decca firmly.

'It's okay, Aubrey,' Charlie called as she stood back up. 'It's only me and Decca.'

The old man grunted and went back inside the house.

'Anyway,' said Decca, 'I'm not here to talk about the neighbours. I'm here to ask you a teensy weensy favour.'

CHAPTER TWENTY-SEVEN

I have to hand it to you, you're putting on a good show. Will there be ice cream at the interval? A programme, perhaps?

I hadn't expected you to go about helping elderly neighbours and joining book groups. Where was this public-spirited persona when women were going missing and lives were being torn apart? You weren't so quick to help then, were you? I see how easy it would be to underestimate you. I see those shy smiles and the lowered eyes. You've fooled a lot of people, but you'll never fool me.

I'm glad you're getting comfortable in your Cornish hideaway. It means the fall, when it comes, will be even greater. Curtains and carpets and plaster and paint. All they do is disguise what's underneath. Old rugs cover the stains almost as well as your new identity covers up your malevolence.

Did you really think that you could hide away down here? In villages like Penderrion whispers and gossip writhe like eels in a barrel. I hope you've rehearsed your back story. I'd hate for you to get caught out before it is time.

I thought that looking for you would be like looking for the proverbial needle in a haystack, but I always knew I would burn it to dust in order to expose you. I am willing to do what it takes to have you answer for what you have done.

All good things come to those who wait and oh, how I've waited. I was always meant to be the one who brought you to justice. If you went missing now, no one would look for you. It would be so simple; but for you to make amends for what you've done there has to be more to it than that.

There's no one to protect you now. No flash lawyers and susceptible juries. I'm all you've got because I'm the only one who knows what you are. And I will be here until the very end.

CHAPTER TWENTY-EIGHT

Charlie Miller

Tuesday, 6 November 2018

Charlie kept glancing at Aubrey as she drove them into town. He was pulling at his seat belt like it was choking him but there was a faint smile on his face. He was wearing a cream shirt and a blue tie for his trip into town. A navy-coloured cardigan was buttoned tightly over his stomach. His coat had seen better days but his hat, a trilby, looked brand new. A special-occasion hat: weddings, funerals, a trip into town. There was a lemony scent that sat with him. Cologne.

He'd not left Penderrion in more than a year. He had no reason to venture out anywhere. He'd been waiting outside her door when she'd opened it this morning, keen, despite his murmurings that he was only doing this to stop her nagging, to have a trip out to break up the monotony of his day. She'd told him that he needed to get checked over by an optician, perhaps get hearing aids, and was surprised when he agreed with her.

Charlie was excited at the prospect of a morning spent with Aubrey. He was easy company and made no demands on her. Apart from the first day she'd met him, he'd not asked any questions about her past and she didn't feel as though he was waiting for her to slip up. As far as she could tell,

Aubrey didn't have an ulterior motive for spending time with her. She wasn't sure she could say the same about her other neighbours.

She couldn't help but feel that Decca had manipulated her. Somehow the older woman had managed to convince Charlie to take part in the skills auction in aid of the new church roof and the repair of the bell tower. And Charlie was annoyed with herself. With Decca, too.

Charlie had been clear and assertive when she'd said that she absolutely could not, no way, not ever, get involved with the skills auction. She was busy with The Buttery, she was still a little sore from the fall, she was nervous around people she didn't know. How many excuses did Decca need? Decca sympathised and conceded that it was virtually impossible for her to do it.

And so it was agreed that she would only offer four hours of her time and limited DIY skills to the highest bidder at the skills auction in aid of the new church roof. It was Aubrey who had been her Achilles heel. Decca had changed the subject from the skills auction to Charlie's curmudgeonly neighbour. Charlie had said she wished the rest of the village would give Aubrey a chance. Though his social skills needed a spit-and-polish he was a funny, smart and warm man. He pushed people away because he didn't know what else to do.

Decca had apologised for not having done more for him and immediately offered her help. He should be embraced by the village, not ostracised, she said.

'Exactly!' Charlie had exclaimed.

He couldn't carry on living like he did. It wasn't safe to live surrounded by all that clutter and piles of old newspapers. It was a fire hazard, if nothing else, Decca had said.

'I couldn't agree more,' Charlie had said.

Decca had said something about following Charlie's lead, and if Charlie was willing to do something so far out of her comfort zone for the good of the community then so could she. The next thing Charlie knew, she was taking part in the skills auction and Decca was offering to take piles of Aubrey's old papers for recycling and make more of an effort to include him in the community.

Bo had been round to Charlie's that morning to give her a pile of flyers advertising the church fundraiser to distribute around the shops of St Austell and to pick up a set of keys to Aubrey's house. Bo and Decca were going to spend the morning cleaning out his house for him and Charlie was excited at the thought that Aubrey would be returning to a house free of clutter this afternoon.

Charlie's name was on the pale blue flyer alongside Jenn's and Bo's. She had a momentary jolt when she saw it there until she remembered that even if someone was looking for her they wouldn't be looking for the name Charlie Miller. Still, it felt uncomfortably like she was raising her head above the parapet, even if it was just to offer four hours of her limited DIY skills.

It wasn't until Bo set off down the track that Charlie wondered how they'd got those flyers printed up so quickly and whether her name had been on them before she'd even said yes to Decca. She felt irrationally annoyed with them all: Bo, Decca, Jenn, Penny. As if they were all using her. They'd been so lovely and welcoming to her and yet she now wondered whether that was only because they needed something.

But now, as she looked over at Aubrey, she realised this was how small communities worked. You gave as much as you could because the time would come when you might have to call in the favour.

CHAPTER TWENTY-NINE

Charlie Miller

Tuesday, 13 November 2018

Another week, and another trip down lanes barely wide enough for two cars to pass. If the roads hadn't curved, dipped and twisted like a kite in the wind, Charlie would have been in Mevagissey in less than ten minutes. But they did. And so, twenty-five minutes had passed before she pulled into the pay-and-display car park at the top of the hill.

As she locked the car and began walking away, a seagull the size of a small dog landed on the roof. It spread its wings to the full length of the car. Charlie hoped it would have gone by the time she got back. She'd rather walk home than confront that thing.

This was a side of Cornwall that Charlie hadn't seen before. There were tea rooms and chip shops and brightly coloured gift shops. An Indian restaurant, a fish restaurant, a bistro and a bar. It was a beautifully blue day with high skies occasionally peppered with birds. There was no wind and, for the first time since she'd been in Cornwall, she could feel strength from the sun. Charlie closed her eyes and tilted her face upwards. It felt good.

She felt good.

She walked slowly along the main street with her phone in her hand, a map visible on its display. There were lots of people milling about with no particular purpose in mind. They squeezed into shop doorways as cars tried to navigate the tight road. She joined them as a red post office van trundled by with Peter at the wheel.

Charlie looked in shop windows that displayed Cornish pasties in ten different flavours, fudge in even more. Crossing the road, she began walking up a narrow hill that looked barely wide enough for a car to drive up, but that seemed normal for Cornwall.

The buildings leaned towards each other, heads together in deep conversation. The incline prompted the ache in Charlie's hip to make itself known. The warmth in the day, coupled with the exertion, or maybe it was the pain, was making her sweat. She slipped off her coat and draped it over her arm.

There were very few businesses that weren't selling some notion of fun amongst these shop fronts. Between the purveyors of fudge were the estate agents, their windows showing everyday houses at extortionate prices. She paused, partly interested, partly getting her breath back.

She was enjoying renovating the house so much that she was considering putting an advert in the parish magazine to offer her services to others. It would be a nice way to earn money and it would keep her busy enough that she wouldn't get morose or start thinking about things she shouldn't.

The *might've-been* thoughts were the worst ones of all. The nights were growing longer and opportunities for introspection, fear and panic were increasing. She told herself that her mind was a muscle like any other. It needed training to concentrate on the here and now. If she could strengthen her weak arms she could strengthen her weak brain.

She was getting used to the sound of seagulls, the change-able weather, and being on her own, but she didn't know if she'd ever learn to live with what she'd done. Surely people had done worse than she had and been able to move on with their lives? What was their secret?

The past was a shadow, sometimes visible, sometimes not, but it would always be there if she was put under a spotlight. She had to find a way to live with it, or forever stay out of the sun.

She saw the shop she'd been looking for in the reflection of the window she was standing at. She turned around, grateful. She might have missed it if she hadn't stopped. She waited for a car to pass and then jogged over the road and pushed open the door. It was smaller than she'd expected but there wasn't a spare inch of space. The charity shop had been advertised in the Parish magazine and, as promised, it held a huge amount of second-hand furniture. It saddened her to see sections of lives discarded, passed over for newer, for big-ger. She wondered what these quiet backdrops had seen in their time.

She tried to visualise the furniture in The Buttery and wished she'd measured the rooms now. The house was small and she didn't want it to feel cluttered. She wanted her house to be comfortable, stylish, and for it to cost less than two hun-dred pounds to furnish. It was going to be difficult.

Charlie settled on a pair of tan leather sofas that had seen better days but could just about be passed off as rustic, and a coffee table that would need either a coat of varnish or roughing up a bit for shabby-chic. She bought a pine bed with no mattress and a set of drawers that almost matched. She paid in cash, extra for a swift delivery, and was excited by her purchases. She was making a statement. The Buttery was her home, and she was going to stay.

The shop assistant seemed to stare at her for an uncomfortably long time. Charlie wondered whether she recognised her, but finally the woman smiled, wished her a good day and gave her a slip of paper to confirm the order.

As Charlie walked back out into the sun, she checked her watch. It was still half an hour until she was due to meet the others. She wondered about walking down to the harbour. She could taste it in the air, smell the pasties baking, and her mouth flooded with saliva. She hadn't eaten yet and was looking forward to a piece of cake with her mid-morning coffee.

An unfamiliar sound, a ringing coming from the bag across her chest, made her frown. It took a moment to realise it was the sound of the mobile phone. She fumbled for it, panicked. The number on the display was Sheffield. Amazing how many thoughts can go through your mind at once. Stupid that her mind tricked her in a split second into thinking it was her mum, then Lee. She was transported back to being Steffi Finn before she could even take a breath.

She hesitated, nearly didn't answer.

'Hello?'

'Hey. It's me.'

Two men walked by, talking loudly, a car laboured up the hill. There was too much noise for her to be able to recognise the voice other than realise that it was a man.

'Hello? Who is this?' she asked.

'Steffi, it's me, Conor.'

Charlie looked around her, fearful that her old name could be heard by those walking by. She'd replied to his letter, giving her mobile number in case of emergencies. It would have made more sense to give him her landline number – at least that could be relied upon to work – but the mobile had the added bonus of her being able to see the number on the display before deciding whether or not to answer. It could also be shut off and put at the back of a drawer.

'Please don't call me that. It's not my name any more.'

She walked down a side street away from the busy road. She heard him sigh as if he thought she was being wilfully difficult.

'Right. Sorry, of course. Well, your name may have changed but some things don't alter and it's really good to hear your voice,' he said. 'It's been too long. How are you?'

She leaned against a wall, suddenly shy, not sure what to say. 'I'm doing okay, I guess. It's early days but, yeah, I'm okay. I'm working hard on the house and keeping my head down. It's good, really good. Actually, I've just bought some furniture for the cottage and I'm about to meet some friends for a coffee, so …'

'Really? That's great. I'm so happy for you. You deserve it.'

'Do I?'

The pause stretched a moment too long before Conor said, 'Of course you do.'

'Right. Well, I'm still finding my feet but it's … it's really lovely here.'

'Yeah? Perhaps I should come for a visit.'

'No.' She pushed herself away from the wall and stood up straighter. 'You can't. We talked about this and agreed not to see each other again.'

'I know. I just thought …' He sighed again.

It would have been the easiest thing in the world to welcome Conor into her life and to slip back in to his, but she couldn't take the risk. It wasn't safe for either of them.

'Look,' she said, 'is there a reason why you're calling? It's just, I need to go and meet my friends.'

'Sorry. Yeah. I was only bringing you up to speed on the house sale. Your buyer still hasn't got a mortgage offer and I'm wondering if you should put the house back on the market.'

'No, I'm happy to wait. Sometimes you just have to trust that everything will work out okay.'

She ran her hand over her hair and looked at her reflection in a shop window. That house was her last link to Pinchdale. There would be no going back once it was sold, and she couldn't help feeling sad about it. The house was the only reason Conor had to keep in touch with her. Once the paperwork was completed they would have no reason to stay in contact. It had been her first house. A house she'd been happy in once. Where she'd had dreams, where she thought she'd bring up her children.

'Right,' he said.

'Right.'

She wanted to ask him how he was, how life was treating him, whether he'd heard from any of her friends. But she couldn't allow herself to get sentimental. He belonged to another life and she had no right to that knowledge.

'Look,' he said, 'I wasn't sure whether to mention anything. I don't want to worry you unnecessarily.'

'Go on.'

'We had a call from someone – a man – who tried to get us to divulge where you were living nowadays.'

'Who was it?'

'Don't know. My colleague spoke to him. He claimed to be calling from your estate agents, but we're almost certain it was the press. We didn't give him your address, though, so no harm done, but I thought I'd better mention it. So, you know, be careful who you speak to.'

Almost at the summit of the hill, Charlie saw the coffee shop Decca had told her about. The New Chapter. It had wooden tables and chairs by the window, but at the back there was a terrace with views over the harbour.

Charlie was early but she needed to sit down and get her thoughts in order before the others arrived. She craved the silence and needed time to take a breath. She wasn't shocked that someone had called Conor's office asking for her address. She wasn't even mildly surprised. All it did was confirm that she'd been right to move away and change her name. The sooner she could sell the house the better because once the house in Pinchdale was gone she would have absolutely no links to Sheffield any more. It was a peculiar feeling. She'd always thought she would die where she was born, surrounded by family and friends. Now she had no idea what the future held for her. She might even move again so that not even Conor would know where to find her.

'Morning,' said the smiling woman behind the counter.

'Morning.'

The New Chapter was part café, part bookshop, part sanctuary. Though there were tables at the front of the shop, there were also armchairs in an array of different colours. The walls were adorned with mirrors and paintings and lined with bookcases that housed more than just books: vases, mugs, clocks and lamps. Candles, notecards and trinkets. Large wicker baskets held rolled-up blankets and the chalk board above them read, *Get comfy and curl up with a book.*

She ordered a hot chocolate – with cream and marshmallows – and a deep slab of rocky road. There could never be too much chocolate in her morning. She chose a purple velvet wing-backed chair next to a round, glass table. If she tilted her head to one side she could see everyone in the room and anyone entering the café. But if she let her gaze explore where it wanted, she could see the glowing white lighthouse and the glistening sea beyond the harbour wall. It was smooth like silk, as if it had never been creased by the wind and the waves. It called to her. A siren, pretending to be calm and inviting, yet hiding its danger from view. She watched a small fishing boat slowly drift inwards. She knew it had fish on board because of the gulls circling overhead, announcing the fishermen's return. It was a scene that probably hadn't changed in a hundred years. This thought gave her comfort. In a life that was full of turmoil it was good to know that the world kept on turning.

Charlie glanced around the room at the Cornwall-inspired artwork on the walls and shelves, and then watched the woman behind the counter go about her business. A tall, good-looking man walked by and let his hand caress the base of her back as he passed. Without looking up, the woman smiled. Their easy nature suggested love.

Love.

Charlie and Conor had been like that once but she wondered if she'd ever truly loved him. They'd been close. Inseparable at first. She couldn't put her finger on when it all changed but, at some point, he stopped making her feel special. All she'd ever wanted was to feel that she mattered to someone.

There were no arguments, no broken hearts. Conor took a job in London without consulting her because it was too good an opportunity to miss. It'd only be for nine months and he didn't see why that would be a problem. He lived there during the week but was home at weekends.

Conor asked her to come and visit. She'd like London if she gave it a chance, he said. They could move down there. Buy a flat together. But she loved her house, loved the street, loved bumping into people she knew. Old teachers, class mates, the man who played the dame in the local pantomime. She wouldn't have dreamed about leaving her little corner of Sheffield. Not then.

Conor had assumed she'd be waiting for him when he got back from London. To protect herself, Charlie had pushed him away. She could see now that it was because of her own insecurities, but she couldn't let herself look forward to him coming home at weekends just for him to go to the football with his friends and leave her behind all over again.

Charlie loved the feeling of being loved. Lee had swept her off her feet and made her believe that everything she said was fascinating. He wanted to put her on a pedestal and worship her. There was no talk of moving away or of pushing her boundaries, only of settling down and starting a family. Funny how he never mentioned his murderous tendencies.

Every time she remembered her love for Lee, she felt dirty. Like she was perverted for having loved him so much when he was capable of such evil. Charlie stood and pretended to busy herself by looking at the brightly coloured artwork by Chris Tate and the bleached wooden framed mirror, made from driftwood. She missed the soothing properties of art in all its forms.

Her eyes meandered about the frame, the smooth edges, and eventually fell on the woman reflected back at her. The mirror showed a stranger. She wore her hair in a ponytail. She hadn't once plugged in her hairdryer since she'd been in Cornwall. The result was the resurgence of curls she thought she'd left behind with puppy fat and braces. But the thing that surprised her most about the woman in the mirror was the determination in her eye. She had colour in her cheeks and looked stronger and healthier than she'd ever seen herself.

'Everything's for sale,' said the woman from behind the counter as she set the mountain of hot chocolate and cake upon the table. 'And we can deliver larger items, too.'

'Thank you. I'm renovating a house at the moment,' Charlie said. 'But I've not got any pictures or anything that gives it that personal touch yet.'

She knew that there was no guarantee that her house sale would go through, and, even if it did, it would take a while before she saw any of the money, but she was thinking about treating herself.

'How long have you been living there?' the woman asked.

'Just over a month.'

'Not long, then. It's good to live in a place for a while to get the feel of it before you decorate,' she said. 'We've been living down here for eighteen months and we've only just got the house how we want it. We got the café ready before we decorated the house and bought stock based on what I'd like to see in our home and, you know, lived with it for a while. Unfortunately, I can't get some of things I really like while our kids are still young and have sticky hands.'

She looked back at the counter where the slim man was making coffee for a customer.

'Between us we've got three kids under ten, with another on the way.'

She smiled and placed a hand on her stomach.

'Congratulations,' said Charlie. 'Four kids? Wow. Sounds like a handful.'

The other woman smiled. 'I'm trying to look at it as a blessing,' she said.

'Well, I've got no kids to worry about,' Charlie said. 'It's budget that's holding me back.'

She reached up and took a turquoise mug from a high shelf; it was lined and pitted and a little rough to the touch.

'I used to make things like this,' she said, half to the woman and half to herself. Charlie had made one for her mum for Mother's Day when she was about sixteen. Two days later Dad had dropped it in the sink and broken the handle but Mum wouldn't throw it away. She had put it on the shelf stuffed with flowers from the garden.

'Well, if you ever start making things like that again, let us know. We're always keen to support local artists. And if you have any questions just give us a shout. Tristan's more of the interior design type than me. He'd be happy to give you any ideas when you're ready.'

'Thank you,' Charlie said. 'For now, I'll just buy this mug.'

'Sure, let me wrap it for you.'

The door creaked open and Decca and Penny tumbled in. They were talking over each other loudly and surely neither of them was listening to what the other one was saying.

Charlie raised an arm to get their attention.

'Ah, there she is.' Decca bustled over towards Charlie, knocking chairs with her shopping bag as she went. Penny followed behind her, righting chairs and apologising to people.

'Are we late or are you early?' asked Decca.

'I'm early.'

'Good. Jenn's picking up Bo. They'll be here soon.'

Penny ordered drinks – a large latte with a shot of caramel syrup for Decca and a green tea for herself. Charlie thought what people drank told you as much about them as any number of psychological tests. Decca's coffee was decadent, comforting and perhaps a little bit naughty, just as she was. Penny's tea was an acquired taste. It screamed out worthiness. Hard work but probably worth it in the end.

'It's lovely here,' said Charlie.

'Yes, isn't it?' said Decca, unwinding a long scarf from around and around and around her neck.

'I wouldn't mind this becoming a regular spot for the book and pudding club, would you? Though I suppose it's book and cake today. Does cake count as pudding?' asked Penny.

'Absolutely,' said Charlie. 'So we're going to meet in the day from now on?'

'Your guess is as good as mine. I expect we'll find out more when Jenn gets here. There was a problem at The Rectory. The official line is that one of the kids has something mildly contagious.' Penny raised her perfectly sculpted eyebrow.

'But you don't think that's the case?' Charlie asked.

'Well, they've gone into school today so they can't be that sick.'

'Pah,' said Decca. 'You're such a gossip. You can tell you aren't a mother. Sometimes you pack them off to school sick or not, for the sake of your own sanity. When my sons were young, they never had a day off sick. And that wasn't because they were always healthy, mind. I was a single mum and I had a job to hold down. Stomach bug, head lice . . . you name it, they went to school with it.'

Charlie grimaced.

'I think it's because of Marcus,' Penny said.

'Marcus?' repeated Charlie.

'He's working from home a lot at the moment. Bit of a drag really; he's normally up in London during the week. My guess is that he doesn't want us over there disturbing his precious peace and quiet.'

'You don't think there's more to it than that, do you?' Charlie asked. She was thinking of the point during their last book club when he said he thought he recognised her, and then there was the fact that Lee's birth date was the code to Marcus's holiday cottage.

Penny shrugged but Decca shook her head. 'Does it matter? We still get to meet up and eat cake, so I can't see a problem.'

Charlie picked marshmallows off the top of the hot chocolate and ate them. She could see plenty of problems.

She wondered about the man who had called Hunt, Fellows & Bartlett asking for her address. Could it have been Marcus wanting to confirm his suspicions? Or was Marcus only one of many people who were on to her?

CHAPTER THIRTY

Steffi Finn

Monday, 15 August 2016

'It's probably nothing,' Steffi said.

She bowed her head, pulling at the tissue in her hand.

The day was overcast and the police station was oppressively warm. She'd dressed absent-mindedly: yesterday's skirt, an un-ironed T-shirt.

Her tights were clinging to her. Suffocating her. She wanted to take them off and ball them up into her handbag, but why stop there? She wanted to take her skin off, to stop the constant crawling over her arms and legs.

They were in a side room on the ground floor of the police station. Steffi had left work after only an hour. Migraine, she'd said. Tina had scowled. Steffi had taken two days off work last week to go to Edinburgh with her boyfriend and now, on her first day back, she was off again. Though Tina had to admit, she had seen Steffi looking better.

She'd walked to the police station, her shoes rubbing. She'd felt a blister on her heel but she wouldn't get a taxi because then she'd have to say where she was going and, once the words were out of her mouth, there'd be no turning back. She'd told herself that, if she walked, she'd have time to come up with reasons why she was wrong about Lee and if she wanted, she could carry on walking straight past the station and into the park. It was a lovely day and a walk was just what she needed. But her feet had stopped at the steps to the station and she'd known what she had to do.

'I'm just wasting your time,' Steffi said.

She thought they must be able to hear the desperation in her voice. For the first time, she hoped that the police would tell her to go home, to stop telling tales. She would have cried with relief if only they could tell her one reason why Lee was innocent.

'Why don't you let us be the judge of that?' said DC Harper.

He sat down heavily across the table from Steffi. His partner, a long-lashed woman who introduced herself as DC Naz Apkarian – 'call me Naz' – wore a plain blue trouser suit with a crisp white shirt. Steffi felt shabby and dull in her company.

Both officers smiled encouragingly, with soft mouths and kind eyes. They spoke quietly so as not to spook her. Steffi wished they wouldn't. She'd hoped they'd scold her for wasting police time.

'Steffi,' Naz said, 'why don't you tell us why you wanted to speak with us today?'

'It would destroy him if he knew I was here. You won't tell him, will you? He'd see it as a betrayal. I suppose it is really, but I don't know what else to do.'

'Who are we talking about, Steffi?' Naz's voice was friendly but Steffi had no friends here.

'My partner, Lee Fisher.'

Steffi coughed, cleared her throat. The deception was choking her but she knew she wouldn't breathe freely until it was out in the open.

Steffi had already been into the station to make a formal statement confirming Lee had been with her the night that

Katy Foster had gone missing. She apologised for the oversight when she'd been questioned at work and said, 'Sorry, I got my dates mixed up. Lee *popped out* for a quick drink in the early evening.' No, she told them, he didn't usually go to bars but they'd had an argument and he just needed somewhere to sit and think.

She could confirm that Lee was home by nine. Oh, yes, no doubt about it. He woke her when he brought her a glass of water. They spoke. That woman, Katy, she'd gone missing after nine, hadn't she? So it couldn't have been Lee. No, not her Lee.

Why would he lie?

But the interview had played on her mind because she couldn't be sure, not as sure as she'd told the detective she was. Her first mistake was asking Lee what time he was home. After all, she couldn't remember the chat that Lee said they'd had. Didn't remember hearing him come home that night.

Lee had been angry. No, not angry, disappointed. He felt betrayed. Was this what she thought of him? Because, if it was, he may as well pack a bag now and leave. He couldn't be with someone who could believe him capable of hurting a woman.

Steffi had cried and she'd begged. She'd been in the wrong, she said. She should never have asked such a stupid question. Please don't go.

He gave her the silent treatment just like Dad used to do.

Her second mistake was trying to make it up to him.

Steffi decided to surprise Lee at his conference in Edinburgh. He was staying at the venue, probably wouldn't be able to call much because the networking went on well into the night at these places. He nearly cancelled at the last minute, complaining that he found these events mind-numbingly boring. Knowing what she had in mind for him, Steffi almost pushed him out of the door.

She took two days' leave from work and boarded the seventeen fifty from Sheffield to Edinburgh on the Wednesday evening. Lee sent her a text saying that he was planning an early night straight after dinner and would call her about nine. She looked at her watch, her train arrived into Edinburgh at nine twenty-nine and then she'd have to get a taxi to his hotel. If she could get him to tell her his room number, she'd surprise him by pretending to be from room service. If this didn't put the spark back in their relationship, then she didn't know what would.

By nine forty she was in a taxi and Lee still hadn't called. She was worried he'd already fallen asleep. Steffi called his phone but it went straight to voicemail.

'Just calling to say goodnight,' she said. 'Call me back when you get this.'

She had a strange mix of excitement and first-date nerves bubbling in her stomach. She wanted things to be right between them, but had never done anything so bold before. She rarely left Sheffield, never instigated anything, didn't do surprises. She hoped Lee would appreciate the gesture.

The Majestic Hotel would have been grand in its day. The foyer was marbled and gleaming. She could see a bar full of people in suits. Men with loosened ties and women who were laughing too loud and too long, in heels too high to be comfortable. Steffi scanned the room in case Lee had found himself cornered, but she couldn't see him anywhere.

She tried his mobile but, again, heard his voicemail without it ringing. She placed her phone back in her bag as she approached the reception desk.

'Hello,' she said, 'I'm here to see my partner but I can't seem to get hold of him on his mobile and I'm not sure what room we're in. Could you check for me?'

'Certainly. Name?' asked the smart, stocky man behind the desk.

'Fisher.'

He tapped away at the keyboard, pushed the mouse around and then looked up at her. 'Sorry, we have that room down as a single occupancy.'

'I know. I want to surprise him. Could you tell me which room he's in?'

'No, madam, I'm afraid I can't give out guests' details.'

Steffi dropped her overnight bag to the floor and leaned on the high counter separating them. *No need to panic*, she told herself.

'Okay. Could you call his room and tell him I'm here?'

It wasn't the entrance she'd hoped for but it would have to do.

'Certainly, madam.' He picked up the phone and they both waited. 'Your name?'

'Steffi.'

He held the sleek black phone to his ear but didn't speak. After a few moments he put the phone back down.

'I'm afraid there is no answer from Mr Fisher's room. It appears he is not in.'

'Perhaps he's in the bathroom?' she suggested.

'I can try again later, if you'd like?'

'Thank you. Is it okay if I wait in the bar?'

'Yes, madam.'

Steffi felt a familiar rush of air in her ears and a tightening around her chest. She had some beta blockers in her bag. Somewhere. Now wasn't the time to get emotional and start panicking.

She ordered a lime and soda and found an empty seat. She looked around. She wouldn't know if any of these people worked with Lee. She'd only ever met his colleagues at a Christmas party last year and only then because she popped in for half an hour before going on somewhere else.

After thirty minutes Steffi approached the reception desk once more. The man saw her coming and cut her off before she could open her mouth.

'Sorry, madam. Still no answer. Perhaps Mr Fisher has gone out for the evening.'

'Where? He said he was going to bed.'

She was worrying about where she was going to sleep tonight, starting to think there was something wrong with Lee. Had he done something stupid? You read about these sorts of things all the time, men in hotel rooms, feeling depressed and lonely. He'd been out of sorts lately and, once she'd got the idea in her head, she couldn't shake it.

'Lee told me he was going to bed straight after dinner and now he's not answering his phone. Could you to go to his room and take a look? If he's not there, he's not there, but if something has happened to him . . .'

The clerk faltered but wouldn't shift.

'I'm sorry, madam, but I—'

'Steffi?'

Steffi turned around to find Lee standing in the foyer with his mouth slightly open.

'What are you . . . ?' he began.

Steffi flung her arms around him and squeezed him to her. Lee held her stiffly, his hands on her waist.

'Oh, thank God, I was starting to worry. When you didn't answer your phone . . .'

'Completely flat,' he said. 'Forgot my charger. What are you doing here?'

Steffi linked her hands behind his neck and leaned back to look at Lee's face. He was smiling but his eyes gave away the fact that he wasn't pleased to see her. If they hadn't had an audience in the hotel foyer, he wouldn't have bothered with the pretence.

Lee smelled of cigarette smoke. It was too deeply woven in the threads of his shirt for it to have been the residue from a passing smoker. He'd given it up two years ago, hadn't he? Or did he have a sly cigarette when he was away with work? She shouldn't be annoyed – or surprised – they were allowed their little secrets. In fact, as much as she disliked smoking, she liked the idea that Lee didn't have perfect self-control.

'I miss you when you go away so I came to surprise you,' she said. 'But then you weren't in your room and the clerk didn't know where you'd gone . . .'

'I didn't fancy eating in the hotel. You poor thing. You must have been so worried.'

'I was. I was starting to think that something had happened to you.'

She let her hands slide down his arms and stood back to take his hands in hers. They were cold, and the cuffs of his shirt were wet. She frowned as he took his hands back.

'Cold out there,' he said.

'Yes,' she said, even though she knew it wasn't.

'I can't believe you came all this way, Steffi. Have you eaten? We could call room service?'

With his icy hand on the small of her back he ushered her towards the waiting lift. 'Here, let me take your bag.'

Steffi could smell him. There was sweat mixed with the cigarette smoke.

'Who'd you have dinner with?' she asked.

'No one. Ate on my own as usual. I hate these conferences. If I'd known you were here I would have waited. I wish you'd called.'

'I did but you weren't answering your—'

The lift doors closed and Lee leaned in to kiss Steffi. His tongue felt thick and stale in her mouth. She reached up and touched his cheek.

'You've scratched yourself,' she said, tracing a red line down his neck.

'Have I? I don't remember doing that.'

'What did you have to eat?' she asked.

'Thai. Super spicy.'

But he didn't taste of Thai food.

He tasted of lies.

Harper put his large hand, fingers splayed, on the table between them as if trying to court her focus.

'What is it, Steffi? Why don't you just tell us what's on your mind?'

'Last time we met,' she nodded towards him, 'you asked me about that night that, um, that woman had died.'

'Do you mean Katy Foster?' Naz was speaking now.

Steffi shook her head, but she wasn't responding to the question. She didn't want to hear the woman's name, didn't want her to be real, with a name, a family, a smile that lit up the room.

'Yes,' Steffi said. 'Yes. Her. So, I told you that Lee was with me. And I don't know for a fact that he wasn't but . . .'

She pulled her bag up on to her lap and reached inside for a clean tissue. She wasn't crying but she didn't know what else to do with her hands. Her mobile phone was on silent, but the display was illuminated, showing that she had just missed a call from Lee.

One missed call.

One voicemail.

'Shit,' she breathed.

She zipped up her bag, but the light still shone through. She dropped the bag on the floor and turned from it. *He knows where I am*, she thought. *He knows I'm about to betray him.*

'Can we keep this between ourselves?' she asked.

'Steffi, what is it you want to tell us?' Naz was keeping her voice light, chatty, like they were old friends.

'That Friday,' she began. 'I'd had a couple of drinks at a colleague's leaving do. I don't normally drink. Lee hates me drinking. His mother was an alcoholic. I . . . I knew better.'

There were voices in the corridor outside but Steffi couldn't make out the words, and then they became fainter along with the footsteps.

'And?' Naz prompted.

'He took the car and was gone for a couple of hours. He said he was back before nine and I was fast asleep. At the time I had no reason to think that he was lying.'

'And now?' Naz asked.

Steffi tucked her hair behind her ear. 'I probably was asleep before nine, so it all stacks up, but the thing is, I don't *remember*.

I got up in the night to use the bathroom about midnight and he wasn't there. At first, I thought he hadn't come home but he was there in the morning and he said he'd slept in the spare room. He probably did, but I can't say for certain.'

The two detectives looked at each other. Naz looked eager, but Harper's face wasn't giving anything away.

'And then there was Edinburgh,' Steffi said.

'What happened in Edinburgh?' asked Naz.

If it wasn't bad enough that she was there telling them that Lee didn't have the alibi he thought he had, here she was trying to link him to something else. Something they'd not even considered.

'He went away for work,' she said abruptly.

'When was this?' Naz asked.

'Last Wednesday. He was at a conference in Edinburgh and I went to surprise him that night. Things have been . . . strained between us. I went up there after work. It was quite late by the time I got to the hotel.'

Steffi looked down at her bag; she could see the glow of the phone again, imagined Lee's name on the display. Lee. Begging her not to do anything stupid. *Don't say a word.*

He'd been watching her like a hawk watches prey all weekend. She'd tried to act normal, to smile, to not give away that she had her doubts, but Lee knew she was suspicious.

'He wasn't there when I got to the hotel,' Steffi said. 'He didn't answer his phone. He told me he'd forgotten his charger, but I saw it in his suitcase.'

'Okay,' said Harper. 'Anything else?'

'He'd been smoking. I found a packet of cigarettes in the hotel bin the next day.'

Harper folded his arms and gave a not-so-subtle glance at his watch.

Steffi leaned forwards over the table. 'When you came to see me at work, I told you he didn't smoke. And he didn't. At least I didn't think so. But that girl, Katy, she met her murderer when she was outside the pub smoking, right?'

Steffi noticed Naz's eyes flicker to Harper's face but neither of them said anything.

'And,' said Steffi, 'his shirt was wet.'

'Wet,' Naz repeated.

'I thought it was odd because it was a dry evening. Warm. I knew he was hiding something. He was . . . *off* with me. He jumped in the shower as soon as we got to the hotel room. At first, I thought he'd met someone else, you know, an affair. And he had a scratch on his neck that he was trying to cover up. It all points to an affair, right? But then . . .' Steffi wiped her nose.

'Yes?' asked Naz.

'Then he started saying some really strange things. He said that if anything were to happen to him, I would regret it.'

'What do you think he meant by that, Steffi?' Harper's voice was warm, encouraging.

Steffi shook her head and shrugged. 'He said that we were in it together and that I wasn't so innocent. I thought he was talking about an affair. I thought he was blaming me for him seeing someone else, but when I asked him what he meant, he just said, "Forget about it, but don't say a word to anyone." And I started thinking about you questioning me about Katy and once I got that thought in my head, I couldn't help it . . . I started thinking that maybe that's what he was covering up. Not an affair. But it probably is just an affair, right? Not that an affair is okay but it's better than . . .'

Steffi stopped, drew in a deep breath and then asked, 'How did she die?'

'Katy?' asked Naz.

'Yes. How did she die? It didn't say in the paper.'

'We're not giving out that information at the moment,' said Harper.

Steffi nodded. 'Was she drowned?'

Naz and Harper kept their faces neutral.

Naz straightened the cuff of her jacket, doing a terrible impression of someone who wasn't giving anything away. 'Why do you ask that, Steffi?'

'I've been checking the news in Edinburgh. There were tributes to a woman. Anna Atkins. She was a single mum, two kids. She went missing the night I went to see Lee. Friends said she'd asked to borrow a cigarette off a man and they'd got talking. They'd gone outside to smoke and she didn't go home that night. Her body was found in the Union Canal.'

Steffi worried the tissue in her hands again. 'It's probably nothing, right? I mean, what are the chances?' she asked quietly.

'Thank you, Steffi, that's really helpful.' Harper was on his feet and heading for the door.

'Wait,' Steffi called. 'Where are you going? Tell me I'm wrong. Tell me that this is all a coincidence and I'm reading too much into it. Tell me that Lee didn't do it.'

Harper took a deep breath but seemed to think better about sharing what was on his mind.

'What?' Steffi asked. 'What is it?'

But Harper shook his head and let the door slam behind him.

CHAPTER THIRTY-ONE

Charlie Miller

Wednesday, 14 November 2018

Charlie had unpacked most of her boxes now and finally found the one that contained her heavy winter coat. She pulled it on and zipped it up to her chin. It smelled stale and dusty and didn't fit as well as she remembered. It hung from her shoulders and the belt didn't cinch her waist like it used to. She closed the door behind her and walked out into the cold evening as the shadows lengthened.

The church loomed ahead of Charlie and she glared at it as if it was solely responsible for her being dragged into the auction. The light was falling quickly from the day. Charlie had hoped to walk to the beach but it was either later than she thought or the impatient evening was seizing control a little earlier today.

If she unfocused her eyes she could almost see the stars beginning to peek through the cloud canopy. Blackbirds circled the church tower like they were extras in a Hitchcock movie. She let her feet carry her forwards. Religion fascinated Charlie. Or was the word confused? She'd been brought up in a household that wasn't just atheist, it was aggressively anti-religion in all forms. Dad said religion was for fools. It made him angry, as if he begrudged people their faith and their contentment. But that was Dad for you. He mistrusted any-thing he couldn't control, including his only daughter.

Charlie went to church for weddings and funerals, a baptism or two. She'd been in cathedrals and mosques and chapels. They were places of calm and reflection for her, and though she'd never felt particularly touched by God, she felt restored. She envied people their faith. She wished that she was able to trust that there was a higher power, a bigger plan; that someone, somewhere, was looking out for her.

On the day that Lee was convicted of the murders of Anna Atkins and Katy Foster, Anna's mum looked down a camera lens and said that she forgave Lee Fisher. She touched a fine gold cross on a chain at her neck and said, 'It's what Anna would have wanted.' Her capacity to forgive had astounded and intrigued Charlie.

Charlie had too much fear of the unknown to give herself to faith, though she used to meet regularly with the prison chaplain, a patient woman with bovine eyes and thick-framed glasses. They spoke about compassion. If the mother of one of the victims could show Lee mercy, then why couldn't she? Why couldn't she forgive him for making her love him, for making her lie for him, for making her complicit? But how would she, *why* would she, excuse him when he had never shown her that he was sorry for what he'd done?

Charlie decided to take a closer look at the church she was going to be fundraising for, and perhaps she would find a crumb of belief that someone had dropped under one of the pews. She pushed open the church door. Though it was getting dark there was still enough light spilling in through the windows for her to admire the grandiose carvings and appreciate the history within the thick stone walls.

The church was larger than she'd expected; even if everyone in the village turned up all at once on a Sunday morning, they wouldn't fill half of it. The dark wood pews were old and smoothed by centuries of prayer, the end of each bench adorned with intricate carvings of human heads and animal faces. She let her hands graze them as she walked down the aisle like a bride without a groom.

Beneath her feet, uneven stone flags paved the way towards the arched window. Charlie was drawn to the light that spilled across the nave. The last of the day's light was being held captive by the stained-glass windows. The flagstones were different shapes here. Some had words on them, lines bidding future generations to remember those who'd gone before. Charlie felt bereft, sad for those who were no longer talked about. The people under her feet had become curiosities for tourists and historians, but at least there had been somebody, once, who'd been touched enough by these people that they wanted the world to remember them. There would never be a headstone to commemorate Stephanie Finn, and it was probably for the best.

She sat on the pew at the front and tried to feel something. Did religion work like that? Perhaps she was too far gone for God to bother with. She'd not made anyone proud with the way she'd lived her life so far. None of it had been intentional. She wouldn't classify herself as a bad person, just easily led, stupid sometimes. Could she be forgiven for that? What did she need to do to make amends? She couldn't bring those women back, and she couldn't rewind time. Perhaps she should offer herself as a sacrifice and let the angry mob have their say.

As darkness thickened around her, she sat and waited. For inspiration? Absolution? She wasn't sure why she'd come.

All she knew was there was something, many things, missing from her life and she didn't know how to go about filling the hole. She had no one to direct or to advise her any more.

Suddenly she needed to get out, away from the dead. She needed to stop looking for someone, or something, to show her how to live her life. She had to stop being scared to live it. No good would come of looking to the past, there were no answers there. She slipped back through the heavy wooden door, annoyed with herself, annoyed with the world.

The stars were already brighter. It was a cold and clear night and there'd be frosted roofs in the morning. She could hear the sound of the waves in the distance, saying, 'Hush now.' She meant to go straight home but a headstone caught her eye and she touched her fingers to it. Karenza Nancarrow. She was only seventeen when she died, but no cause of death was given. It was always sad to read of a life cut short. It was natural to want to blame someone for the injustice. She felt it herself. Why didn't Karenza live to a ripe old age? Why wasn't that part of God's plan? Were there headstones in Sheffield and Edinburgh with Katy and Anna's names on them?

Many of the graves were covered in lichen and some were crooked and sunken. Half a dozen of them were at such an angle that it defied gravity they were standing at all. A Celtic cross was adorned in ivy; stones worn smooth with the seasons threatened to keep the identities of those buried there to themselves. The approaching night didn't help.

Charlie wished she'd brought a hat as she pulled up her coat hood and stuffed her hands into her pockets. Her fingers touched something cold and hard and she flinched. It was a coat that she'd bought five or six years ago and hadn't worn for two.

Cautiously this time, she reached in and explored the depths of the pocket. A chain. She pulled it out and looked at it in the half light. It was a silver dove necklace. She smiled at the sight and then just as quickly frowned. When she thought she'd lost it Lee had been furious with her. It had been a gift from the early days of their relationship – the first gift – before they'd even decided if they were in a relationship or not. He used to shower her with trinkets and love notes. She lifted it up, letting the dove fly around her fingers. It was traditionally a message of peace, though she hadn't realised that when Lee had given it to her. It seemed apt that it should reappear now.

He'd brought it back from Derbyshire where he'd been at a team-building event in the Peak District. He'd said he would've bought her diamonds but the shops were scarce. She'd laughed and said she didn't need diamonds as long as she had him. He'd made her lift her hair and close her eyes while he put it around her neck. And then he'd asked her to be his girlfriend.

'Is everything okay?'

Charlie gasped and turned, quickly, toward the voice.

Marcus stepped on to the path in front of her and Charlie took a step backwards. Her heel found the edge of a grave and her ankle twisted. She cried out as she fell, landing on her hip.

'I didn't mean to startle you!' he said, rushing towards her. 'Here.' He held his hand out to her but Charlie pushed herself up on to her knees and then, holding on to the headstone, pulled herself to her feet.

'You didn't hurt yourself, did you?' Marcus asked.

'No. No, I'm fine.'

'You're a bit accident prone, aren't you? First the ladder and now this. But then you're asking for trouble walking around graveyards in the dark, don't you think?'

It was impossible to read what was behind Marcus's eyes.

'What about you?' Charlie asked. 'What are you doing here?'

Marcus chuckled. 'Church warden. My turn to lock the church up for the evening. You?'

'Exploring the village. I've volunteered to help with fund-raising for the church. Thought I'd better take a look at what I'm raising money for.'

'What do you think of it? It's quite beautiful, isn't it?'

'Yes. Yes, it is. Well, I'd better get home. It was good to see you again, Marcus.'

'Wait a minute. I'll walk with you,' Marcus said.

'No, really, I . . .'

Marcus opened the church door and peered inside before closing it again and locking it.

'We can't leave it unlocked any more. A few years back someone started a fire in the northern aisle of the church.'

'So I heard. Why would anyone do that?'

'We never found out why. Or who, for that matter. Makes you wonder what goes on in people's minds, doesn't it?'

Charlie nodded. Every moment in Marcus's presence made her wonder what was going on in his mind. He was being perfectly civil despite her misgivings that he'd recog-nised her that first evening. Perhaps his desire to stop the book group meeting at his house wasn't personal. Perhaps the coincidence over the combination number for the cottages was simply that – a coincidence.

They walked together along the path. Charlie looked down at her hands and noticed that she'd dropped the dove necklace when she stumbled. She glanced over her shoulder, wondered about going back for it, but it was too dark to see anything now, and she wanted to get away from Marcus as quickly as possible.

The necklace had held sentimental value for her. It had been given at a time when she was in love, but none of that mattered now. Her knowledge was a filter that distorted the past when she looked at it. None of the happy memories existed any more. They were all lies. Her life had been built on deception.

'Is anything wrong?' Marcus asked.

'No, I'm fine.'

She was by the gate now where a single light illuminated their way.

'So, how are you finding Penderrion?' Marcus asked.

'Good. It's beautiful here.'

'Are you thinking of staying here long?'

'I don't know. Would you have a problem with it if I did?'

'Now why would you say that?' Marcus asked.

Charlie shrugged and folded her arms across her chest. She was careful not to look at him.

'Well, for a start, I get the impression you don't like me very much.' She smiled as if she was making a joke of it.

'Me?' He seemed genuinely surprised. 'I don't know whether to be offended by that. It was never my intention to make you feel unwelcome, Charlie.'

He held her gaze for an uncomfortably long time.

Through the still of the night they heard a door slam and the rattle of a door knocker. Footsteps. Marcus looked away momentarily and Charlie stepped towards the church gate.

The footsteps were getting louder. Charlie pushed her way through the gate and closed it behind her.

'Hiya, I saw you out of the window.' Penny came into view. 'You got time to come in for a cup of tea?' she asked.

Charlie joined Penny on the lane. 'I really should be getting back. Another time, though.'

She heard the gate open and close and felt Marcus walk up behind her. He was standing too close.

'It looks like we're going to have to keep an eye on this one, Penny,' he said.

'Why's that?' Penny asked.

'She's taken another fall. Just found her sprawled out over a grave. One of these days it'll be the death of her. Lucky I was there to help.'

Penny linked arms with Charlie. 'Are you all right?'

Charlie managed a smile. 'Marcus crept up on me and—'

'I'd hardly call it creeping, I—'

'Goodness me, Marcus. Have you got nothing better to do than going around scaring women in graveyards? You'll get a reputation.'

Penny squeezed Charlie's hand and Charlie squeezed it back.

'Me?' asked Marcus. 'I'm just doing my civic duty. You never know what danger lurks around the corner. It's my job to keep everyone safe.'

CHAPTER THIRTY-TWO

Steffi Finn

Tuesday, 16 August 2016

Conor peered out of a crack in the plush, lined, curtains.

'He's sitting on a wall, smoking. Are you sure he's a journalist?'

'He's been there all day,' said Steffi. 'Rings the doorbell every hour or so, but Dad's threatened to throw a bucket of water over him if he does it again.'

'Never thought I'd say this,' said Conor, 'but I'm loving your dad's style.'

She'd surprised herself by dialling Conor's number before anyone else, and he'd come straight away. She didn't know who else she could trust. In a way she was rewinding to a simpler time when she was part of a healthy relationship where the biggest disappointment was the fact that her boyfriend never put the toilet seat down.

Steffi was sitting cross-legged on the floor of her parents' living room and pulling at the ends of her hair. She had until the end of the week to find somewhere else to stay. Dad didn't see why he should have to close his curtains in the middle of the day just because she had bad taste in men. He glared at her every time they had the misfortune to be in the same room.

Mum hadn't got out of bed all day. She wasn't feeling well and there was no hiding from the implication that it was Steffi's fault. When Steffi had turned up in tears, Mum had said everything that a parent should say, about how it'd all pass in time, and that Steffi wasn't to know what Lee was like. 'He hoodwinked us all,' she'd said. But then she asked if anyone minded her having an early night, and she hadn't got out of bed since.

'Christ almighty, Steff. I can't get my head around this. It's . . . I mean, well . . . I wish you'd told me what was going on,' Conor said. 'I could've done something.'

'There was nothing to tell you. I only went to the police yesterday morning and I was hoping I was wrong. I started to doubt him when the police came to my work and asked me where Lee was on the night Katy Foster went missing, but Lee explained everything away. It all seemed so plausible and I thought I was imagining things. Of course, now I know that I was just a naïve idiot and anyone with half a brain could have seen through him.'

Conor pulled at the neck of his T-shirt that was sticking to him and sat heavily on the edge of the armchair.

'Shit, Conor, that was your cue to say, "No, Steff, you're not an idiot. He had us all fooled." Remember?'

'Sorry. You know I don't think you're an idiot. I just think that maybe you trust too easily. I don't know what to tell you. I'm here for you, and I support you all the way, but if the police came to my work and questioned where my other-half was on the night someone went missing, there'd be significant alarm bells going off, you know? I'd be looking for signs, I'd be questioning them. I'd—'

'I'm sure that your girlfriend is going to be thrilled that you wouldn't trust her.'

'Not being funny, Steff, but where has trusting everyone got you? For what it's worth, no, I wouldn't trust her. She's a little bit . . . intense, you know? I think it comes with being an actress. I never quite know whether she's being completely open with me or just playing a role. And that's okay, because I'm not completely open with her either. It's not a bad thing to be a little bit guarded until you're sure you know what the other person is capable of.'

'So you do think I'm an idiot?'

Conor shook his head but said, 'Only a bit. And you're right, he did have us all fooled. He's that bloke on the news that all the neighbours describe as "a lovely man who kept himself to himself". And then he turns out to be a serial killer with bodies in the basement.'

'We don't have a basement.'

'Good job. Have they actually charged him with murder?'

Steffi shook her head. 'Not yet.'

'Christ, Steff. What can I do to help?'

She smiled weakly. 'I don't know. Nothing really. I just wanted to talk to someone who wouldn't judge me. Dad is hardly speaking to me and I don't want to go home so I have to find somewhere else to hide out behind closed curtains on one of the hottest days of the year.'

'Oh.' Conor grimaced. 'I would have you stay at mine but it's . . .'

'Yeah, I know, your girlfriend wouldn't like it.'

'She's there most of the time now and the house just isn't big enough for . . .'

'That's okay. I wasn't hinting that I wanted to stay with you. The last thing you need is for me to make life difficult for you. I'm really happy that your relationship is going so well.'

'Are you?'

She wasn't sure she should answer that question honestly. She'd had an irrational dislike of this woman ever since Lee had come back from Max's party singing her praises. Though, she had to admit, being admired by Lee no longer meant what it used to.

Steffi pulled her knees up under her chin. 'Well, mostly. Right now, I'm jealous of anyone who isn't in a relationship with a murderer.'

Conor moved away from the window and sat next to Steffi on the floor. He put his arm around her shoulders and she leaned into him.

'I've never liked Lee,' Conor began, 'but—'

'*Now* you tell me.'

'It never once crossed my mind that he could do something like this. They're not saying it could've been an accident, are they? They definitely know it was murder? I mean, I thought he liked being in control a bit too much. The fact that he never drank . . . I never once saw him let his guard down. I've been drunk in front of him a few times. I bet he loved that. Do you think he was motivated by the fact that his mum was an alcoholic? Because both of these women had been drinking when they disappeared, hadn't they? He never gave the impression he was bothered about people drinking in front of him. I noticed that you'd stopped drinking but I thought you were on a bit of a health kick. I never thought . . .'

Steffi let him talk himself out. It's what everyone did. Her dad, her mum, they talked and talked until the words were all out in front of them like the pieces of a jigsaw puzzle. Once they found all four corners they would try to put the rest together to make some sense of it all.

'You know I could face charges for providing a false alibi?' Steffi said.

'No chance. You're the one who brought them the information they needed to link him to that woman in Edinburgh.' He squeezed her shoulder and kissed the top of her head. 'They'll probably give you a bloody medal.'

The doorbell rang.

'Get the bucket of water ready, Phillip,' Conor said.

Steffi laughed for the first time in days. It wasn't just that she didn't have much to smile about, but she felt guilty finding any enjoyment from her life when two women had lost theirs at the hands of the man she'd defended.

Voices murmured up the hallway and, judging by the lack of swearing, it wasn't the journalist this time. Steffi got to her feet as DC Harper and DC Apkarian walked in.

'Afternoon, Steffi.' Naz held out her hand formally.

Harper nodded from the doorway.

'Hi,' said Steffi.

Naz looked at Conor, raised her eyebrows in an unasked question.

'Oh,' said Steffi, 'this is Conor Fletcher, one of my oldest friends. You can speak in front of him. He knows everything that's happened.'

Naz shook Conor's hand. Nodded at him.

Harper remained by the door. His silent presence took up so much room that everyone turned to face him when he scratched his chin.

'Steffi, we need to ask you a few questions,' he said. 'And I think it would be better if you came down to the station.'

'Has something else happened?' asked Steffi. 'God, you haven't found another body, have you?' She dropped on to the sofa and pulled on the neck of her jumper like it was crushing her windpipe.

'Do you have reason to believe there are others, Steffi?' Naz asked.

'No. God, no. It's a possibility, though, right? You must have thought it too.'

Harper walked into the middle of the room and stuffed his hands in his pockets.

'Let's talk about this at the station,' he said.

Conor put his hand on Steffi's shoulder. 'She's been through a lot. Can't you ask questions here?'

Steffi saw Harper's jaw clench before he calmly said, 'It would be a lot easier at the station.'

'For you, maybe. But not for Steffi,' Conor replied.

'It's okay,' Steffi said. 'I don't mind. If you think that's for the best . . .' She stood up again, nodding to herself. 'Bag,' she muttered, looking about her. 'Bag. I'll need my bag.'

'I'll get a solicitor to meet you at the station,' said Conor.

'Don't be daft,' said Steffi. 'I don't need a solicitor.'

She caught the glance that passed between Naz and Harper. 'Do I?'

Naz took a deep breath. 'Actually, Steffi . . .'

CHAPTER THIRTY-THREE

Interview Room 3

Tuesday, 16 August 2016

Naz put her jacket back on. Despite the warm evening, the interview room was cold. Harper rolled up his sleeves. Neither the cold nor appearances bothered him in the slightest.

'Okay, Steffi,' said Naz, 'you do not have to say anything. But it may harm your defence if you do not mention when questioned something which you later rely on in court. Anything you do say may be given in evidence. Is that clear?'

Naz sat back in her seat to signify to Steffi that the formalities were done and now they could get back to chatting like old friends. Steffi nodded too quickly. She looked nervous, anxious for this to be over. It was the first time Naz had seen her without make-up and she was surprised at how young and vulnerable she looked.

There was a portly solicitor by Steffi's side. Naz hadn't met him before; he wasn't one of the regulars at the station. Steffi's friend, Conor, must have called him. Hal Baxter was a doughy man with a bald head that reflected the overhead light. He was impossible to age but Naz considered him a good few years past retirement. His hands were peppered with liver spots, his signet ring cutting into the fleshy part of his pinkie finger.

'Steffi, we'd like to talk to you about the night that Katy Foster went missing,' Naz said.

'Of course. I've already made a statement,' Steffi said. She half turned to Hal so he knew she'd complied with everything that the police had asked for so far. She seemed desperate for him to know that she was a good girl, despite what the circumstances might suggest.

'Yes, and we just need to be clear about a few things, that's all. Why don't you start by telling us what you remember about the evening of Friday the first of July?'

Naz and Harper didn't need to assign good cop/ bad cop personas. Each played to their strengths and 'making people feel comfortable' wasn't on Harper's list of attributes so Naz automatically led on interviews.

'Okay, sure, well . . .' Steffi leaned forward in her chair, her hands clamped between her knees. 'So, I was a bit late home from work because we went for a drink for Suki's leaving party. I perhaps had one too many, and when I got home Lee was annoyed with me. I knocked over some flowers and it caused a huge argument.'

'About what, exactly?' asked Naz.

'I don't know. I was . . . a little bit, well, drunk, and I don't remember everything clearly. Lee didn't have a great childhood; his mother was an alcoholic and died when he was a teenager. He blames the drink, you see. So when he asked me whether I'd been drinking I said "no", because I knew he'd be disappointed in me, but it was obvious that I had been. He got angry and accused me of lying to him and not loving him enough to manage to say no to alcohol and . . . I don't know. He shouted a lot, I cried a lot, and then he told me to sleep it off and he'd be back when I was sober.'

'Did he physically hurt you?' Harper asked.

'No.'

'Has he ever?'

'Never. He's not like . . .' Naz watched as realisation made the words dry on Steffi's tongue. She was about to protest that Lee wasn't like that, but then remembered that maybe he was.

'Can you remind me what time Lee left the house that evening?' Naz continued.

'Yes, it was just before eight. I remember lying on my bed and looking at the clock, thinking that it was amazing it was still light at eight o'clock. I didn't see Lee again until I came downstairs the next morning at seven thirty.'

'And why was that?' Naz asked.

'Well, like I said before, I'd had a few drinks – which wasn't like me. And I'd not had anything to eat so it affected me more than it would usually. I went to bed and must have fallen asleep about, I don't know, maybe eight thirty? When I woke in the night to use the bathroom Lee wasn't in bed with me.'

'What time was that?' Naz asked.

'Around midnight.'

'Weren't you worried about Lee when you realised he wasn't there?' asked Naz.

Steffi didn't answer straight away. She glanced at Hal and then shrugged as if she knew the truth wouldn't paint her in a good light.

'Not really. I knew he was angry with me so . . .' She wrinkled her nose. 'I thought he was sleeping in the spare room to punish me.'

'Okay,' said Naz. 'Makes sense. And that was something that happened a lot, was it? Sleeping in the spare room, that is?'

Naz took a sip of coffee. It was cold and bitter but it was caffeinated and she needed help to get through the rest of the night.

'No, not a lot,' Steffi said. 'The bed's always made up in case one of us has to get up really early in the morning, or one of us is ill, but never because we've fallen out. We don't normally argue, you see.'

Naz tapped her fingernails on the table and frowned. It was strange that, given they'd just arrested Steffi Finn's boyfriend for murder, she was still trying to paint their relationship as healthy. Naz had never been so glad that she was single.

'So, you woke up around midnight and went to the bathroom. Is this an en suite or . . . ?'

'No, we only have the one bathroom, and it's across the landing from our bedroom.'

'And the spare room, where you thought Lee was sleeping – where is that?'

'Next door to the bathroom.'

'Right. So, when you got up to use the bathroom, why didn't you check the spare room to see if he was in there?' Naz asked.

Steffi tucked her hair behind her ear and looked at her hands. 'I was scared to wake him. I didn't want to make things worse.'

Naz paused for a minute as if she was mulling that over. If Steffi was telling the truth, and Naz suspected she was, what kind of relationship was it where you were scared to wake your boyfriend up?

'And I wasn't feeling great,' Steffi said, filling the silence. 'I was more concerned with not being sick. Like I said, I'm not much of a drinker.'

This seemed to wake Harper up. 'More concerned with not vomiting than whether your boyfriend was home safe? My wife fusses if she doesn't know where I am. She worries I've had an accident. And you say you weren't worried at all?'

'If I'd stopped to think about it I suppose I would have been, but I wasn't going to go looking for another fight by waking him. I had no reason to think that he was in any danger so I assumed that he was in the spare room, because, where else would he be?'

'Okay, so you didn't see him at all between eight o'clock on the evening of Friday the first of July and seven thirty the following morning?' Harper said, folding his arms.

'That's right.'

'And did you see anyone else? Make any calls? Receive any?' he asked.

'No. I just went to bed and slept.'

'And you didn't leave the house at all? You weren't tempted to follow Lee and see where he was going?'

Hal flexed the fingers on one hand as if he had cramp from writing. 'Stephanie has already said what happened. I think she has been perfectly clear. Is there anything else you would like to ask her about that night?'

Naz smiled at him as sweetly as she could manage. 'We just want to be clear about alibis. Or lack of. So, the Red Toyota RAV4. Can you confirm that this is your car, Steffi?'

'Yes.'

'Did you drive that car on the day that Katy disappeared?'

'No. I walked to and from work.'

'Do you look after it?'

Steffi looked momentarily confused. 'I'm not really a car person but I get it serviced and MOTed when it needs it, so . . .'

'What about cleaning the car?' Harper asked.

'Sometimes. Not as often as I should, but occasionally I pay the people in the supermarket car park to clean it for me.'

She gave another little shrug. Steffi was eager to please but couldn't see where this was heading.

Or pretended not to.

'When was the last time you cleaned it yourself – you know, with the old sponge and bucket?' Harper asked.

She looked up as if she was thinking. 'Not that long ago. A couple of weekends ago, maybe? Yeah. I think that's right.'

'And why was that?' Harper asked.

'What do you mean?'

'Well, was it dirty? Why did it need cleaning at that precise moment?' he said.

'There was a funny smell. I couldn't smell it, but Lee could. We were talking about selling the car and so, well, it needed cleaning properly.'

'According to your neighbour,' Harper said, 'it was early on Sunday morning. She remembers it well because it woke her up and she looked out of the window to see you with the hoover. She can't recall ever seeing you clean your car before that day.'

'Like I say, the guys at the supermarket . . .'

'Strange, though,' mused Harper. 'That the only time anyone has seen you cleaning the car was in the weeks following the disappearance of Katy Foster. You can see how we might be wondering if the two things are linked.'

'But they're not. There was a strange smell. Lee wanted to sell the car and I decided to clean it. There's nothing more to it than that.'

Steffi was sitting up straight now, agitated by the way the questioning was going.

'The thing is, Steffi,' Naz said, 'we found a hair matching one of the victims in the boot of your car.'

Steffi let out a long breath and shrank back into her seat. They all sat in silence and Hal shuffled in his chair but his discomfort wasn't due to the melded plastic. Harper sat forward, resting his elbows on the table while Naz studied Steffi's reddening face, the twitch of her nose, the way her eyes had become shinier with a thin film of tears.

'Who knows how much evidence you got rid of by cleaning that car, for the first time in months, in the early hours of Sunday morning?' said Harper.

'Honestly, that's not what I was doing. I . . .' She looked at Hal, her eyes imploring him to do something, but he was mute.

She opened her mouth but the words got stuck in her throat and she gasped to get oxygen into her lungs. And again, and again, like she was a balloon being inflated. Steffi put the back of her hand across her mouth and started to deflate.

What started as a whine became a silent scream.

Naz glanced at Harper but he was unmoved. It was part of the job to know when you were being played, but despite the accusations that Lee levelled against Steffi, Naz couldn't get the measure of this woman. If she had something to do with the murders she was covering it well. Still, every avenue had to be explored. Every lead. Tears ran down Steffi's face. She hunched over and buried her forehead in her arms.

'Steffi?' Naz's voice was professional but kind. There would be no hugs from her but that didn't mean she relished every part of her job. 'Here.' She pushed a box of tissues in Steffi's direction.

'Can you tell us why you're crying?' Naz asked.

Steffi took a tissue and blew her nose three times. She shook her hair like she was resetting herself and sniffed sharply.

'I . . . It just sunk in what you said, about there being a hair in the boot of the car and me trying to get rid of . . . evidence. Does that mean that . . . ?' She blinked hard and two more tears appeared on her cheeks.

'I was thinking maybe it could be there because Lee gave her a lift, but then I realised that you said "boot" so, well, people don't get into the boot of cars by choice, do they, um, so there's a chance, a probability really, that she was . . . not alive when she was put in the car. So there was a dead woman in my car. A body. In my car. It's a lot to take in,' she said.

'Tell us why you went to Edinburgh, Steffi,' Harper said, changing the subject suddenly.

Steffi frowned at him. 'Edinburgh? I went to surprise Lee.'

'Do you often surprise him when he goes away on work trips?' he asked.

'Well, no, but it wouldn't be a surprise if it was something I did often, would it?'

'What was different about this work trip?' Harper asked.

'We'd not been getting on and I thought that this might be a way to get things back on track.'

Red blotches appeared on Steffi's neck and chest.

'How long had things been difficult between the two of you?' Harper asked.

'Only since that argument on the night I got drunk. He said he'd forgotten all about it and didn't want to talk about it any more, but he became distant. Less affectionate. It got, perhaps, a bit more strained after you came to talk to me about the night that Katy Foster went missing. For a second,

I wondered whether he could have had anything to do with it and maybe he saw that I doubted him.'

'Maybe?' Harper pushed.

'I don't know. I felt like he watched me carefully after that. Always asking what I was thinking.'

'Why do you think that was?'

'I suspect he was worried I'd tell you that I didn't remember him coming home that night.'

'If you had concerns,' Harper said, 'why go to the trouble of following him to Edinburgh?'

'Because . . . Look, it crossed my mind that he'd been acting differently since that night, but it could have easily been because we'd argued, it didn't have to be because he'd killed someone. It's difficult to believe that the person you love is capable of something like that. I was just trying to get us back to where we used to be.'

'Okay, so what happened when you got to Edinburgh?' Naz asked.

'I, um, called him from the taxi but he didn't answer his phone. When I got to the hotel he wasn't in his room either. I was just asking the receptionist to check if Lee was okay when he turned up and said he'd been out for dinner.'

'Can you remember what time this was?' Naz asked.

'About half past ten? Quarter to eleven?'

'Okay. Your train arrived in Edinburgh at nine thirty. What were you doing in the time between arriving in Edinburgh and Lee returning to the hotel?'

'I had a drink in the hotel bar and waited.'

'You didn't go for a walk around Edinburgh? Take in the sights? I hear it's a beautiful city.'

'No. I thought we might explore a bit over the weekend but not that night.'

'You must've been angry when he wasn't where he said he'd be, right?' Naz asked.

'Angry?' Steffi looked genuinely confused. 'Not angry, no. I was more concerned for him, really.'

'Concerned?' asked Harper. 'But you weren't as concerned on the first of July when he wasn't in bed with you when you woke up?'

'This was different. At home, he could be in the spare room but in Edinburgh he only had that one room.'

'You'd gone all that way; it must have been, what, four hours on the train? And it wouldn't have been cheap either. And then, when you arrived expecting to find him bored and alone in his hotel room, he was out enjoying himself. I'd have been pissed off with my boyfriend,' said Naz.

'Well, yes, I suppose I was a little bit frustrated. But only because things weren't going according to plan; and if I couldn't track him down I had nowhere to sleep for the night. I thought he just had his phone switched off. I felt a bit stupid for going all that way without a back-up plan.'

'The receptionist,' said Harper. 'He remembers you and says you appeared agitated but doesn't recall whether you stayed in the bar while you were waiting for Lee. We're waiting on the CCTV footage now so we'll be able to see if you were where you say you were.'

Steffi nodded. 'I promise you, I didn't leave the bar at all.'

'Not even to go looking for Lee? You didn't, maybe, see him chatting to Anna Atkins?'

'Of course not. You can't think that I—'

'Steffi,' said Naz, 'Lee isn't denying that he met Katy or Anna. But he says he didn't hurt them. He says you're very possessive, jealous even. He thinks you killed those women after you saw him talking to them.'

'I would never do that. Why would I do that? He's lying.' Steffi's voice was getting higher and louder with every word uttered.

'Lee says he's never known you take so much time over cleaning the car and he thought it odd at the time. He thinks you knew there was evidence in the car. He's suggesting that you were the one who killed Katy Foster.'

Hal let out a small bark of a laugh. 'That's ridiculous.' They all turned to him as if surprised he was still there.

Naz said, 'Steffi, Lee says he went straight to the spare room when he got home the night that Katy was killed. He says he can't be sure that you were even home because he didn't see you until the next morning. He says you lied about speaking to him that night to give yourself an alibi. He thought you were doing it to protect him but now he realises you were doing it to protect yourself.'

Steffi pinched her lips together.

'By your own admission,' Naz continued, 'you don't have an alibi for the time that the murders were committed. And we also found a pair of earrings belonging to one of the victims under the spare tyre in the boot of your car. Can you tell me how they got there, Steffi?'

Steffi shook her head and dislodged the tears again.

'No,' she said. 'You have to believe me. He . . . he . . . He's had plenty of opportunity to plant those earrings, to come up with an alternative story for what happened to those women and why the signs were pointing in his direction. Because if they were pointing to him, they were pointing to me too. He knew that if I ever dropped him in it, I'd be in trouble too.'

Steffi looked from Harper to Naz and back to Harper again.

'Can't you see what he's doing? He knew I doubted him and he knew I didn't have an alibi. He tricked me into cleaning the car so it would look like I was getting rid of evidence. I played into his hands by following him to Edinburgh. He's sacrificing me to save himself. He knew I was going to come to you. He set me up.'

CHAPTER THIRTY-FOUR

Ben Jarvis

Thursday, 15 November 2018

Ben dragged all his worldly belongings out of his bag and on to the bare mattress. He'd be sleeping in his clothes tonight with his coat as a pillow. It wouldn't be the first time.

The best that could be said about the new flat was that it was 'within budget'. But with no references and not much money to put down as a deposit, this was one of those times when beggars really couldn't be choosers.

The flat was above a Chinese takeaway and not far from the supermarket Steffi had shopped at. In the cold, late evening, and with his stomach rumbling, the decision to come down to Cornwall on the strength of a conversation with the solicitor seemed idiotic. Especially seeing as it was almost three weeks ago. She could have moved on by now or been warned that someone had been asking questions about her whereabouts. Perhaps he should have acted on it immediately. Or not at all. St Austell was bigger than he'd expected. He'd hoped it would be a quaint little seaside town. Population one hundred. He was wrong.

His good mood of earlier had gone. When he'd first arrived at Truro bus station he'd dropped his duffel bag at his feet and taken a good look around him. The late-afternoon sun had painted the buildings peach. Kids with school ties and long limbs at awkward angles had barrelled across the square causing shrieking seagulls to take to the skies. A busker had been making the most of well-disposed shoppers outside Marks & Spencer. Coins clinked in his guitar case as people walked by.

Ben had been struck by the thought that Steffi could walk past at any moment. She wouldn't recognise him but he was sure he'd recognise her. Wouldn't it be nice if it could be that easy? He'd felt a stirring in his chest. A thrill. He was getting closer.

But that positivity had waned now.

He looked at the framed photo on the window ledge. It had been taken at his daughter's graduation. Ben was on one side of her and Amanda on the other. Separated. That was the official term for them now until one of them filed for divorce. It was apt, really, because they were separated by a gulf of sorrow that neither of them knew how to bridge.

The grief twisted in his chest. It was like being punched repeatedly while his hands were tied behind his back.

When his daughter died, he spent hours looking through her posts on Facebook. It was as if he could hear her voice, picture what she was wearing, and doing, in the moments while her fingers typed on her mobile phone. He felt closer to her. He looked through photos she'd taken and photos she'd been tagged in. But soon they became the only thing he could see and his real memories were replaced with false ones. Snapshots of events that he wasn't invited to, smiles he'd never been on the receiving end of.

Online she'd had hundreds of friends, but he'd met less than thirty of them. How could he have been cut off from so much of her life when she took up so much of his? Perhaps that was the way it was meant to be. You raised your children to be independent of you, and the more successful you were, the more it hurt.

Ben rubbed his face. He was in desperate need of a shave. His dad used to tell him that a good shave was the equivalent of two hours' sleep. He hadn't spoken to his folks in a while. Grief fucks everything up. His parents lost their only grandchild. It was natural they would be destroyed too but he couldn't take the sobbing of a man he'd never seen cry when he was growing up, couldn't bear his mother leaning on him for support.

He'd been expected to be strong for them all. For his parents. For Amanda. For the countless friends and relatives who wanted to share a slice of his grief so they could have a good cry, post something pathetic on Facebook. They did grief like they were giving blood. Just a sharp scratch and then it was all over. Lately he'd become possessive of his grief, didn't want to share it with anyone. It was his to nurture, to protect. It was all he had left.

Lack of sleep, lack of food and lack of hope had made him fractious. The smell from the Chinese takeaway was driving him insane. He had a bruised apple and half a bottle of lemonade, but he needed something more.

He checked his pockets for keys then walked outside into the sharp, cold, night. It was fully dark now but the roads were still busy. A group of men came out of the pub opposite, laughing about something or nothing. Ben envied their camaraderie, their easy laughter and beer-warmed bellies. He went into the off-licence and bought four cans of the cheapest lager they sold. He needed some help to get to sleep tonight.

With the blue carrier bag banging against his knee he walked back past the entry to his flat and pushed open the door to the Chinese takeaway. The woman behind the counter pulled her gaze from the television on the wall. A travel documentary. Somewhere exotic.

'All right?' she asked, though her eyes were back on the television before Ben could answer.

Ben ordered a spring roll and the chicken chow mien before sitting on the covered, faux-velvet bench that faced the counter. The woman had taken his order through to the back and then returned to her seat to watch the screen. Ben studied the wall by his side, which was covered with posters for local events.

There was a jazz night at a local pub, a Slimming World class, a dog in need of a new home. There was a car boot sale at a place he couldn't pronounce and a fundraiser for a church in a place called Penderrion.

Ben stood up to take a closer look at an advert for a second-hand car. A car would be handy, but could he afford it, really? On the other hand, could he afford not to? It would be difficult to get to some parts of Cornwall by bus.

He could ask his parents for a loan but he hated having to ask for help. He could pay them back when the divorce settlement came through, though. No. He shook his head. If he was going to buy a car he would go to a garage, not the local takeaway. He took his seat again, his eyes lazily taking in the posters and flyers.

He looked at the clock above the television. It was only ten o'clock but it felt much later, he'd been awake since four thirty. His eyes were drawn back to the board. Something had lodged in his mind. He looked for, and found, the pale blue flyer for the Penderrion church fundraiser on Saturday night. It was a skills auction in aid of a new roof for the church.

Help us raise the roof!
Five pounds for a ticket, which entitles the ticket holder to a drink and a buffet. Bid on LOTS of LOTS, including a three-course meal for six cooked by Jenn Ferrers, a portrait of your pet by local artist Bo Pietersen or four hours of DIY from Charlie Miller.

Miller.

He said the name out loud.

'Miller.'

It was a satisfying name. 'Miller. Miller. Miller,' Ben mumbled.

The woman dragged her gaze away from the television for a moment, appeared to decide he wasn't any crazier than the usual crowd she got in at closing time and went back to watching her programme.

Wasn't Miller Steffi's mum's maiden name? Miss Maggie Miller? He remembered thinking it was a name that was satisfying to say. He was sure it began with an M. He tried to recall the school website where he'd read the dedications to a beloved teacher. Some of whom were calling her by her maiden name from thirty years ago. He'd look it up when he got back to the flat. That's if he could summon the energy before falling asleep.

He was certain that Steffi Finn would be using a new name by now. But would she really use a name that she had links to? Unless it was a double bluff . . . He was tired and reading too much into things. Even if she was using the name Miller, wasn't Charlie a man's name? It seemed likely, given that this person was offering their DIY skills. It hardly sounded like the kind of thing Steffi Finn would be up to, but long shots were all he had right now.

'Excuse me,' he said.

The woman dragged her eyes from the television once more.

'How would I get to Penderrion from here?' Ben asked.

'Up to the roundabout,' she pointed as if he could see through walls, 'turn right and it's down there about four or five miles. You'll see a turning off to your left. The road's always getting cut off when there's bad weather, though, so pick your day.'

'Okay, thanks.'

He could manage to walk five miles, but was it worth it to see what was, in all likelihood, a sixty-year-old bloke offering to put up a shelf for a fiver? Right now, as tired as he was feeling, the answer was probably no.

Then again, there was something about that poster that had caught his eye.

Always trust your instincts, he thought.

CHAPTER THIRTY-FIVE

Charlie Miller

Saturday, 17 November 2018

This time, Lee's date of birth opened the security box to reveal two sets of keys.

Maris and her family had deposited their keys when they left Chi an Mor, as directed. Jenn had asked Charlie to go in and check whether anything needed fixing. Any loose blinds, toilet seats, rickety chair legs or dripping taps were her domain now. And then she'd said as an after-thought, 'Oh, I don't know why I didn't think of it before. Why don't you make use of the bathroom in the cottage while yours is out of use? There's really no point in it sitting empty.'

Charlie protested, but only long enough for politeness' sake. It wasn't that her bathroom was out of use, only that she didn't like to use it. It was cold, damp and every now and again clumps of plaster fell into the bath from where she had loosened the crucifixes. She suspected that Marcus wouldn't like the idea of her bathing in his luxury holiday cottage and there was a small part of her that was thinking about this as she said 'yes' to Jenn with a smile.

Penny had been in that morning, stripped the beds and emptied the bins. Charlie took a book – *I Capture the Castle* – from the bookcase and went into the bathroom, locking the door behind her. The bath was bigger than her bed and the space around it bigger than her bedroom. She slipped off her boots and felt warmth on the soles of her feet. Either someone had forgotten to switch the underfloor heating off or someone had switched it on especially. *Penny*, she thought.

She turned on the taps and let the water thunder down. She hung her brand-new, still-with-the-label-on towel over the heated towel rail and began to undress. She'd ventured out of the village that morning for what her mum would have called life's little luxuries: a soft grey dressing gown, a matching towel and bubble bath promising the healing properties of *Sea Kelp*. Charlie knew there wasn't a bottle big enough to heal her wounds, but she was willing to begin the process. Penderrion was getting to her if she thought that anything with 'sea' in the title could be soothing instead of threatening.

Reading in the bath used to be Charlie's idea of luxury. She'd only do it when Lee was away, otherwise he'd get annoyed with her for wasting time she could be spending with him. She used to think it was sweet of him. Now, just washing without being watched was indulgent enough.

The steam circled around the spotlights in the ceiling as the water roared into the bath. Goose bumps erupted up her arms even though the room wasn't cold. She wrapped her arms tightly around her naked torso and looked to the door. Even if someone got into the cottage, they couldn't get into the bathroom so why was she so nervous about getting in the bath? For some reason she'd never felt so naked.

Exposed.

Unguarded.

In prison she'd showered with no privacy. It was a perfunctory act, not something to be savoured. But a bath . . . ? A bath encouraged eyes to close and minds to wander. She wasn't ready for where her head would lead her if she gave it a chance. Charlie was still learning how to relax. Her jaw ached from grinding her teeth and her shoulders ached from the tension she kept there. She wasn't expecting the bath at Chi an Mor to have mystical healing properties but it had to help.

Charlie had a love-hate relationship with water. Though she craved a bath, or a long hot shower, she would happily never set foot in the sea again. Since that time she nearly drowned, and perhaps even before then, Charlie hated swimming. Certainly, she couldn't remember a time when she found it enjoyable. That's what memory did – disregarded the thoughts that no longer supported your current beliefs.

So much had changed. Almost everything she thought she knew was a lie. Some people embraced change but change had always been Charlie's monster-under-the-bed. The unknown fear always being the greatest. She was ill-equipped for this life. Everyone else had had twenty, thirty, forty years of growing into the person they were today. She'd only been Charlie Miller for six weeks.

Charlie Miller, the DIY enthusiast who was sinking what was left of her money into a house that wouldn't thank her for it. 'Urgh!' she shouted into the empty room, her voice amplified by the tiled walls. She couldn't let herself get morose. What did she expect? Things were going to be difficult for a while but she wasn't going to be a victim of her circumstances.

Charlie stepped into the bath. It was a little too hot and it stung as she folded her body into the water. She sat with her knees bent under her chin until the water level rose to just below the overflow. She turned off the taps. The foam popped about her but otherwise, silence.

She leaned backwards until her shoulders found the edge of the bath. It took both a physical and a mental effort to straighten out her legs and submerge her body in the hot water. Excess water tipped into the overflow and rushed away.

Minutes passed. Heat dispersed. She let some water out of the bath and topped it up again. She looked down at a body she didn't recognise. There were no mirrors at The Buttery and she'd only washed herself in the sink since she'd arrived in Penderrion. The days of checking herself in the mirror before getting dressed for work or admiring herself as she got dressed for an evening out were far behind her. Now her body was a vehicle for getting things done. It didn't matter whether she was exfoliated, tanned and waxed. She thought of the hours that she had wasted worrying that her stomach wasn't flat enough, her breasts not big enough.

Even with everything she'd been through she wouldn't go back to that time. It took something as momentous as going to prison for her to get her priorities straight. In some ways she'd been unlucky falling for Lee, in other ways it was inevitable after the way her dad had treated her. Everything that had happened to her had led to this – the realisation that she was going to be okay on her own.

She needed to see this as the start of a new life where what she *did* mattered more than what she *wore*. Where her worth was no longer measured by other people's opinions of her.

The first time she'd seen the headlines she'd laughed out loud, but only because it was so ludicrous. How they described her couldn't have been further from the truth, and yet there it was in bold black letters. They said she'd had an affair with Lee while she was still living with Conor, but it hadn't been like that. Her relationship with Conor had been over long before that, but he hadn't finished moving his things out of the house. They'd parted ways after a mutual decision, not because she'd callously ditched him in favour of a new man. There was never any mention of Lee's ex-partners. Sex sells newspapers, but only if you're a woman.

They said she was volatile. They said she was jealous. They said she was evil.

She'd provided an alibi for a murderer. There was no getting round that fact, but the papers implied that she knew what he'd done when she said they had been together – that she was enabling him to kill again. They failed to report that she'd believed him when he said he'd been in the house at the time of the first murder and made her think she'd forgotten speaking to him because she was drunk.

They didn't know that she'd been full of good intentions, believing that the police were trying to wrongly accuse the man she loved. That as soon as she realised what he'd done she went to the police. God, she was naïve. She knew that now, and perhaps she should have realised sooner what Lee was capable of.

The papers had stitched her up, made her look guilty. Strangers hated her as much as the families of the victims did. Charlie didn't want to be hounded any more. She didn't want to start receiving hate mail again, didn't want to be spat at in the street.

Even here she was unable to drop her guard completely. She still wasn't certain that Marcus knew who she was, and Charlie was thankful that Penny had turned up at the graveyard when she did. Who knew what Marcus would have said to her if they hadn't been interrupted? Charlie didn't think that Marcus would've hurt her. He was a businessman, not a thug. He had too much to lose.

To confront him would be to force his hand, and Charlie wasn't ready for that. Instead, she was going to win him over. After all, she'd done her time. She'd paid the price.

Hadn't she?

She took a deep breath. Now she could relax, wash her hair. Clean herself. She methodically moved up her body, scrubbing and rinsing. She massaged conditioner into her hair and then let her head sink down so that her ears were below the water. She felt her hair float out behind her and the water run across her eyes. She held her breath and let herself be taken under the bubbles.

At once, images of Lee's strong hands on slender necks, holding them under, eyes open, mouths gasping. Charlie sat up quickly and hot water sloshed over the side of the bath. They were the images that had haunted her dreams for months even though she'd never seen them. In her dreams she was often the one holding them down, sometimes she was the one being held under. She never saw Lee's face in any of them though she could always feel his presence.

Charlie clambered out of the bath, half fell, but steadied herself on the sink.

She dried herself with the new towel. It left small grey fibres of fluff over her wet body. She pulled on her clothes and dragged a brush through her hair. The bath had been short-lived, but necessary. She still had a little time before she had to pick up Aubrey and take him to the auction. Enough time to calm herself down.

She wiped around the bathroom checking that she'd left nothing behind. If it hadn't been for the steam-blurred mirror in the bathroom, it would have looked as if she'd never been there. Turning off the lights she gathered her things and headed outside.

She was nervous about seeing Marcus at the auction and, more than that, she was dreading the humiliation of no one bidding for her skills.

'Please,' she muttered into the night. 'I don't care who it is, just make someone bid for me.'

Would it matter if she dropped out? It wasn't entirely a lie if she said she had an upset stomach. It was doing somersaults right now.

The security light came on outside the front door of Chi an Mor as she opened the key safe. Something caught her eye that she could have sworn wasn't there before. Wrapped around the other keys was a silver chain. Charlie pulled at it, turning the key as it unravelled.

She looked around her. She could hear dogs barking down the lane. It was dark and there were no street lights at this end of the village. Anyone could've been watching her from the trees. Anyone could be hiding around the corner.

Charlie looked back at the chain in her hand. It was a fine silver necklace.

And on it was a single, silver dove.

CHAPTER THIRTY-SIX

Charlie Miller

Saturday, 17 November 2018

Darkness had dropped two hours ago. As she stared out of the church-hall window, all Charlie saw was a reflected ghostly version of herself with Aubrey at her shoulder. The hall was filling behind them – friends greeting friends, new acquaintances being made. There was a lot of chatter and occasional bursts of laughter.

Her stomach clenched. It was hard to judge how much of her fear stemmed from the thought of the auction and how much was thanks to the dove necklace that had been left as a message for her at Chi an Mor.

She had no way of knowing how many people knew the code for that box, but she was sure that Marcus was the only one who could have seen her with the necklace at the graveyard. He had meant for her to be scared but, instead, she was furious. His house, his rules. She knew men like him. Dad. Lee. They liked to control through fear, and she'd spent most of her life trying to guess what mood they'd be in and altering her actions accordingly.

By putting the dove necklace in the key safe Marcus was showing her that he'd been watching her. He knew what she'd dropped in the graveyard and was showing her that he could have walked straight into Chi an Mor if he wanted to. Who was to say he hadn't been sitting on the other side of the bathroom door while she was naked? No matter what he thought he knew about her, he didn't have the right to intimidate her. She wouldn't let him. She'd taken the necklace home with her and placed it on the mantelpiece. Doves were a symbol of hope, and she refused to be bullied any more.

'I hate this time of year,' Aubrey said, bringing Charlie's attention back to the room.

'Hmmm?'

'The day never stays around long enough for me to do anything with it.'

He looked handsome tonight. He was wearing the new glasses that she'd helped him choose, his new hearing aids, and he had trimmed his beard for the occasion. Even the tufts of ear-hair had been dealt with. Charlie had been surprised when he said he wanted to come with her. Perhaps the world didn't look quite as scary now he could see it clearly.

Charlie scanned the room; it was almost full but she hadn't seen Marcus yet. It was a better turn-out than she'd expected. For a moment she allowed herself to believe that more people meant more people who could bid on her, and then she decided that, when no one bid on her, the humiliation would be even worse. And, no doubt, Marcus would be there to see it.

'Aubrey? Would you do something for me?' she asked.

'Depends what it is.'

'I need you to bid on me. I'll give you the money. If no one else is bidding for me I want you to offer ten pounds. Okay?'

He smiled. 'Won't be any need,' he said.

'Still, I'd appreciate it if you could.'

He raised his eyebrows and his shoulders. It was as close as she was going to get to a 'yes'.

Charlie recognised a handful of people but most of those streaming through the door were strangers to her. She kept her face down, in case someone recognised her, but no one was paying her any attention. Why would they?

'I first came here nearly seventy years ago,' said Aubrey. 'It was the Golowan Festival. Course, they don't have it now. Bleddy health and safety. Though I think they've started doing it again down in Penzance. We'd set the bonfires. Burning barrels of tar and rolling 'em down the hill. Had to jump through the dying flames of the bonfire to ward off the evil spirits. Might not manage it nowadays, though.'

'It sounds . . .' She was going to say *fun*, but instead said, '. . . dangerous.'

He chuckled but Charlie saw his eyes glaze over as his memories led him away.

She looked again for Marcus. She'd be surprised if he missed this event seeing as he was so involved with the village and the church.

Penny and Bo were serving drinks. Tea and coffee only. If people wanted alcohol, they had to bring it themselves. Decca was having a terse conversation with a harassed-looking man that Charlie didn't recognise.

Aubrey sniffed loudly.

'You okay, Aubrey?'

'Thinking,' he said.

'Penny for 'em,' she said.

'Cheapskate,' he said. 'They're worth their weight in gold.'

They heard the *duff, duff, duff* of a finger tapping on the head of a microphone, followed by the *screech* of feedback. Chatter died to a hum.

A small, bearded man took the stage and welcomed everyone to the church hall, thanking them for coming out on such a cold night. Charlie frowned. This must be the vicar. Shouldn't he be wearing a dog collar? Have white hair? This man in Converse and a Ramones T-shirt didn't fit with her expectations. She shifted in her seat. It wasn't that she was disappointed, just disquieted.

Charlie felt the gust of cold air before she heard the door close. She turned to see Jenn and Marcus walk in. Jenn mouthed 'sorry' at Decca, and Marcus squeezed the shoulder of a stocky man wrapped in tweed.

'And without further ado I'll hand you over to Decca, who has agreed to be our auctioneer for the night,' the vicar said.

Everyone clapped. A cheer went up from the back.

'Thank you for coming . . .' began Decca's voice through the speakers though she was loud enough that she didn't need a microphone.

'Tonight, you lucky folk have fifteen lots to bid on. After eight lots we'll take a comfort break. And by "comfort" I mean a chance for you to get yourself a cup of tea and help yourself to the buffet.' She motioned to the tables where egg sandwiches were flattened smooth beneath cling film. There were foil trays of crisps, pork pies and cocktail sausages. The food spanned a narrow spectrum of pink to beige.

'There are lists on the tables telling you what's coming up during the evening so bid wisely and bid generously. Remember it's for a terribly good cause.'

Charlie looked around for the list so she could see when her lot was up.

'Lot number one, then, is half a day of DIY from our newest resident, Charlie Miller. Good at plastering, decorating, can put up shelves, hang pictures. Any of those little jobs you've been putting off, now's the time to bid. Who's going to start me at ten pounds?'

The room went quiet and Charlie began to sweat.

'Anyone? Ten pounds? You wouldn't normally get an hour for that, and Charlie is offering four hours.'

Silence.

'Ten pounds anywhere?'

Discomfort sat heavy in the room. Charlie stole a glance at Aubrey, willing him to speak up, but he was studying a bruise on the back of his hand.

'Chaps, those jobs your wife nags you about? This is your get-out-of-jail-free card. Bid now and it's in the bank for the future.'

Please, someone, please.

'Come on, it's for a good cause. Five, then; do I hear five anywhere?'

'Here!'

Charlie let out a sigh of relief and, with a smile on her face, looked to the back of the room where the voice had called out. Marcus was looking back at her with his hand in the air. Charlie's smile slipped away.

'Thank you, Marcus. Any advance on five?'

Aubrey raised his walking stick. 'Aye. Ten.'

'Ten! Marvellous. We have ten with the gentleman with the stick.'

'Gentleman with the stick?' Aubrey murmured to Charlie. 'She knows who I am. She's been watching too much *Cash in the Attic.*'

'Any advance on ten, then? Is that fifteen, Marcus? Fifteen it is, then.'

Decca pointed in Aubrey's direction. 'Twenty? Do I see twenty?'

Aubrey shook his head.

'No? No advance on fifteen?' She pointed a pen towards the back of the room. 'Is that twenty? Twenty to the lovely Bo.

'Perhaps this is a good time for me to point out,' began Decca, 'any ladies who are nervous about having strange men in your house with a hammer, this is the lot for you. Stand up, Charlie.'

Charlie sank down in her seat but there was no point pretending she wasn't there.

Oh, God.

A deep breath and Charlie stood up. She smiled, or at least stretched her lips into the requisite shape.

'As you can see,' said Decca, 'Charlie is a lovely young woman and . . . Ah, is that twenty-five? Thank you.'

Charlie looked around but Marcus's arms were folded. Whoever had bid for her had already lowered their hand.

'Thirty anywhere?'

This time Marcus raised his hand.

'Thirty-five?' asked Decca.

Charlie saw Peter, the postman, raise his hand and then lower his head to the man next to him as he said something in his ear.

'Thank you, Peter. You do know you can't get Charlie to deliver your letters for you, don't you?'

There was laughter and Charlie smiled. She would rather do work for Peter than Marcus, if at all possible.

'Forty?'

Marcus hesitated for a moment then nodded.

'Can I get fifty?'

Charlie looked at Peter, who shook his head.

'Anyone?' asked Decca.

Charlie was regretting having said yes to this auction. Why hadn't she considered that Marcus might bid on her? She could always refuse to work for him. Pay him back the money he'd bid, though she could scarcely afford it.

'Ah, fifty, thank you,' Decca said. Charlie turned in her seat to see who Decca was looking at.

'That's fifty with the gent in the blue striped shirt then. Any more? Marcus?'

Charlie didn't recognise the other man. Relieved, she saw Marcus shake his head.

Decca scanned the room. 'Going then. For fifty pounds to the handsome man with the salt-and-pepper hair.' She fanned her face theatrically and people laughed. Someone wolf whistled.

'No? Are you sure? Four hours of Charlie's time going for fifty pounds. Going . . .' Decca paused. 'Going . . .'

One last scan of the room to make absolutely sure she couldn't squeeze any more money out of anyone.

'Gone.'

CHAPTER THIRTY-SEVEN

You're smiling more now and looking . . . what is it? Happy? Hopeful? Good. You're not the only one who is looking to the future with high expectations, Steffi. The only difference between us is that your future is short. Your future is not yours to spend.

Two dead bodies.

A man in prison.

There'll be more casualties before this is over.

You can change your name, but you can't change the person you are inside.

I can see straight through you.

I think about it all the time. Your face as you realise who I am.

Your tears, your confessions, how I'd love to hear them, but I know it can't be like that. We don't have the luxury of sitting across from one another and speaking our minds. Once you realise why I'm here, you'll lie, you'll lash out, you'll try to run away. If I've done my job right it'll be too late by then, and the trap will be set.

You think you're special. And you are, but not the way that you think. Take the auction, for example. You were up first. I wouldn't have planned it like that; I'd have made you wait until the tension was too much for you to stand. I'd have made you sweat. All of those people bidding on you, clambering for you. And you give yourself to the highest bidder. What does that make you? Bought so cheaply. So easily.

Did you worry that you'd lost your charm? Did you think that no one wanted you any more? Oh, quite the opposite. We all want you.

And there's the problem. It strikes me that I'm not the only one watching you. Who was that man who won you at auction? Someone else whose life you destroyed? I don't know what he wants from you but we can make an educated guess, can't we? Their motives won't be as pure as mine, though. I serve a higher purpose. I am reason. I am justice.

Time is running out. I have to act soon before someone else beats me to it. I found you first. You are mine.

It is time to start the final act.

Are you ready?

CHAPTER THIRTY-EIGHT

Charlie Miller

Monday, 19 November 2018

The two delivery men swore their way through the narrow doors, tilting the bulky items first one way, then the other. The sofas were larger than Charlie remembered and they made the room look smaller. She would need to get new cushions, but the furniture looked like it was meant for this room.

The men dropped the coffee table between the sofas and then sweated their way up the stairs with a headboard and wooden planks that would transform into a double bed once assembled. The new mattress would be delivered soon, and the carpets were already down.

Charlie signed her new name, without having to think about it, on the bottom of their delivery note and thanked the delivery men profusely. They didn't return her enthusiasm, just clambered back into their van with all the trepidation of men about to navigate narrow lanes with a large vehicle.

She was suddenly excited. She was making friends and she'd already made a small difference to Aubrey's quality of life. She'd stood up to Marcus, made some money for the church fund and someone had made an offer on the house in Pinchdale. It had only been two months since she'd been released from prison and yet, she really felt like she was getting her life back on track.

Charlie sat down heavily on her very own, new-to-her sofa. The leather creaked as she slid herself sideways and lay down upon it. The sofa had absorbed the chill of the day. She sat up again and beamed. Sofas, carpets, a bed. All she needed for perfection now was a roaring fire.

The Buttery was becoming a home.

She was enjoying walking about in bare feet, relishing the feel of the springy new carpet. The house was definitely warmer now it had a new window but she was yet to feel like she could remove a layer of clothing without shivering. An open fire later would finally chase the chill from the room. Jack had swept the chimney before the carpets went down. Unfortunately, she'd overlooked the most important thing: wood. She'd go foraging behind the house and in the woods to see if she could find any that was dry enough.

She looked around the room.

For obvious reasons she didn't have any photos to put up, but she'd like to get a painting or two. The white-painted walls gave off the scent of a fresh start and the fusty, unloved smell had almost gone.

During the break in Saturday night's auction Charlie had to choose between introducing herself to the man who'd bid for her or putting herself in Marcus's way.

The man with the striped shirt slipped out the door, he'd already got what he came for and clearly didn't fancy staying to bid on a portrait of a pet. According to Decca, he didn't have enough cash on him – he hadn't expected the bidding to get so high – but he was going to swing back round to Penderrion this week with the money. All Charlie knew about him was that his name was Ben and he would call to make arrangements.

She spied Marcus by the buffet table, all hands-in-pockets and chest puffed out with self-importance.

'Marcus?' She placed a light hand on his shoulder and he turned to face her. Oh, how she longed to take that smug look off his face.

'I wanted to thank you,' she said.

'For . . . ?'

Some of his composure slipped. She noticed that he'd cut himself shaving and the blood had dried brown on his shirt collar. She wasn't going to let him get the better of her. The only way to deal with bullies was to stand up to them or to take the wind out of their sails.

'For starting the bidding for me. It's thanks to you that it went as high as it did. I'm sorry you missed out. If you need any work doing, you'll have to hire me in the usual way.'

His mouth opened but nothing came out. A slight frown creased his brow.

'I've learned a lot in the short time I've been here,' she said. 'For a start I've learned who I can rely on. It's hard starting somewhere new but, as long as people let me, I'm going to embrace this community. At the churchyard the other evening you asked me if I was planning on staying long in Penderrion. Well, something happened earlier tonight – I won't bore you with the details – but I was reunited with a lost necklace and it felt like a message, a message of hope. It made me realise that it's time to put down some roots. It looks like we're going to be neighbours for a very long time.'

He nodded. One cheek twitched into a smile.

She wasn't going to hide from him. She wasn't going to hide from anyone, and, for the first time, Charlie began to believe that she deserved her second chance.

She grabbed her coat and rushed outside to look for logs. On the off-chance that there was a secret stash in the outbuildings she checked there first. It was dark and cold in there, and she let her imagination off the leash. She thought about the potter's wheel she'd seen when she'd first moved in. She used to love making things and could do so again. She'd need a kiln. She'd have to get electricity and some heating.

She hadn't planned on doing anything other than keep her head down and work on the house. It felt self-indulgent to consider starting a hobby again. It had been years since she'd done something creative with her hands.

Vases and bowls, she'd made them mostly for her mum, but she'd kept some for herself, too, which she'd dotted around her teenage bedroom, proud of what she'd created. When she moved out, her dad had thrown them all away and turned her room into a home gym. Somewhere for the treadmill to catch dust and ironing piles to grow.

She thought about the plant-pots mum had on her kitchen window ledge in turquoise and blue and wondered where they'd gone. Conor had arranged for a house clearance company to come in. More landfill, more charity-shop stash, and nothing concrete for Charlie to touch, hold and smell. There was nothing to fuel her memories apart from her own threadbare recollections.

She'd known that this would happen, of course. She knew that she wouldn't be able to put photos of her old life on window ledges and fireplaces. She couldn't have any-one stumbling upon them, looking at them, following the breadcrumbs to who she really was. But, did it have to hurt this much? Shutting down her emotions and keeping busy seemed the only way she could get through this.

It was hard not to let her imagination run wild now there was interest in her house in Pinchdale. Three months, maybe more, to get the surveys done. The paperwork. But by February she should have enough money to renovate these buildings and turn them into a workshop. She could sell her pottery through that café in town; she could take a course in furniture making. There was so much potential for Charlie Miller.

If she'd never met Lee, she'd still be living in Sheffield and would probably never have left. She'd never had the desire to fly abroad, explore new things. She'd been too scared of what she would find, of the plane falling from the air all because she was greedy enough to want more from her life. No, Steffi was the kind of girl who was careful not to ask for too much and was grateful for the little she had. Charlie knew where that level of apathy had got her and wouldn't make the same mistake twice. If she wanted a better life for herself she would have to craft it herself.

She brushed the brick dust from the arm of the coat, shuddered when she realised she had cobwebs in her hair, imagining spiders running down her neck. She stamped her feet and headed towards the path that went behind The Buttery down to the beach. She knew the steps were closed off, gradually eroded by the seasons until the last storm decided to put an end to the path altogether. She was in the mood to explore her surroundings. On the way back, she'd collect wood for the fire. Then, hands stiffened by cold, she would spend the afternoon relaxing while the fire warmed her bones.

There seemed to be nobody in Penderrion except Charlie today. It was cold and there was a hat-stealing wind on the rampage. There were plumes of smoke trickling into the sky from the tall chimneys of the rich houses, suggesting that people were staying indoors. She'd checked on Aubrey, taken him his weekly shopping, and covered his knees with an extra blanket. He seemed to have lost a little of that bluster she'd encountered on the first day she met him. Partly, it was because his bark was far worse than his bite. Mostly, however, it was because his confidence had taken a knock when he'd fallen. She'd managed to get him out of the house to the opticians and again to the auction but he wasn't confident leaving the house on his own.

Charlie knew that Decca had gone to visit her sister again but she thought she would have seen Penny walking the dogs or Jenn out with the kids. There was a storm forecast for this week and everyone seemed to be taking cover already. She stopped and looked about her. She was completely and utterly on her own. She didn't mind it. It was beautiful here and it was nice to be able to take in her surroundings without having to watch what she was saying. Strange, though, that she found herself wanting to see someone, to make a connection with another person.

The generous trees laid a red carpet before her. She kicked at the leaves, watching her toes disturb the burnt oranges, the fiery reds. The smell of gently decaying foliage was heavy in the air. The branches conducted an orchestra that only they could hear.

Charlie looked beyond the path, through the columns of trunks. She'd never been an outdoorsy girl. She hadn't been one of those tomboys who'd climbed trees and made dens. She'd been the kind of girl, and then woman, to take pleasure from staying inside with lit candles, a good book, a film. It had been a long time since she'd taken a walk in the weak autumn sun and let the wind blow her wherever it fancied. She'd not expected to want to walk outside for no reason, with no purpose except to get some fresh air. And that was the thing: the air did seem fresher here. The sky seemed bolder, the wind stronger. In turn, she was feeling bolder and stronger too.

The wind picked up and the leaves hissed at her. She looked over her shoulder, to see how far she'd come, and thought she saw a movement. She strained to see, even took a couple of steps back up the path for a better look, but all she saw was a squirrel scampering up a tree. There were many things moving round the woods today but none of them wished her harm.

Charlie smiled to herself and started humming a tune to a song she didn't know. She kept walking towards the sea, the wind blowing straight in her face. She spotted a fallen branch. If it wasn't too heavy, she could drag it home and chop it up for the fire. At the very least she could drag it to the side of the path to pick up on her way back.

The wind rushed at the trees, shaking the branches, throwing the leaves around in a tantrum. The trees hushed and shushed until the wind calmed down.

She bent and lifted the end of the log. It was a little damp underneath, she wasn't sure it would burn well. Hadn't she

CHAPTER THIRTY-NINE

Charlie Miller

Monday, 19 November 2018

She could feel the heat on her face, but her hands and feet were cold.

Tongues of orange light licked her eyelids. Shadows danced across her eyes. She could smell the smoke of a wood fire and hear the crack and spit of damp logs burning. It made her think of country pubs after autumn walks as the warmth bled back into her fingers and toes.

She tried to open her eyes but they were weighted with fatigue and her lids would only part a little. Through her eyelashes she could see a crescent of light, a roaring fire, and someone walking past her with their head down.

She breathed in to fill her lungs with enough power to push some beseeching words out of her mouth, but she forgot which words she wanted to use, and the air left her lungs with a wheeze.

There was the taste of blood in her mouth. She licked her cracked lips and they stung. Her nose was throbbing and she couldn't breathe through it. She was lying on her back covered by a heavy blanket. When she tried to lift her arm, the blanket fell away.

She slid her hand up the side of her face, past her temple and into her hairline.

There was a hard lump under the skin.

Throbbing.

Her hair was matted and sticky with . . . what? Blood?

She groaned and heard the creak of floorboards. Someone was in the room with her.

Help, she thought. *Help me.* But the words wouldn't come. She was so very sleepy but she had to stay awake.

Charlie tried to remember.

Had she been in an accident? She wasn't in hospital. Someone's house, then? Not hers, surely, or she would have recognised it. She didn't have a fire, did she? Her mind ticked over slowly, stuttered, stopped. She remembered being outside and the wind was blowing. She could smell the sea, feel the crunch of leaves under foot. She remembered Lee coming up behind her. No, it couldn't have been Lee. Who then? Marcus? It was someone strong. Taller than she was. She remembered something hitting her from above.

She remembered Marcus saying, *We'll have to keep an eye on this one . . . Accident prone.* Or had that been a different day?

Charlie tried to sit up but her head was too much of a burden and she instantly felt sick. She had to get help. Vomit burned the back of her throat. She couldn't breathe. She let her muscles go limp and swallowed the bile away.

Groaned.

Her body started to shake. She tried to control her limbs, but she gave in and let her body do what it must. One moment hot, cold the next, shivers up and down her body.

Charlie was tired, but she must open her eyes. Stay awake.

But the world was slipping away from her.

CHAPTER FORTY

Charlie Miller

Tuesday, 20 November 2018

The rain was in a rush. Charlie could hear it chattering on the roof and gushing in the gutters.

She opened her eyes, closed them, opened them again and tried to focus.

No matter how many times she blinked she couldn't recognise where she was. She looked to the grey skies out of the window but there was no way of knowing what time it was, only that it was the day. Like a tide, she couldn't tell whether it was coming in or going out.

The pine drawers had a vase of flowers on them. No, not a vase. A jar. Carnations. She hated carnations; she wouldn't have bought them for herself, so who did? She was in a bed, the same shade of pine as the drawers. The covers were soft with age and they looked familiar. Something was scratching at the back of her mind as if she was trying to open a door but her hand kept slipping off the handle.

By the side of the bed was a glass of water on top of a taped-up cardboard box. Black writing in a familiar hand in broad letters across the side. *Summer Clothes*. Mum's handwriting.

'Mum?' she croaked.

Her lips were sore and her skin felt like she'd spent too long in the sun. Her head ached. No, not ached, pounded. And her nose was tender. She touched it too hard and sucked air sharply through her teeth. It was swollen.

Charlie could hear someone coming up the stairs. The steps were light but the floorboards loose and unforgiving. She pushed herself up on to her elbows and her head peeled away from the pillow. There was dried blood where she'd been lying.

At least that explained why she felt so groggy and her memory was in shreds.

The footsteps stopped outside the bedroom door.

'Hello?' she called out.

She felt more curious than scared.

The door creaked open, slowly, and a woman's face came into view.

'Oh, good. You're awake,' the woman said.

She smiled broadly as if she was pleased to see Charlie.

'What time is it?' asked Charlie.

The other woman came into the room and sat on the corner of the bed. 'Don't worry about that now. How're you feeling?'

'What happened? I . . . can't remember. Who are you?'

'Me?'

She looked surprised, then hurt.

'It's me. Penny. I'm . . . I'm your friend.' Her voice was full of concern, her eyes wide and her bright red lips pursed.

'Sorry. God, yes. No, I remember you. Of course I do. Sorry. I'm feeling a bit groggy. For a minute there I just couldn't place you, but . . . Yes, of course. Penny. I remember now. What happened? Did I hit my head or something?'

'Yes, when you were in the woods behind the house.'

'Right. My head. But how?'

'It was really windy. A branch fell on you. The tree must have been damaged in the storm. I found you when I was out for a run. Don't you remember?'

'I do,' Charlie said. 'Actually, no. The last thing I remember was hearing someone behind me.'

'I found you half covered in leaves with a branch on top of you. I don't know how long you'd been lying there but you were freezing. It was lucky I found you. I was trying to fit in a quick run before the weather changed and almost turned back but thought I'd just get to the end of the path. If I'd taken a different route . . .'

'It's all a bit . . . hazy.'

'Perhaps we should've taken you to a hospital after all. In general, I try to steer clear of them unless it's an absolute emergency. I thought if you just had a good night's sleep . . . You were lucid yesterday. Don't you remember talking to us? You were adamant you didn't want to go, but I don't know how much memory loss is normal. You've obviously got concussion.'

'Am I at home?' asked Charlie.

'Yes.'

'The Buttery,' said Charlie. 'Right. But I don't . . . I mean, I recognise some of it, but . . .'

'You were sleeping on a camp bed before. We put the bed up for you. There was a mattress delivered yesterday afternoon, and I found some bedding in one of your boxes. I hope we didn't overstep the mark.'

'No. That's so kind of you. Thank you for the bed, for finding me . . . for everything. Who did you say helped you?'

'It was that man from the auction. If it wasn't for him, I would've had difficulty getting the mattress up the stairs.'

Charlie remembered a tree branch on the ground. The wind. She'd gone for a walk and was planning to light a fire when she got home. Her memories were playing hide-and-seek with her but they were there, just out of reach. Perhaps if she closed her eyes and counted to ten, she'd find them.

'The man from the auction?'

'Oh, bless you. You really are confused, aren't you? Yesterday you were telling me all sorts of odd things, like how you were hiding from people and that Charlie was your pretend name.' She laughed.

How much had she told Penny? How much of it could she take back?

She remembered coming back to the house and lying on one of the sofas. Penny had fussed around making tea, asking questions, bringing blankets. There'd been a man with Penny who Charlie didn't recognise but she didn't question why he was there and his presence hadn't unsettled her. She'd felt sick but her vision wasn't blurred. She was too tired to go to the hospital so told them she hadn't felt dizzy at all. She tried to speak clearly, and to focus on them when they talked. She'd felt like a drunk person pretending to be sober. She'd thought the man was a friend of Penny's, a neighbour she hadn't yet met.

Everything was unravelling. The past had caught up with her more quickly than she'd expected.

'The man who helped you with the mattress,' Charlie said. 'Did he say who he was?'

Penny looked worried. 'Are you okay? Did we do the right thing by keeping you home yesterday? I mean, we almost called an ambulance but—'

'Penny, did he tell you why he was here?'

'I'd suggest getting you to the hospital now but I wouldn't be happy driving in this weather—'

'Penny, please. The man. Who was he?'

'Don't worry. It was just Ben from the auction. He's lovely, actually; he'd walked all the way from St Austell to pay what he owed, but Decca wasn't there because she's had to go to her sister's again and so he was on his way here when he heard me shouting and came running down the path.'

'Oh, God, Penny, what if that branch didn't fall on me? What if he hit me with it?'

'Who? Ben? No. It was the wind. Ben didn't turn up until after I'd found you and he helped me get you to your feet and check you over. He was genuinely concerned, so I hardly think that—'

'Someone was there, Penny. I'm sure of it. I remember looking behind me and thinking I saw someone hiding behind a tree. I should have been more careful, should've realised that I wasn't safe here. It's not just this,' she said, motioning towards her head. 'There have been other things, too. I should have taken more notice of the signs.'

'What are you talking about?' Penny's smile had frozen on her face.

'Penny, I'm not who you think I am.' Charlie swung her legs out of the bed and pushed herself to her feet. She swayed and Penny grabbed her arm to steady her.

'What are you talking about? Come on, let's get you back into bed. You're not well enough to—'

'Penny, please listen to me. I thought it was only Marcus who had worked out who I am but this man, Ben ... It's not a coincidence that he turned up in Penderrion on the night of the auction. You have to let me explain.' Charlie looked at Penny's trusting face, wishing she didn't have to tell her, wishing she could have kept it from her for ever. 'I didn't want to lie to you, but I thought I was protecting myself. I hoped I'd be able to put it all behind me but I realise that that was never possible. I can't run from my past.'

Charlie slumped back down on to the bed and looked down at her hands. She felt Penny's weight rock the mattress as she sat by her side but Charlie couldn't look at her.

'Penny,' she said, 'I'm not Charlie Miller. My real name is Steffi Finn.'

Penny sat in silence. The only interruption was the rattle of the glass in the window frames as the wind demanded to be let in.

Charlie told Penny about Lee, about Katy Foster and Anna Atkins. She told her about the all-consuming guilt, her time in prison and how she wished it had been longer so that people would think she'd been punished enough. Finally she described her attempts to start again in Penderrion.

The first words out of Penny's mouth were, 'You're not serious?'

'I wish I wasn't, but . . .' Charlie replied.

Penny looked to the window where the wind and rain were tussling outside. Her face was difficult to read, but at least she wasn't running from the house in horror. Eventually she placed a thin smile on her face and said, 'It's going to take me a minute to process all this. It's a bit of a shock, that's all.'

Charlie got to her feet and this time felt stronger, as if her lies were no longer holding her down. She pulled her dressing gown off the back of the bedroom door and wrapped it around her shoulders. She didn't know how long she had until Ben came back. At least, this time, she'd be ready for him. She glanced around the room. It wouldn't take her long to pack up all her belongings.

'But,' Penny began, 'I'm not sure I understand where Ben fits in.'

Charlie walked over to the window, half expecting to see him there looking up at her, but there was nothing except the wild lashing of branches fighting against the wind and the rain. She could just see the lights on in Aubrey's cottage. He was the one thing that she couldn't take with her.

'If Ben knows me as Steffi Finn, and has gone to the trouble of tracking me down, he's not here to offer me his support, is he? Either he's here because Lee has sent him or he's linked to one of the murdered women somehow. When I was in prison I got a lot of hate mail from people who said my sentence was too short. They said I'd had more to do with the murders than I'd let on. I even got letters from women who were in love with Lee and believed him when he said that I'd been the one who killed Anna and Katy.'

'Hasn't Lee confessed to the murders?' asked Penny.

'No. Even in the face of the evidence, he maintained that he'd been fitted up by me and by the police. He might've got a shorter sentence if he'd pleaded guilty to the charges but he wouldn't drop the "wronged man" act. He admitted meeting both women, and Anna had his skin under her nails from where she scratched him. Katy's hair was in the back of the car, as were her earrings, and Anna's necklace was found in the lining of the suitcase he took to Edinburgh. I mean, it couldn't have been any clearer and it didn't take a jury long to reach a guilty verdict, but there are still those who refuse to believe the facts. For a time I was genuinely concerned that the police would believe Lee when he said that I was the guilty one. Luckily CCTV put me in the clear in Edinburgh and there was nothing linking me to the women at all.'

'So why did he blame you?'

'Partly to save his own skin, but also because he thinks it's my fault. I started the chain of events that led to him going out to that bar where he met Katy. It was me he was angry with really, and he was also angry at his mother for choosing alcohol over him for his entire childhood. I let him down when I came home drunk that day. I was no better than his mum. He couldn't forgive me for that and, when the police questioned him about that night, he panicked and tried to divert their attention to me instead. It wasn't until I caught him out in Edinburgh that the police began to get a clear picture of what he was capable of.'

'And Ben?' asked Penny. 'What's he capable of?'

'I don't know, but I'm sure he attacked me with that branch, Penny, and I'm scared he's going to come back to finish what he started. I suppose I should call the police and explain everything. Perhaps they can track him down before he hurts anyone.'

Penny nodded slowly. 'Okay – and it's not that I don't believe you – but, when I found you in the woods there was no-one else there. Ben didn't turn up until after I did. If he'd hurt you why would he have come back? And why stay around and help out? It doesn't make any sense. And . . .' She took a deep breath.

'What?'

'It's just that when you fell off the ladder you thought that someone had been behind you but it was just a broken catch.

Couldn't it be that the branch simply fell? I understand that, with everything you've been through, you'd think the worst but sometimes there's a simple explanation. Is there any possibility that Ben is just who he says he is? I mean, are you sure about calling the police and accusing him of assaulting you when no one saw him do it?'

Charlie went back to the bed and sat back down again. She couldn't think straight. She'd felt threatened on several occasions since she'd been in Penderrion but Penny was right, there was nothing concrete that she could tell the police.

'But what if I'm right? What if I don't do anything and I'm not so lucky next time?'

Charlie noticed that Penny wasn't looking her in the eye. The way she viewed Charlie had changed. Everything had changed. Charlie's ability to stay hidden had changed.

It was over.

Charlie's new life and her pathetic attempt at fitting in and making new friends were over. Aubrey, Decca, Jenn, Bo. They'd all know soon enough. Secrets didn't stay secret for long. It was a wonder Marcus hadn't told Jenn what he knew already. Perhaps he had. Maybe she was already keeping her distance.

Charlie had to decide whether to stay and face the music or to pack her things and flee.

And if she was right about Ben, how long would it be before he came back to finish what he'd started?

CHAPTER FORTY-ONE

Charlie Miller

Tuesday, 20 November 2018

The rain pounded on the roof of her car as Charlie took the keys out of the ignition. It was so loud she found it difficult to hear her own thoughts. The wind rocked the car from side to side. She should have known that the engine wouldn't start.

The engine had bleated weakly. It had clicked and coughed. And then it had died. A week ago Charlie would've called it a flat battery due to an oversight, such as leaving the lights on, but not today. This man – Ben – had anticipated her next move. Now he'd found her, he wasn't going to let her escape.

She lay her head on the steering wheel. Her shoulders slumped in defeat. She should've taken the car maintenance course when she was in prison. Her plastering technique wasn't going to help her now. Her eyes filled with tears. Even if the car had started, where would she have gone? He'd found her once, he could find her again. And if not him, there'd be someone else.

She sat back in her seat, the windows steaming up, and listened to the rain strumming impatient fingers on the roof. Had she really thought she could start again and put the past behind her? She was sure that Marcus knew who she was but she'd hoped to reason with him. If he'd wanted to hurt her he'd have done something by now instead of just glowering at her, intimidating her. Ridiculous of her to be so focused on Marcus that she hadn't noticed the stranger who had bought her at auction. He didn't need to hit her with a branch; she would have gladly gone to his house like a lamb to the slaughter.

Her head ached, and it wasn't just from the concussion. None of this was making any sense. Who was Ben, and how had he known about the dove necklace or the code to the holiday cottages? Was he working with Marcus? Peter? Jenn? Decca? Penny? Bo? And what had this got to do with Lee? She was missing a piece of the puzzle.

She'd read everything she could about Lee's case, in part to torture herself. She wanted to read about Anna and Katy, to make them real to her, not just victims of Lee's anger, but she couldn't recall ever having read about anyone called Ben. She wondered where he was now. Was he watching her from the shelter of the trees? Could she persuade him that she wasn't as bad as he thought she was? If she could just explain . . .

She un-clicked her seat belt and stepped out of the car into the rain. She didn't run, didn't look over her shoulder. If she was being watched she didn't care. By the time she reached the kitchen door her hair was stuck to her face and rain was dripping off the end of her nose.

The house smelled of wood fires and coffee. She could hear the crackle of the logs and gravitated towards the warmth and comfort that the flames offered. She slipped off her coat and wiped her face on her sleeve. Charlie placed another log on the fire and sat on the floor in front of it, hugging her knees. With each gust of wind down the chimney the flames crouched and leapt; she could have watched the fire for hours, mesmerised by the dance.

Penny had left Charlie's house as soon as she was able. She was careful not to look as if she was rushing but Charlie noticed how she didn't stay a moment longer than was necessary. She'd made sounds about walking Decca's dogs but Charlie doubted she would really take them out in this weather.

So far only Ben, Marcus and Penny knew who she was. Though she didn't know exactly how much Marcus knew and who he'd told. He would tell Jenn, Penny would tell Decca, and Ben would tell the world. She really should go over and explain it to all to Aubrey before he heard the gossip from someone else.

She'd only got a brief glimpse of Ben at the auction and had hardly noticed him at all when he'd been in the house yesterday, thinking him to be a friend of Penny's, but she could have sworn she'd never seen him before. The name Ben didn't ring any bells either, though he could have easily changed his name – *she* had. She wished now that she'd read all the hate mail she'd received in prison. Perhaps they would have explained what Ben wanted from her. She wanted to look at articles related to Lee's case and see if there had been anyone called Ben involved but she hadn't been able to find her mobile anywhere.

She checked the pockets of her coat but they were empty. Her phone wasn't in the kitchen or the bedroom and, when she tried to call it from her landline it didn't even ring. It was a small cottage – a two-up two-down, as Gran would have called it – and there weren't many places it could be. She would ask Penny whether she'd seen it – if she was still talking to her. Maybe she'd dropped it in the woods.

She lifted the landline and slumped on to the sofa. Her head still hurt and the nausea was overwhelming when she moved too fast, but she could still remember important phone numbers. Like Conor's.

She had no means to run. Nowhere to hide. The only way she was going to survive was if she asked for help. If nothing else, if something happened to her someone should know why and who. Charlie had kept Conor at arm's length. His life didn't need complicating by an ex-con ex-girlfriend, but he was one of the few people who would understand without her having to explain everything, and one of the only people she could trust. She wiped her nose on the back of her hand and tried to steady her breathing. She couldn't do this on her own. And perhaps she didn't have to.

She dialled Conor's mobile number and waited. She was trembling. Conor would know what to do.

The silence stretched and then the ringing stopped. Charlie took a quick breath in, ready to speak, but the voice on the other end of the phone was distant.

'Hello, this is Conor Fletcher, please leave a message after the tone.'

'Shit.'

A pause.

A beep.

'Conor, hi, it's . . .' Charlie hesitated. She was Charlie now, but she'd been Steffi when she used to mean something to him.

'It's me,' she said eventually, hoping that the sound of her voice would be enough for him to recognise her. Even now she couldn't bear to use her old name.

'I know I said I wouldn't call, but there's a problem and I don't know who else to turn to. They know who I am,

Conor. I'm okay, but someone attacked me yesterday. His name's Ben. I don't know his surname. If anything happens to me there's a woman called Penny in the village who should be able to describe him to the police. Oh, and there's a lawyer called Marcus. I can't remember his surname, but he's Jenn's husband and he seems to know who I am. Look, call me back, yeah, on this number. Not my mobile. I don't know where it is. I'm sorry to get you involved but—'

'Thank you for calling. To re-record your message please press—'

Charlie looked at the phone in frustration and slammed it down. She had to hope Conor picked up the message before it was too late.

He had been so good to her. They'd seen very little of each other in the lead-up to her trial, and nothing since, but he'd arranged her father's funeral, arranged for the sale of her parents' house, and hers too. If she could turn back time, she would have appreciated what she'd had when they were together. Instead of letting them drift apart when Conor went to London, she would have gone with him.

There had been a moment, when she'd been staying in the hotel getting ready to give evidence when Conor had looked at her the way he used to do. She'd been confused, scared and so desperate to be loved that she had kissed him. She wasn't proud of it. Nor of what that simple kiss inevitably led to. Even as Conor murmured, 'We shouldn't do this,' she was pulling him to her. She needed to feel someone else's hands on her body. Lee was not going to be the last man to touch her. She needed to give herself to someone else.

It would have been easy for her to accept Conor's offer to wait for her if she went to prison. But she cared deeply for him, and he had someone at home – someone better than her – who cared for him. Charlie couldn't let Conor go into hiding with her. He had a career, a loving family and, according to Lee, a gorgeous girlfriend. He didn't need her dragging him down. She couldn't do that to him. She pushed him away and told him that it had meant nothing. The fact that he continued to help her was a testament to his character, not hers.

Charlie didn't know if he was still with that same girlfriend, whether they'd married, or even if he still lived in the same house. Their brief phone calls never strayed to the personal.

She swallowed back the tears that were threatening to bring her to her knees and stood up, wanting to take action but not knowing how. The weather, the car, the fact that Conor wasn't answering his phone, everything was conspiring against her to keep her isolated. She could still call the police and explain that someone was out to hurt her, but even as she tried to form the words she realised how empty they sounded.

What would Charlie say? That a man had turned up at the skills auction and made a donation to the church? That he might have hit her with a tree branch, though it could have been the wind? Or should she tell them he'd helped get her home safely and then assembled her furniture? Everything he'd done in front of others had been faultless. So how would she explain that she knew he meant to harm her? That he had a link to her hidden past though she just didn't know what it was yet?

The wind blew the rain against the living-room window as if it was throwing gravel at the glass. It made Charlie jump. She watched the leaves fly past the window at high speed.

The clouds were dark and heavy even though it was not yet midday. The only light came from the fire but Charlie didn't move to switch on the lights. The storm that was building outside fascinated her.

The phone rang and she snatched it up.

'Conor?'

There was a gasp on the other end of the phone. An audible swallow.

'Charlie? It's me, Penny.'

'Penny, hi. Sorry, I was expecting a call from someone else. Are you okay?'

'I don't know. I . . . the, um . . .'

Charlie took a deep breath. Here it came, the judgement, the reason they couldn't be friends any more, the plea for her to leave the village. She should've been expecting it as soon as Marcus asked if he knew her from somewhere.

'Just say what's on your mind,' Charlie said.

'He's been in my house.'

'Who?'

'I knew something was wrong as soon as I opened the door.' Penny's voice cracked; she was crying. 'After I left your house I took the dogs for a quick walk but when I got home . . . My things are everywhere. I think Ben's been in my house.'

Charlie sat forward suddenly. 'Has anything been taken?'

'No, but he's been through all my stuff, there are letters on the table. Bank statements. Private letters. My drawers are open and there are clothes all over the place. Do you think it's Ben? I mean, who else can it be? And why me? He seemed so nice yesterday. Do you think it's because I know what he looks like? Oh, goodness, I've seen his face. That's it, isn't it? You don't know what he looks like, but I do – I spent hours with him. He's warning me off. Charlie, I think he wants to hurt you.'

Of course he did. But then Penny would lead the police right to him because she could tell the police who he was and what he looked like. If Ben was serious about hurting Charlie, he wouldn't want any witnesses.

'Penny, listen to me. I want you to get in your car right now and go to the nearest police station. Don't wait for them to come to you – go straight there. Ben might still be nearby. Okay? Tell them everything that has happened. Tell them all about me and who I really am.'

'I can't leave you,' she said. 'What if he tries to hurt you? Let me pick you up first.'

'No, go straight to the police,' said Charlie.

'I'm not leaving you,' Penny said. 'That's not what friends do.'

Charlie hesitated. She wanted Penny safely away but she didn't want to sit and wait for whatever Ben had planned. Besides, this might be her only chance to escape the village.

'Okay. But when you get here, stay in the car and beep your horn. I'll come out to you.'

Perhaps she didn't have to face this alone after all. If she had been the only one in danger she might have waited for the inevitable – after all, with her car out of action she had no way to escape – but threatening her friends was unacceptable. She couldn't just sit here and wait for him now.

Charlie went upstairs as quickly as her aching head would let her and switched on the light, banishing the gloom into the corners. She grabbed two jumpers, some underwear and a toothbrush. She was just stuffing them into a bag when the lights went out. The darkness seemed denser than before she'd switched them on. She froze. Listened. Outside she could see that the whole of Penderrion was without light. Mud was sliding down the lane. The clouds were purple with rage and chased each other across the sky, hurrying to be gone and dragging others behind them like stubborn children.

The rain was still pelting down and smacking the ground. The river on the horizon was thicker and fuller and faster. The trees stood firm, but thinner branches bowed under the wind and rain.

She wondered about Aubrey. Did she have time to check on him before Penny got here? If they weren't coming back for a couple of days – at least until the police picked up Ben – who would keep an eye out for Aubrey? Perhaps she could get Penny to ask Bo.

Charlie went down the stairs slowly. In the gloom it was hard to see where the steps were.

Her eyes were on the window as she rounded the corner into the living room.

Otherwise, she would have seen the man sitting, quietly, in front of the fire.

CHAPTER FORTY-TWO

Charlie Miller

Tuesday, 20 November 2018

The man rubbed his hands together and blew on them.

'Horrible weather out there,' he said. 'I'm soaked through to the bone.' Meeting Charlie's startled look he said, 'And look at you! You're trembling. Why don't you come and get warm by the fire?'

Charlie had only caught a glimpse of him at the auction but now she was looking at him closely, she still didn't recognise him. He looked strong, broad across the shoulders, with hair that was beginning to grey at the temples and deep brown eyes. She'd seen the families of the victims in court and she was sure he wasn't one of them.

'Who are you?' she asked.

'You'll have to forgive me for barging in like this. I thought you and I should have a little chat. I popped by yesterday but you were in no fit state.'

He stood and thrust out a hand. 'We haven't been properly introduced. I'm Ben Jarvis.'

Charlie ignored the gesture and flattened herself against the wall, as far away from him as she could get.

Ben let his hand hover for a moment longer then shrugged and sat back down.

'What do you want?' Charlie asked.

'Did Penny tell you about me? I bet she did. She's very chatty, isn't she? Told me all about how you two are the best of friends, as if it was something to be proud of. Still, despite all your new friends, someone's got it in for you, eh?' He pointed to Charlie's head. 'I mean, you must have pissed someone off.'

Every time Ben looked away, Charlie glanced around the room for a weapon or for something to protect herself with. A half-empty glass lay on the coffee table but she wasn't sure she had the strength to break it.

Ben stood up again and took a step closer to the fire with his hands outstretched. He was restless. The light illuminated his face and showed the shadows beneath his eyes.

'I've been looking for you ever since you left HMP Hillstone. Sorry I missed you getting out, by the way. My plan was to meet you at the gate but they don't like to give exact dates, do they? Not when people might wish you harm. What did they do? Release you in the middle of the night?'

Keeping her eyes on Ben, Charlie took a step towards the door.

'Where do you think you're off to?' Ben asked without turning to face her.

'People are on their way,' Charlie said. 'They'll be here any minute. You should leave.'

'Me? Why? What is it that I've done wrong? I'm just a friend checking up on you after yesterday's nasty accident.'

She glanced over her shoulder. Penny would be here soon. When Charlie didn't go outside would she come inside to see what was taking so long or would she call the police?

'Pardon me for being so ungrateful, but it was you who caused that *accident* by hitting me with a branch in the first place,' she said.

'Did I? I don't recall doing that. Did anyone see me hitting you?'

'So, it was just a coincidence that you appeared not long after Penny found me, was it?'

'What can I say? I'm a regular Good Samaritan.'

Charlie took another half-step towards the door but Ben appeared to know exactly what she was doing.

'You won't benefit from the heat if you keep stepping further away from me. Don't make me force you to stay,' he said.

'How did you track me down?' Charlie asked.

'I can't give myself too much credit. I've had to rely on a lot of luck to lead me to you. God knows I was due some, though. Word to the wise, you would've been better off hiding out in a big city. London, Manchester, Birmingham. I'd never have found you in London; but here, well, it's not like you blend in, is it?'

'The police will be here any minute.'

'Come on now, Steffi. Don't insult me. We both know that I'm never going to fall for that.'

'Don't call me Steffi,' she said. 'It's not my name.'

'Ah, yes. Charlie Miller. Mother's maiden name, right?'

Charlie blinked hard. 'How did you . . . ?'

'Her death was mourned by many of her students. You should read some of the lovely things they said about her. Her old students remembered her back in the day when she was still Miss Miller. I was lucky really, because I probably wouldn't have bothered to look into your family history. I would never have expected you to use a family name. What were you thinking, Steffi? Careless. Anyone would think you wanted to get caught. Although, and I take my hat off to you here, Charlie was a good choice. It made me think you were a man, and I almost didn't come along to the auction. Come on, sit down. You're shivering. Why don't you come and get warm by the fire?'

Ben was being calm at the moment but Charlie didn't know how quickly that might change. She walked towards him slowly and sat on the other sofa as far away from him as she could get – not because he'd asked her to but because, if she didn't, she might faint. Her mind was still too slow. She wasn't scared, an eerie tranquillity had settled over her as if this was what she'd been waiting for. Now that the fear had a name and a face, she could reason with it, run from it. She could confront it.

'You know,' she said, 'I'm not lying. Someone is on the way. If you're here to hurt me—'

'They'll have a job getting into the village,' Ben said. 'The road is completely blocked. That picturesque little stream you've got down there has washed the road away. There are trees down all over the county. I walked over the fields. Tough going in this rain, though.'

Charlie looked out of the window. If he was telling the truth there was no way for her and Penny to leave the village and, even if she could get to a phone, it would delay the police getting to them.

Ben turned away from the fire so that he was facing Charlie. 'You changed your hair. I wouldn't have recognised you in the street because I was looking for a blonde. If it wasn't for everything coming together . . . Cornwall, Miller . . . I don't think I would've spotted you. When you stood up in that village hall, though, I knew. You still do that thing that you used to do in court with your ear. Always fiddling with it. I'm surprised anyone else has recognised you, though.'

'What makes you think someone else recognises me?' Charlie asked.

'Well, it wasn't me that knocked you out in the woods, was it?'

'Right.' Charlie almost laughed. 'And it wasn't you who made sure my car wouldn't start, or broke into Penny's house either?'

'Nasty bump on the head, that,' he said. 'Looks like you're imagining things. Mind if I put another log on the fire? I can't seem to get warm.'

'You haven't told me what you want.'

'What everyone wants.' He sighed dramatically. 'Answers.'

'Is Ben even your real name?' Charlie asked.

He smiled. 'Yes, it is. Unlike some people, you see, I've got nothing to hide. You had me worried yesterday. I honestly thought you were going to die. Your friend was insistent that you didn't need an ambulance; she's got a thing against hospitals, hasn't she?'

'Wouldn't it have been easier for you if I'd died?'

'Died? God no, what good would that do anyone? I wanted to look you in the eye. I've got a lot of questions, see? And I think you might be the only one who can answer them. Well, you and Lee but I'm not getting anywhere near him for another nineteen years at least. I would've waited for better weather, or for you to get over your accident, but I knew you'd bolt as soon as you could. Either that or someone else would get to you first.

'I used to write to you in prison but you never wrote back. Rude. Very rude. You must have known how much I was hurting and you didn't even take the time to respond. What else were you doing with all that time on your hands? How difficult would it have been to write a note?'

'I hardly think you've come all this way to chastise me for being a bad pen pal,' Charlie said.

'Did you even read my letters?'

Charlie shook her head. 'Didn't want the fan mail to go to my head.'

Charlie still didn't recognise Ben but she could take a guess. 'So, what is it? You've come to make me pay for covering for Lee? You've come to make me see that if I'd gone to the police sooner I could have saved Anna? Well, you could have saved yourself a trip because there's nothing you can say that I don't already know.'

Ben tilted his head to one side and narrowed his eyes. He looked her up and down as if he were measuring her.

'I think we've got our wires crossed,' he said eventually. 'I'm not here because of Anna. I'm here because of my daughter. Remi Jarvis.'

CHAPTER FORTY-THREE

And a new player enters the game.

It was only a matter of time before others made themselves known. But that's okay. He might even have helped. The pieces on the chess board are lined up and now you realise you're in battle. Which way should you run?

It's cruel really, the way we're all playing with you like a cat with an injured mouse. We should put you out of your misery.

You are crumbling in front of my eyes. Telling tales to anyone who'll listen. No one will believe your sob story but too much has been said now to let this go on for even a day longer. You've started blabbing and now you'll never shut up. The whispers are circling the village. The storm is blowing the news down chimneys, writing it on leaves that it drops from the skies. By nightfall they'll all know who you really are. They won't stand for it.

In the end it was your desire to see the best in everyone that was your downfall. You trusted us all, invited us into your home, came into ours. Why weren't you more cautious? I'd have been suspicious if I were you.

I understand you better now. You are desperate to be liked. You were so nervous that no one would want you at the auction that you begged an old man to bid on you. You're easily hurt when people let you down, aren't you? And you hate it when people aren't who they appear to be.

I know that better than most.

CHAPTER FORTY-FOUR

Charlie Miller

Tuesday, 20 November 2018

Charlie didn't know the name Remi Jarvis.

She watched Ben. He watched the flames. Under his eyes he had the deep bags of a man who hadn't been sleeping well. Tiredness could make him slow or it might make him quick to anger. Charlie was trying to work out which path he would take.

'She's been missing since May 2014. Four and a half years,' he said. 'But I know she's dead. I tried to hope – I did – but, as the weeks went by, I couldn't keep kidding myself. No body. No leads. No suspects. As far as the police are concerned, there's nothing more they can do unless more information comes to light, but no one's treating this as a missing person's case any more. She's not used her phone or her bank cards since she went missing. All the police have is some blurry CCTV footage of her leaving the bar with a man of average height. He was wearing dark clothes with no distinguishable markings. It hardly narrows it down, does it? I'm the only one still looking for that bastard.'

Charlie tried to swallow but her mouth was dry. She didn't see how this could have anything to do with her but, at the same time, unease unfurled in her chest.

'Remi could light up a room,' Ben continued. 'She was the one thing in my life I was really proud of, you know? I couldn't be that much of a failure if I'd produced a girl like that. She was smart and kind and funny. Pretty, too. Not like these girls you see on the telly, all false eyelashes and lip-fillers. She was . . . flawless. Sorry, I don't get to talk about her any more. My wife has moved on. Says we can't keep wallowing in the past, but no one else knew her like we did. If I can't talk to Amanda about her, then who can I talk to?'

A log crumpled in the grate and sparks flew upwards. The power was still off and the flames made shadows dance on the walls.

'You can talk to me,' said Charlie. 'Why don't you tell me about her?'

She hadn't expected to feel sympathy for the man who had attacked her and then appeared in her house. But this was a man who had experienced life-shattering loss. How could she deny him a chance to be heard?

Ben said, 'She was twenty-five when she disappeared. My only child. Maybe I put too much on her, had too much of my happiness resting on her shoulders. I never held her back, mind. I encouraged her to spread her wings and take every opportunity she could. I wanted to give her what I never had. I didn't go to university or have foreign holidays. I didn't start living my best life until she came along. I worked hard for her so I could buy her nice things. I paid for piano lessons and she was up to grade six by the time she was fourteen. I'd never heard a child play like she did. I could've sat and listened to her play all day long. And then . . . then she was gone and nothing was ever the same again.'

Charlie had to choose her words carefully. 'Remi sounds like a lovely young woman and she was lucky to have a dad like you. I wish I could say something that would make it better but I don't know how I can help you. I . . . I didn't know her.'

Ben stood up quickly and lunged at her. He stepped over the coffee table with one easy step and pushed Charlie against the back of the sofa. He rested a hand on either side of her shoulders.

'No? What about that boyfriend of yours?' he shouted.

Flecks of spittle landed on Charlie's cheek.

'I don't know. The police never . . . This is the first I've heard of her. I swear. But I'm listening now, aren't I? Tell me why you think that Lee has something to do with this.'

'Why are you sticking up for him?' Ben's face was inches from hers.

'I'm not. I'm only saying I don't know how you've linked Lee to your daughter's disappearance.'

'Murder,' he said.

Ben stood, turned away from Charlie, walked to the fire and then came back to stare into her face again.

'Her friends all said the same thing. They'd gone out the back of the bar, into the beer garden, for a cigarette. There was this good-looking guy there, smoking. Remi started talking to him and her friends left them to it. They seemed to know a lot of the same places in Sheffield, talked about places that had closed down. Restaurants that they'd been to. She was drunk, but so were her friends. No one realised that she'd not come back inside. We checked all the hospitals. Called friends. Hoped that she was staying with someone maybe, or was injured somewhere. Can you imagine what it's like to pray that your daughter is injured and in hospital? When that's the best news you can hope for?'

Charlie shook her head. 'I can only imagine how terrible it was for you.'

'I kept going back to that bar, other bars too, looking for this guy, but there were no leads. I felt sure it had to be a jilted ex, but the boyfriends I knew about all checked out. I couldn't help but think there must be someone I didn't know about.'

Ben paced the floor. The muscles in his jaw were twitching.

'It wasn't until Lee Fisher's case went to trial that I noticed the similarities. I felt for the families of the girls. I knew what those parents were going through. A reporter said that Fisher had lured the girls away when he'd been outside bars smoking with them. They went as far as to say that the smoking ban was putting women in danger as they had to go to isolated places to smoke. It just . . . it clicked. I knew it was him.

'The last person to see Remi alive was that bastard she was outside smoking with. I went to the police but they didn't take me seriously. These two killings were close together and both women's bodies turned up in the next few weeks, whereas Remi went missing a couple of years before and her body hadn't turned up. They saw nothing to link the cases. They said I was clutching at straws.'

Charlie turned her head away. It wasn't such a big leap and she could see why Ben had made it but, if the police hadn't seen any links between the cases, she didn't know how she was meant to help.

'I don't know what you want from me,' she said.

'You can drop the innocent act because there's only you and me here now. You knew what he was doing, didn't you?

You knew what he was capable of. What was it? Were you egging him on? Did you get a kick out of it? What happened four years ago? Why did he kill my daughter? And then why did he stop for two years?'

Charlie put her hand over her mouth against the rising bile in the back of her throat.

She knew that Lee was capable of terrible things but she didn't want to believe there were other victims that she didn't know about. She didn't want to acknowledge the possibility that she'd fallen in love with a murderer.

If he'd killed Remi, who was to say there weren't others in the time they were together? She'd thought her drinking had caused him to get angry, to lose control, but what if he'd always had it in him to kill, but the opportunity hadn't presented itself in a long time? What if there were others, like Remi, that he'd managed to hide? Had he just run out of time to hide Katy and Anna's bodies?

'I had no way of knowing,' she said, as much to herself as to Ben. 'I still don't. What you're saying . . . Do you have any evidence that Remi's disappearance has anything to do with Lee?'

Ben sat down heavily on the sofa opposite Charlie and looked up at the ceiling. The anger seemed to drain from him and he deflated in front of her. Charlie tried to control her breathing and swallowed hard.

'Remi didn't turn up to work one day. Her boss said it wasn't like her, but they'd assumed she was sick and had forgotten to call in. Apart from leaving messages on her answer phone they didn't know what else to do. On Thursday a colleague from HR called my wife, and that's when we raised the alarm. Days. Days and we never knew that she . . . I mean, was she scared? Did he hurt her? You'd think that you'd feel a shift in the universe when your child is no longer in the world, but I didn't. Nothing had changed. She was probably killed on that Saturday night but I carried on as normal day after day, not even knowing. I wouldn't believe it at first. And then, of course, there's no body so there's always the tiniest chance that she's not dead at all. Some days I try and kid myself that she's alive and living it up in Bali. Even if I never saw her again, I'd be all right with that, but I know she'd never let me feel this way if she could help it. She was the loveliest girl; she'd never let me and her mum hurt like this.'

'Ben, please believe me. I would help you if I could. What you're saying . . . well, maybe you're right but that's for the police to decide.'

'I want to know what happened to my baby girl and I want to know where he buried her body.'

'I swear I don't—'

'Did he drown her?' he asked. 'Because that's what he did to the others, wasn't it? If you tell me what you know, I won't tell the police how I found out. I'll just say I've received new information and tell them where to start looking. And if you don't tell me what I want to know . . .' Ben left the threat hanging in the air between them.

Charlie felt like she might vomit. Ben was glaring at her. If she knew what he wanted to hear she would tell him, but she'd never heard of Remi Jarvis. She couldn't recall having read about her disappearance in the papers and was sure the police hadn't mentioned her in relation to Lee's case.

'Tell me where she is and I'll leave you alone. I'll walk away from here today and you'll never see me again. I need to lay my daughter to rest.'

Charlie felt the room sway. She blinked hard. 'I'm sorry you've lost your daughter. I can't begin to understand how that must—'

'You covered for him. You knew what he was up to.'

'I didn't.'

'You expect anyone to believe that you didn't know your boyfriend kept dead bodies in the boot of your car?'

'I didn't know he'd killed those women. I—'

'Lies!'

'I knew he was hiding something. Sure, I didn't want to believe he was capable of something like that, but I wasn't covering for him.'

Ben was suddenly on his feet. He slapped Charlie's face.

'Stop your lies.'

Charlie put her hand to her stinging cheek and raised her voice to match his. 'I have never heard of your daughter!'

Ben grabbed her by the throat and lifted her from the sofa. She grappled with his hand, trying to prise his fingers from her neck. He held her firmly but he wasn't choking her. Yet.

'You're a convincing liar, I'll give you that much. I came here to talk to you yesterday. I thought we could piece it together, see if you could help me pinpoint Lee's movements around the time Remi went missing. I thought, between us, we could spot what the police had missed.'

'Please,' Charlie gasped. 'I don't know anything about Remi's disappearance. I swear. You say she went missing in May 2014, right? I'd only just met Lee. I had no idea what he was up to.'

'I helped bring you home when you were hurt. I put up your bed. I carried you up the stairs. I stayed around to make sure you were okay, and then I saw it, just lying there on your mantelpiece, and I realised you were nothing more than a lying bitch.'

The angrier he got, the more his hand was tightening around her windpipe. Charlie was gasping for air.

'Please . . . I don't know what you're talking about.'

Ben reached inside the neck of his jumper with his free hand, fingers grasping for a fine silver chain with the outline of a dove.

'If you didn't know my daughter then why do you have her necklace?'

CHAPTER FORTY-FIVE

Charlie Miller

Tuesday, 20 November 2018

The room was dimming at the edges of Charlie's vision. She was fighting for breath, didn't want to pass out.

'The . . . the necklace was a gift.'

Ben threw her to the floor and crouched over her.

'Gift? Or was it a trophy? I read about him keeping his victim's jewellery. Katy's earrings, Anna's necklace. What kind of man collects jewellery? Now tell me the truth. Where did you get it from?'

'Lee gave it to me.'

'When?'

'I don't know.'

'Where did he get it from?'

'I don't know.'

'Where is my daughter?'

'I don't know!' Charlie lay on the floor and sobbed. 'I swear I don't know.'

She had curled into a ball and cowered as Ben threw a glass at the wall. He wanted answers that Charlie couldn't give him.

'What did that bastard do to my daughter? Did he drown her like he drowned the others? Did he? Tell me!'

There was a sudden bang that made the window shake. Three hard knocks on the glass. Charlie raised her head from the floor to see a face at the window with his hands cupped around his eyes. Aubrey.

Ben took one last look at Charlie on the floor. 'Maybe it would jog your memory if someone you cared about got hurt,' he spat. 'I hope you never have to go through what I go through every single day.' And then he ran from the house, leaving the back door swinging open in the wind.

Charlie put her hand to the back of her head. It came away tacky with blood.

'Aubrey?' called Charlie. 'Is that you?'

'Bleddy hell,' he said, hobbling into sight. 'Y'okay?'

She looked at the blood on her fingers and stood up. 'Yeah, I'm all right.'

The wind took advantage of the open doorway to dash into the corners and tried to blow out the fire like a candle on a birthday cake.

'Who was that?' he asked, pointing out of the window at Ben's retreating figure running down the lane towards the church. 'He took off like he had the devil after 'im.'

Charlie took a deep breath to calm her hammering heart. 'He's the man who bid for me at the auction. Turns out he wanted a bit more than a shelf putting up. I'm just glad you turned up when you did.'

'Good job you talked me into getting those hearing aids, eh? Went outside to see whether this wind had left me with any roof tiles and heard shouting and glass breaking. Knew there was summat up.'

'Thank you, Aubrey.' Charlie kissed him on his forehead and squeezed his shoulder.

She'd thought Ben was going to kill her. She supposed he still might. The threat hung in the air. His last words to her were that he would help jog her memory, but if she didn't know what had happened to Remi, nothing Ben could do would make her remember.

'Who was he, then, this idiot?'

'He's someone who thinks I know more than I do. It's a long story but the fact is, I have an ex-boyfriend who did some horrendous things.'

'This boyfriend hurt you, did he?'

'Not me.' Charlie licked her dry lips. 'Not physically. There's no easy way to say it, Aubrey, but he's in prison for the murder of two women. I didn't suspect anything and, when the police asked me, I told them that Lee had been with me the night of the first murder. I . . . I was wrong and I ended up going to prison for providing a false alibi.'

Charlie stared out of the window and waited for Aubrey's reaction. She hadn't wanted him to know, but there was no point concealing her past any more. When he didn't say anything she turned to face him.

'I said,' Charlie raised her voice for him to hear, 'I went to prison for—'

'I heard what you said.' Aubrey flapped a dismissive hand at her. 'I can hear everything now I've got these things in my ears. What I don't understand is what it's got to do with the fella who was in here a minute ago.'

'Oh,' Charlie said. 'Ben? He thinks that Lee – that's my ex – he thinks Lee killed his daughter.'

'What do you think?'

'I think,' said Charlie, 'that he's right.'

Charlie touched her neck. It was sore from where Ben had half-choked her, but, worse than that, it burned at the memory of where that dove necklace used to touch her skin. The necklace had been the first gift Lee had ever given her. She recalled that there'd been no gift box, no receipt. He'd produced it from a pocket and put it around her neck. Before hers, the last pulse it had rested upon was Remi's. It had been taken from a woman's dead body.

She stood by the window, mind wandering, until a flash of lightning caused her to flinch. She should call the police, tell them what had happened. The threat was no longer in her mind, Aubrey had seen Ben and so had Penny.

Penny.

It had been almost an hour since Penny said she was on her way round to pick her up. Ben had said the road was blocked so Penny couldn't have driven straight to the police like Charlie had urged her to.

'Aubrey, have you seen Penny?'

'Not today. Why?'

Perhaps she'd called the police and was waiting for them at the house. But what if Ben was heading there now?

Maybe it would jog your memory if someone you cared about got hurt.

Penny had told Ben that she and Charlie were best friends. If it was him who broke into Penny's house, he already knew where she lived.

'Shit!'

Charlie lifted up the phone to call Penny but the handset was silent. She pushed at buttons but there was no dialling tone. The bad weather must have taken out the phones.

'What is it?' asked Aubrey.

'I think he's gone after Penny but the phones are down.'

'What d'you want me to do?' he asked.

'Stay here. Keep checking the phone. As soon as that line gets reconnected, I want you to call the police and send them straight to Penny's. Tell them I think that Ben is going to hurt her.'

Charlie ran from the house as the thunder sounded. The rain was heavy and the wind stronger. Charlie ran down the lane towards Penny's, she could see the church spire through squinting eyes against the rain. The wind buffeted her from side to side. She didn't know whether it was rain or tears trickling down the side of her face.

Charlie had to stop, take a deep breath. She was weak but she had to keep going. She looked at the holiday cottages, but they were empty. Decca wasn't home either. There was no one she could call for help. She started moving again, half walking, half jogging. There was no time to waste.

She was breathing hard as she reached Penny's door and pushed it open. It opened straight into a small living room. Charlie tripped and knocked her hip on the table. She bent over it, still fighting the concussion, the nausea. She tried to harness her fear so that it could carry her forward.

'Penny?'

Ben was unstable and he was emotional. There was every chance that he would hurt Penny to get back at her. To get her to remember.

Maybe it would jog your memory if someone you cared about got hurt.

'Penny! Where are you?'

A chair was on its back and an empty glass lay on its side in the middle of a circular rug. There were letters and papers scattered over the low coffee table. Some were handwritten. Charlie looked into the kitchen but no one was there.

'Penny!'

Her pulse was hammering in her ears.

Charlie dragged herself up the stairs. Clothes were thrown all over the bedroom and drawers lay at angles. The sheets had been pulled off Penny's bed but there was no one in the house. She went back downstairs and picked up the phone. Silence, just like there had been at The Buttery. The phone lines were still down.

Charlie turned around slowly. On the mirror, written in bright red lipstick, were the words, THEY ALL DROWN.

CHAPTER FORTY-SIX

Charlie Miller

Tuesday, 20 November 2018

Charlie ran into the lane, spinning around looking for some-one. Anyone. The power was still out and all the houses were in darkness. The few neighbours she had would be hunkered down behind locked doors, if they were in at all. She shouted, hoping someone would hear her.

'Help! I need help! Someone, help!' But her voice was whipped away by the wind and blown out to sea.

Ben said he didn't have a car, and Penny's was still in the driveway, so he'd only gone as far as he could get on foot. The river had burst its banks, and it was too close to where other people could see him. If he was threatening to drown Penny, he must have taken her to the beach. The cottages that overlooked it were empty this week and no one would be walking there in this weather.

Charlie staggered towards The Rectory and hammered at the door. She pressed the doorbell over and over again. The house was in darkness, just like the rest of the village.

'Jenn!' she called. 'Open up!'

She walked backwards from the house, looking up at its sombre windows. She thought she saw a movement behind a curtain.

'Help! I need help! It's Penny!' she shouted. 'Jenn? Are you in there? Marcus?'

But if someone had been at the window they weren't there now. She turned and ran back to the lane. There was no one to help her. She had to do this on her own.

Lightning split the sky in two and Charlie instinctively ducked as she opened the gate to the coastal path and slipped through it. She heard the rumbling of thunder in the distance.

The trees scattered water upon her as she ran. Her heart hammered through fear and exertion. She stumbled over wet leaves and branches strewn in her path and paused to catch her breath. The stream by her side was racing her to the sea. Twigs and leaves overtook her and sped away.

It seemed to take longer than before for the sea to come into view and, when it did, it wasn't the same water that she'd walked beside with Penny. This was an angry grey writhing mass that covered most of the beach, frothing at the mouth like a rabid dog. Charlie couldn't tell if the tide was coming in or going out, but there was only a small sickle of sand visible and no sign of Penny.

A gust of wind tilted her to one side and she had to grab at a gorse bush to steady herself. It cut into her hand but she didn't cry out. Adrenalin was driving her, and it was numbing the parts of her that felt pain. At the gap in the rocks, Charlie jumped on to the beach. She landed heavily and fell on to her side. What was left of the sand was strewn with driftwood, plastic bottles, blistered seaweed and bright blue netting that had been dragged from the depths of the sea. Charlie staggered to her feet and looked around her, but the rain was directly in her face. The wind was so strong that she could hardly catch her breath. Her clothes were sticking to her and her jeans were heavy. There was no sign of Ben or Penny. The only part of the beach she couldn't see from here was the inlet beyond the rocks.

The sounds of waves on rock were thunderous and she couldn't hear any voices or movement. Her jumper flapped behind her as she leaned into the wind. She caught a glimpse of yellow where the rocks jutted out into the sea. She ran towards the small inlet calling Penny's name, but the words were thrown back in her face by a storm that didn't want her to be heard.

'Penny!'

She put her arm in front of her face to stop the spray from stinging her eyes. Her thighs were aching from propelling herself forward on the sand and, though she was going as fast as she could, it was slow progress. The water was splashing into the side of her feet, her legs.

The wind kicked sand into her eyes, but she still didn't turn her face. Charlie's eyes were locked on the space beyond the rock where she knew she'd find Penny. She tripped on a rock and fell heavily. Sand coated her chin and lips. Charlie spat it away and clambered onwards.

A line of rocks, black with rain and seawater, rose before her. She began to climb them, but her hands and feet slipped. Clutches of purple mussels clung tight to dark crevices and she tried to do the same. She banged her knee but didn't stop. She didn't have much time, and neither did Penny.

She pulled herself up the rocks, knowing that she couldn't get a purchase with her feet. Her arms were throbbing with exertion and her hands were numb. She got to the top and saw Penny sitting on a rock in her thin yellow raincoat with the sea whipping up around her.

'Penny!'

The water was rushing around her and a deep cave behind Penny was already being hollowed out by the water. There was no sign of Ben.

Penny was grey with the cold and she had her arms wrapped round her knees. The water level was rising. The tide was coming in and they had to move fast.

Charlie jumped down into the water but her heel caught a rock and she was flung face-first into the water. The temperature of the water shocked her and for a moment her chest seemed crushed by the cold. She snapped her head out of the sea and gasped for breath, but a wave hit her full in the face and she choked on the salt water. Her eyes were burning and her hair was plastered across her face, but she pulled herself up and waded towards Penny. Charlie fell upon her in relief.

'Penny, where's Ben?'

Penny looked up at her. Her eyes were vacant. They were bloodshot and wide.

'We need to get out of here. Where is he?'

'I'm cold,' Penny said.

'I know, but it's okay now. We need to move. Come on.'

Charlie looked all around her again in case Ben was behind them, but either he wasn't there or he wasn't ready to show his face yet.

Charlie took hold of Penny's arm and began to drag her, but Penny slipped out of her grasp and started shaking her head rapidly.

Something was stopping Penny from moving.

'I thought you'd never get here,' Penny said. 'I was scared that you'd be too late.'

'I came as quick as I could. Ben doesn't want to hurt you. He's trying to scare me and show that he could hurt someone

I care about if I don't give him what he wants. He thinks I know something about his daughter's disappearance. Come on. There's nothing to be scared of. We need to get out of here now.'

Penny's teeth were chattering. Her trademark red lipstick was absent and her lips were turning blue.

'Penny, did you see which way he went?'

Penny lifted her gaze to Charlie's. Her eyes went from distant to hard. 'As if you don't know,' she said with a small shake of the head.

'Where's Ben? Is he still here?'

Charlie looked again into the caves, looked up the rocks above them. She couldn't see Ben anywhere and couldn't work out how he'd managed to get Penny down here and then slip past Charlie on the path. She could only have been ten minutes behind him, fifteen at the most. She grabbed Penny's hand. It was as cold as the water around them. Colder than ten minutes in the sea would be.

'Ben nearly ruined everything,' Penny laughed. 'Who cares about that now? This has got nothing to do with him.'

'What's going on, Penny?'

'Haven't you worked it out yet? I'm talking about Lee Fisher. It's all about him. You were the one who put him away, but I'm the one who's going to set him free.'

CHAPTER FORTY-SEVEN

Charlie Miller

Tuesday, 20 November 2018

The rain stopped but the wind was still flinging waves at the rocks, and Charlie with them.

She was holding Penny's hand and her nails were digging in to Penny's cold skin.

At first Charlie thought she'd misheard her and then she hoped that she had.

'What are you talking about?'

She had to shout to be heard over the sound of the crashing waves.

'Lee doesn't deserve to be in prison for something that you did. We're going to be together when he gets out.'

Charlie's legs buckled and she let go of Penny's hand as she sank into the water. She pushed at the water and got back to her feet. Penny wasn't making sense.

'Penny, no. You can't—'

'His lawyers are working on an appeal and this is the evidence they need to reopen the case.'

'What evidence?'

'You tried to kill me when you realised that Lee and I were in love. You dragged me to the beach and tried to drown me.'

'He's lying to you, Penny. You've got to listen to me. I know he's convincing but think. Think. You can't do this.' Charlie thought of what Decca had said the first time they'd met, about how long it took for hypothermia to set in at these temperatures. If Penny had come down here as soon as she called Charlie, she'd been here for an hour.

'Let's talk about this in the dry, yeah?' Charlie took hold of Penny's arm again and looked about her. The tide was almost fully in and she was finding it difficult to stay on her feet. The water was at her chest now.

'The police are on their way,' said Penny. 'I called them and said I was scared of you. I said you'd found out about me and Lee. I thought you'd rush straight over when I didn't turn up to pick you up. You were meant to panic that Ben had hurt me. Doesn't matter now. You're here before the police, and that's the important thing. They'll be here soon enough.'

'No they won't. The road is out.'

'They'll find a way.'

'Penny, you're freezing. We need to get you in the warm. The police don't need to find us here. It'll have the same impact if they find us in your house. Yeah?'

'What took you so long?' she asked.

'Ben turned up. As soon as he left I came to find you. Penny, you've got this all wrong. Please don't do this. You know I'd never hurt you. Lee is manipulating you. I didn't hurt those women, Lee did.'

Penny's whole body was shaking.

'I know the story you told the police, but they couldn't see through you like I can. I read all about it at the time and how you didn't have an alibi either. Lee told me how jealous you were. He was trying to leave you, wasn't he? I know all about it. And then you punished him by telling lies to the police, by planting evidence. Pretended you were an innocent bystander.'

'Fine. If that's what you want to believe. Just come with me. Let's get inside where we can talk about this. If you really believe that I'm capable of drowning people then this is the worst place to be. Right?'

'The police will see that you're up to your old tricks again and they'll have to let Lee go free. And then we can be together and I can help him piece his life back together. I won't let you destroy anyone else's life. Lee and I both know what it's like to have you tear our lives apart.'

'I would never hurt you, Penny.'

'No? You still don't know who I am, do you? I knew I was taking a risk, but it was only a small one. I didn't even have to change my name like you did. I was right under your nose and you didn't notice a thing.'

Charlie stared at her. 'What?'

'I was so desperate to impress you,' Penny said. 'Conor never shut up about you. I knew one word from you could end our relationship and things were going so well for us.'

Charlie tried to step backwards but the waves kept pushing her, pushing her, towards Penny on the rock.

'You're Conor's girlfriend?'

'Ex-girlfriend, thanks to you. Do you remember that night we were due to meet at Max's party? You had somewhere better to be.'

'I was ill,' Charlie said.

'Conor was disappointed and ended up getting far too drunk. I was the designated driver, of course. Lee and I were the only sober ones there and we spent the evening talking. We had a deep connection.'

Charlie's teeth were chattering. The rock was almost covered with water now. Penny stood and swayed as her stiff limbs tried to find some strength.

'I'd always planned on luring you to the beach to show the police how you tried to drown me just like you drowned Katy and Anna. But I panicked. I thought I was out of time. Marcus was suspicious and kept asking questions about how well I knew you and where you were from. And then Ben bid for you at the auction. You're not worth the amount he paid for you so I knew he had an ulterior motive.' Penny was shouting over the din of the waves. 'I lost my nerve. But then I saw the opportunity and I took it. When I hit you with that branch—'

'It was you?'

'I was going to say you'd attacked me when I confronted you. I was going to rough myself up a bit – hit my head on a tree, that sort of thing – and then call the police. It had to look like I hit you in self-defence, but then Ben turned up before I had time to make it look like we'd had a fight. I've been watching you, waiting for an opportunity for you to be alone, but you hardly went out. You were surrounded by all this beautiful coastline and you didn't even go for a walk.'

'But, Penny, why?'

'The letters that Lee wrote to me from prison are on the table in my house. Your fingerprints are all over them. I got you to hold them when you were still delirious from the accident. Your fingerprints are on the lipstick I used to write on the mirror, too. I'll tell the police that you discovered my relationship with Lee, perhaps even moved down here because of it, and you tried to kill me. When I escape from your . . . clutches,' Penny laughed at this, 'and tell the police, they will see that it was you all along. Be sure your sins shall find you out.'

It was almost too much for Charlie's mind to process.

'Do you want to know something funny?' Penny continued. 'It was you that drove me into Lee's arms in the first place. We hardly spoke after that night at Max's party. We were both in relationships and I didn't want to jeopardise what I had with Conor. I almost felt sorry for you when I heard about the court case. I was surprised that Lee had been arrested, but I accepted that there was enough to link him to those poor women. But then something happened, didn't it?'

'Did it? Look, we need to get out of the water, Penny.'

'I know what you did, Charlie. You slept with my boyfriend on the day the trial started.'

Charlie gasped. 'Hold on. It wasn't like that,' she said. 'I was vulnerable, I was . . . Oh, God, Penny. Yes, I slept with him. I shouldn't have done it. It was unforgiveable of me and I am so, so, sorry. I feel terrible about it and wish I could take it back. My life was falling apart and I was desperately clinging on to Conor but that's no excuse for what I did.'

The look of hatred on Penny's face was starting to make sense now.

'We were so happy together. We have such different personalities but it seemed to work. No one had ever treated me that well before. He respected me, he was kind to me, he loved me. And then your selfishness ruined everything. Conor's a good man and he couldn't cope with the guilt of what he'd done. He confessed everything to me. I told him that I could learn to forgive him, that we could work through it, but he said he needed space and that was it. It was all over. My future gone.'

Charlie could hardly look Penny in the eye. She knew what she'd done, and was ashamed of herself, but it was so much easier on her conscience when she didn't know who Conor's girlfriend was.

'I don't know how to show you how sorry I am, but if you come with me now I promise to try,' said Charlie.

'So you can kill me too, to shut me up?'

'I'd never hurt you, Penny.'

'I've met women like you before. You're the type who uses men,' Penny said.

'No. It's not like that.'

'You used Conor and you used Lee. I went to see him in prison and he explained everything. He told me all about your jealousy and suddenly it made sense. You ruined both our lives and thought you could swan off and leave us to pick up the pieces.'

'Lee lied to you. I understand why you want to make me pay for what I did but this isn't the answer.'

Penny glanced over her shoulder. There was still no sign of the police, or anyone coming to help either of them.

'How did you know where to find me?' Charlie asked.

'Conor had all the information about The Buttery on his desk when I let myself into the house to get the last of my things. Lee asked me to keep an eye on you. He said he knew you'd try to hide but you were bound to keep in touch with Conor. When Conor bid on an auction property down here, I knew this was where you'd go. He'd never shown any interest in Cornwall so it wasn't for him. It was a risk, but I moved down here straight away and then I waited. I didn't think you would suspect someone who'd moved down here before you. I probably knew about this place before you did.'

'Lee isn't who you think he is. *I'm* not what you think I am. But we're both in danger if we stay here any longer. If we both drown there won't be any justice for anyone.'

Penny's lips were blue, she was freezing, but if she wouldn't get off that rock there was nothing Charlie could do except get help and hope she wasn't too late. She turned around and tried to move away. If she could climb up to the path, she could go for help.

'Go on then!' shouted Penny. 'Run. I'll tell the police that you left me here to die.'

'You won't tell them anything because if you don't leave now, you'll drown!'

'I don't care. They'll still know it was you and then Lee will be released. His freedom is all that matters now.'

The waves were too strong and Charlie felt her feet being taken from beneath her. She tried to swim against the tide, but her attempts were feeble and she was pushed towards the dark cave. She pulled as hard as she could and the sea rewarded her by spitting her out again so that she could get a grip on the rocks. She held fast but the sharp stone was cutting into her hands. She was too waterlogged to pull herself up.

Charlie kicked off her shoes and was able to ride the next wave to get a foot on the rocks. She fell and grazed her cheek but pulled herself out of the water. The urge to lie there and rest was powerful, but she had to carry on. Had to get help. Lee wouldn't win this time.

But as she got to her knees and looked to the path, a cold hand grabbed her ankle and yanked her back towards the water.

CHAPTER FORTY-EIGHT

Charlie Miller

Tuesday, 20 November 2018

Charlie held on to the rocks with clawed hands and felt her nails tear. She kicked out instinctively and her heel connected with Penny's face.

Penny fell backwards and was immediately swallowed up by the water.

'Penny!'

Charlie stared into the churning sea. She couldn't walk away and leave Penny to drown but the other woman had disappeared and the waves had removed all trace of her.

Suddenly Penny's face bobbed up to the surface and she gasped for air. Charlie slid down the rock, one hand gripping the cold hard stone and the other outstretched.

'Take my hand!' she cried.

Penny reached a hand out of the water but began to slip back under. She wasn't close enough for Charlie to get hold of her. Penny's mouth filled with seawater and she began to cough.

'Swim for the rocks,' Charlie shouted, but Penny was being dragged further away from her.

Charlie wouldn't let another person die because of Lee. She couldn't bear another death on her conscience. Penny didn't know what she was doing. She was vulnerable, easily led, and she had believed every lie that Lee had sold her. Not so long ago, Charlie had been the same.

Charlie half stood and then dived into the water. She put her head down and screwed up her eyes. She held her breath and pulled as hard as she could towards Penny. She had to save her because she hadn't been able to save the others.

She saw a flash of yellow rain mac through the water and grabbed a handful of it.

Penny sank beneath the water and Charlie kicked hard and dragged her up again.

'I need you to help me help you,' Charlie shouted. 'If we swim together . . .'

Penny pivoted in the water, her arms thrashing about, and Charlie was left holding her coat. A terrific wave towered above them and crashed down upon their heads. The world went from loud and thunderous to quiet and muted.

Charlie was held under by the waves. She felt herself tumbling, not sure which way was up. Gravity didn't exist under the water. She held out her arms, hoping to touch the ground or feel the air but all she felt was the water bubbling around her. With eyes wide open she searched for the light, a direction in which to pull towards, but there was no discernible difference between up and down.

Her lungs were beginning to burn. She was fighting the urge to cough, to breathe in. It would all be over so quickly if she sucked it in. She thought of Anna and Katy. Was this the feeling that they fought at the end, this desire to fill their lungs? What about Remi? She imagined Lee's hand on their heads, and it was as if he was in the water with her.

No. She didn't want it to end this way. Not with Penny believing that she was guilty and the police believing that she'd lured Penny to the beach to drown her.

Her arms were weak, her legs too heavy, but she wouldn't give up. Her knees were at her chest as her feet touched something rough. She pushed hard and broke from the water. She sucked in the salty air and blinked hard against the stinging in her eyes. A wave hit her on the side of her face and she went under the water briefly. She came back to the surface and screamed Penny's name.

The waves were high, and Charlie couldn't see Penny. She could be hidden behind any of them. Charlie clung to Penny's coat as if it would suddenly be filled with her long limbs.

'Penny, where are you?'

The waves spun her towards the rocks. She looked up and saw figures on the cliffs above, but they were too far away for Charlie to see who they were. She raised her arms.

'Help! We're here. Help!'

The air took on a deeper base note. *Thud, thud, thud.* Charlie looked into the grey sky as the waves lifted her upwards. A helicopter came into view and seemed to pause above her.

'Thank God.'

Her first thought was that they were saved. Help had arrived and everything was going to be okay. But then she realised that there was nowhere for the helicopter to land. The tide was high and there was no beach. It would be suicide for anyone to come into the water to help her and Penny.

She didn't want it to end like this. All she'd wanted was to put the past behind her but instead she was forced to pay a price she hadn't known was needed.

'Penny!'

There was no sign of the other woman.

Charlie hoped the police would be able to sift through the trail of lies that Penny had left behind, to discover what had really happened.

She hoped Ben would get justice for Remi.

She hoped Lee never walked free.

She hoped that people wouldn't think too badly of her, or of Penny.

She hoped.

She hoped.

She hoped that death wouldn't hurt.

CHAPTER FORTY-NINE

The Royal Cornwall Hospital

Friday, 30 November 2018

Naz had to take two strides to every one of Harper's as they marched down the hospital corridor.

It was cold outside but her winter coat was causing her to sweat. She stepped to one side to allow a hospital porter to come by, but Harper pushed on regardless. Naz was in no mood to break into a run to catch up with him.

The hospital was both noisy and quiet at once. So many visitors, staff and patients were moving through the building that conversations and footsteps had welded together to become a low hum. She wondered how many people's hearts had stopped here today, and how many had restarted, or even beat for the first time. She thought about the tears of heartbreak and the tears of joy, and of how different they should look under a microscope because they came from different places, were made by different emotions.

Naz didn't think of herself as a sentimental woman, but hospitals brought out the vulnerability in her. She hated them for it.

Two women bustled by and Naz heard the end of a conversation.

'. . . I always said there was something fishy about her.'

'Oh, for the love of God, Decca. You did not!'

Further along the corridor, Harper stopped and looked behind him. He'd finally noticed that he was on his own. Naz slipped off her coat and walked towards him. She wasn't used to feeling guilty so didn't recognise what was causing her slow step and her reticence to reach the ward. But there was a part of her that wondered whether Conor Fletcher was right. Could she have done something to stop this from happening?

A young woman had died but they had so nearly lost two people. Strictly speaking this wasn't her case and she was bound to ruffle some local feathers by being here. But they'd called her and said that the patient was insisting on talking to her. She had some information that she'd only tell Naz. Harper tagged along, because that's what partners do, but Naz was wondering how much trauma would be visible – both physically and mentally.

The local police had interviewed everyone in Penderrion who knew Charlie and Penny. Had they suspected anything? What did they know about the dead woman? Had she been acting strangely in the days leading up to her death? They were now trying to follow the links to the Lee Fisher case to see what lessons could be learned.

Naz and Harper followed the signs down the labyrinth and, at last, turned a corner into the ward they'd been searching for. It was quieter in here, despite people crowded around the beds ignoring signs saying, 'two visitors only'. A nurse pointed them to the correct room and they walked past the curtained bays, six women in each. Some were sitting up chatting to visitors, others lay still and alone.

'Y'okay?' asked Harper. 'I've never known you to be so quiet.'

'I hate hospitals,' she said. 'Is this it?'

They stopped and Naz looked through the glass panel on the door. 'Looks like she's got visitors.'

'Shall we?' Harper pushed open the door and stepped to one side to allow Naz to enter first.

There were three women standing around the bed. She recognised two of them as the women she'd overheard in the corridor.

'Hello,' Naz said. She couldn't see past them to the bed. 'I'm DC Naz Apkarian and this is my partner, DC Angus Harper.'

One of the women, who had her hair pinned up in a messy grey bun, said, 'Police? Good lord, do you have to do this now? Visiting hours have only just started. This is the first time we've been allowed to see her since they dragged her out of the sea.'

'Decca,' said a rasping voice from the bed. 'Don't.'

Naz stepped further into the room. She tried to keep her face neutral as she looked at the pale and weak-looking woman lying beneath a crisp white sheet.

'Hi. I hear you wanted to talk to me.' Naz paused and then said, 'I don't know how you like to be addressed.'

'Charlie. Not Steffi any more.'

'Charlie it is, then. How're you feeling? You look like shit, by the way.'

'Battered but—'

'She gave us quite the scare,' Decca said. 'We thought we were going to lose her, and I'm not convinced we're through the woods yet. Look at you, so pale. Are they feeding you, my love? Would you like us to bring you anything to eat?'

'For goodness' sake, Decca,' said one of the other women, 'be quiet for a minute, will you? Let Charlie speak.' She was expensively dressed and wearing shoes that couldn't be comfortable to stand in. No wonder she sounded like she was in a bad mood.

Charlie smiled, 'S'okay, Jenn. Hurts to talk.'

'That'll be the tubes they stuck down your throat,' the one with tattoos said. 'That and all the salt water you swallowed.'

Charlie lifted her hand from the bed to get Naz's attention and whispered, 'Have they found her?'

Naz shook her head. 'There's been no sign of Penny's body.'

She looked at the other women, wondering how much they knew. As if reading her mind, the one called Decca said, 'Don't worry, we know everything. We've known about Charlie's past since before this happened.'

Charlie coughed from the bed and flapped her hand from side to side. 'No,' she breathed.

'Sorry, darling, but yes. Aubrey had kept every newspaper going back years. Bo and I were taking them to the recycling when we spotted a photograph that looked a little familiar. We took it to Jenn and we agreed that, on close inspection, this Steffi Finn looked remarkably like our new friend Charlie Miller.'

'Sorry.'

'What for?' asked Jenn. 'None of it is your fault. We looked up the case on line. Bo remembered that pitiful excuse for a man and the way you'd been accused of all sorts. We were just biding our time until you felt you knew us well enough to confide in us.'

'Penny?' asked Charlie.

'Well, here's the thing,' said Bo. 'It was your story to tell and we knew you'd tell it when you were ready. We never told

Penny. I just never quite trusted her. She hadn't been in the village long and I always got the impression she wasn't planning to stay. She was never invested.'

Naz glanced at Harper; he raised a single bushy eyebrow but said nothing.

'Jenn,' Charlie wheezed.

Jenn went forward and sat on the bed. 'Yes?'

'Marcus. He knows about me.'

'I know he does, darling. He recognised you straight away, though it took him a day or two to remember exactly where from. Of course, he didn't think to tell me what he'd discovered. He took it upon himself to keep you away from our family, thinking he was keeping us safe. If he'd bothered asking, I would have told him that we didn't need protecting.'

She glanced over her shoulder at Naz as if she wasn't sure she could speak freely in front of her. 'Charlie, there's something you should know.' She cleared her throat. 'Marcus heard you hammering on our door on the day of the accident. He saw you through the window but decided against letting you in. He could see you were distressed but . . . oh, Lord knows why, but he didn't answer the door. The kids were home because of the storm. The power cut had scared Tilly so I was building a blanket fort with her in the bedroom. When I asked Marcus who was at the door he said, "No one," and I didn't even question him. If he'd let you in, none of this would have happened and Penny wouldn't have . . . I know we're not meant to feel sorry for her after all she's done, but she was our friend and . . .'

'It's okay,' Charlie said. 'I don't blame Penny. Or Marcus. No way of knowing . . .'

'But if Marcus had let you in—'

Decca put her hand on Jenn's shoulder and she stood up and walked over to the window to stop anyone seeing the emotions playing across her face.

Naz took a step closer to the bed. 'You asked to talk to me, Charlie. Would you like your friends to leave so we can have that chat?'

'Stay,' Charlie said.

'Is it about Penny?' asked Naz.

Charlie shook her head and Naz threw another glance at Harper, who still hadn't said a word since they'd stepped foot inside the room.

'Ben,' Charlie said.

'Ben Jarvis?' asks Naz. He'd voluntarily turned up at the local police station when he heard the news and told them everything that he knew.

Charlie nodded. She was looking tired. Her eyes closed for a moment and Naz thought that she was falling asleep, but she was just gathering her strength to tell them what she had to say.

'I thought he'd attacked me. In the woods. But it was Penny. Ben saved my life. He thinks Lee . . .' She paused to take a deep breath. Naz leaned closer.

'Ben thinks what, Charlie?'

'He thinks Lee killed his daughter, Remi, before he killed Katy and Anna. He wants to know . . . where her body is.'

'Ridiculous!' said Decca. 'How would you possibly know that?'

Charlie's eyes didn't leave Naz's. 'Lee gave me Remi's necklace. As a gift. He brought it back from a trip. I think I know where Remi's buried.'

CHAPTER FIFTY

Charlie Miller

Tuesday, 12 March 2019

Charlie pours four glasses of wine and carries them on a tray into the living room.

The fire crackles in the hearth and the candles illuminate the corners of the room.

'Isn't this nice?' Decca says.

Charlie catches sight of her reflection in the driftwood mirror. Her brown hair dye has faded and the tips are glowing golden in the firelight. She isn't trying to hide any more. Charlie has spent as much time trying to hide from herself as she has from others. For now, she's going to let herself be and see what she'll become.

It turned out that the prison had been monitoring Lee's letters and Penny was one of his stranger correspondents. There was much talk of revenge and 'making things right' and how they would be together one day. Lee's letters to Penny had urged her to 'do what you think is for the best', though he swore he meant that she should leave Charlie alone to live her life. There was nothing in his letters that expressly asked Penny to set Charlie up or to stalk her. But, as Penny had said, in his early letters he had asked her to use her contact with Conor to find out where Charlie would be living after she was released.

Charlie had a lot to thank Aubrey and Conor for. When Conor hadn't been able to get through to her he had called the police. Usually it wouldn't have been a priority – there was chaos all over the county with the storm and most of their resources were deployed elsewhere – but five minutes later they received a call from an old man telling them to scramble the coastguards to Penderrion because someone was in trouble in the sea. And just then a message got passed through from the front desk about a woman who'd called from that same village to say she believed someone was trying to kill her.

Aubrey had hobbled on walking sticks to Penny's, where he'd seen the lipstick-scrawled message, and then on to Bo's house where he'd demanded to use her mobile phone. 'They've gone to the beach,' he'd said. 'They'll die in this weather.'

The helicopter and coastguard got there just in time. For Charlie, at least. They had no trouble locating her, thanks to the bright yellow raincoat she was clinging to.

Remi's remains were found not far from the hostel Lee had stayed in on that team-building course he'd told Charlie about. His boss confirmed Lee had been in Derbyshire for a meeting that week, but that he'd gone on his own and stayed on for a couple of days to go hiking in the Peak District.

The storm that had claimed Penny's life and made an attempt for Charlie's had battered the Derbyshire countryside too and Remi's shallow grave had been disturbed. It was early days, but there was little doubt in anyone's mind that Lee had murdered her. The police were now looking into other cases of missing persons. Who knew how many other victims there were?

Charlie's house in Pinchdale had finally sold. To Marcus. He said it was a bargain and he was trying to expand his property portfolio. Charlie was certain this had more to do with Jenn and perhaps his own guilt at how he'd treated her. Either way, they both benefited: she had a tidy sum of money in the bank and he had acquired a property at well below market value. He'd already had it refurbished and had a tenant lined up.

The money had enabled Charlie to hire Jack to do her bathroom and finish her kitchen. She was in the process of turning the outbuildings into workshops. Jenn was offering art holidays at the cottages now and they were all booked for summer. Staying at the cottage, they had the option to do pottery with Charlie three mornings a week. The rest of the time she would either be working on her own art or working at The New Chapter café. She was covering maternity leave for the owner, Imogen. Who knew where it might lead?

'Now,' says Decca, 'what do we make of this week's book?'

'I loved it,' says Bo.

'Dreadful,' says Jenn.

'You hate anything that's not a classic,' says Decca. 'It's time to live a little.'

Charlie smiles. She loves her book group, her new home, her new friends. And she has come to realise that not all of her past needed discarding. Some parts of it were worth holding on to.

Conor had visited her at the hospital.

They'd both cried. Conor kept apologising, over and over. He said that he knew that Penny was unstable but he'd never thought for a second that it could lead to this. They hadn't split up because of Charlie, he'd said. They'd split up because Penny was jealous, unreasonable, and too intense. He regretted having confessed to her about them sleeping together. He'd only told her so that she knew there was no going back. He'd not heard from her again and had assumed she'd moved on. He had no idea that she was in touch with Lee or that she'd moved to Cornwall.

He begged Charlie to forgive him. Charlie told him there was nothing to forgive. If she hadn't been so adamant that she needed to cut all ties with her old life, Penny's link to Conor, and to Lee, might have been uncovered sooner. He was too dear to her for her to lose him again. Good friends were precious and she would never take them for granted again.

Charlie was particularly close to Aubrey and viewed him more as a beloved member of her family now. She was getting a carer's allowance to look after him. In the days after she was home from hospital, he was the only reason she got out of bed. If she hadn't had someone to look after she would have curled up in a ball and tried to block out the world. She owed him her life. It was the one time that seeing the best in people had paid off.

She was determined to honour her promise to keep him out of an old people's home. There was a rota now, in the village, for who was going to take him his Sunday lunch. Decca, in particular, had grown fond of him and – when she wasn't out for dinner with Jack – she liked to argue politics with Aubrey.

Charlie had expected journalists, letters and phone calls but none came. Penny's death was only mentioned in passing in a local paper among the list of those who'd lost their lives in the recent storm. Charlie hadn't been mentioned at all, and neither had Steffi Finn. This community looked after their own, she was told. She was one of them now and she wasn't the only one with a past she'd rather forget.

Still, one problem remained. Thanks to Lee's correspondence with Penny he now knew where Charlie lived. There were many years left before he would be considered for parole, so he wasn't an immediate threat, but there would come a day when he would be free to come looking for her. Perhaps she'd have to find another name, another place to live.

But for now she wouldn't worry about what the future held. She was going to make the most of each day as it came.

CHAPTER FIFTY-ONE

Pinchdale Telegraph

Thursday, 4 July 2019

LEE FISHER FOUND DEAD

Notorious murderer Lee Fisher has been killed in prison, the Pinchdale Telegraph *has learned today. He was due to stand trial next month for the murder of 25-year-old Remi Jarvis.*

Fisher, who was serving two life sentences for the murders of Katy Foster and Anna Atkins, was found unresponsive in his cell in the early hours of yesterday morning. Attempts to revive him failed. The prison has refused to confirm reports that he was murdered by another inmate.

Ben Jarvis, Remi's father, has long believed that Fisher was responsible for more murders than the two he had initially been convicted of. Remi's body was found in Derbyshire's Peak District where Fisher had been attending a work function. Her badly decomposed remains had been identified thanks to DNA testing.

Remi was separated from her friends while on a night out in Derby city centre. It is believed that she met

Fisher outside a bar and accepted a lift home from him. She was never heard from again. Callous Fisher dumped Remi's body in a remote spot in the Peak District and took an item of Remi's jewellery as a trophy. This proved to be the link the police needed to tie him to the young woman's murder.

Steffi Finn, who had been Fisher's girlfriend at the time that Katy and Anna were murdered, was said to be key to discovering what happened to Remi Jarvis. A close friend of Ms Finn told us that she had reached out to Remi's father when she realised the significance of the necklace. Ms Finn had served ten months for providing a false alibi for Fisher. The *Pinchdale Telegraph* has reason to believe she left the country immediately upon release from prison and went to live with family in Australia.

Ben Jarvis said of Lee Fisher's death, 'I wish he'd stood trial for my daughter's murder but I can't say I'm sorry he's dead. I'll be forever grateful to Steffi Finn who helped me convince the police to search for my daughter's body in the Peak District. Perhaps now we can both move on with our lives.'

ACKNOWLEDGEMENTS

I count myself lucky to have such an amazing agent who is incredibly supportive and insightful. Imogen Pelham, at Marjacq, thank you for everything you do for me. And thank you to all the team who support me in so many ways. Sandra, I hope you don't mind but I stole the line about someone 'with the face of a man who used to be handsome' from you at York Festival of Writing.

I am so grateful to my amazing editors – at Harvill Secker and Berkley – who have helped me immeasurably in writing this story. Sara Adams, Jade Chandler, Danielle Perez, Liz Foley, I have benefitted from your wisdom and I thank you. The rest of the team there work so hard behind the scenes and it would be remiss of me not to give them a special mention and my heartfelt thanks. Noor, Mia, Kate and too many others to name, I appreciate everything you do and I simply had no idea that so many people would be involved in bringing my books to life.

For this book I got invaluable advice from Rachael Hodges about police procedure. Thank you for your patience, Rachael! Where there are mistakes, they are mine alone as I bent the rules to suit the story.

For everything else; the sanity check, the solidarity, the laughter and the love, I must thank the amazing writing community that I have met since this journey began. Roz Watkins, Fran Dorricott and Sophie Draper (aka The Doomsbury Group) have kept me going when times were tough. And I don't know where I'd be without the support of The Ladykillers. The wider writing community, the bloggers, the readers, the reviewers, those who champion the books they love – I am always amazed at how generous you are with your time. And to the book festivals and the booksellers (especially in Derby) – thank you!

Thank you to my friends who have helped with childcare when deadlines loom, or just to give me a well-needed break – particularly Pete and Michelle, and Kayte.

As this book is set in Cornwall, my second home, I must thank my in-laws for welcoming me into the fold. One of the first gifts my mother-in-law gave me was a t-shirt saying 'Everyone Loves a Cornish Girl'. I thought it meant I wasn't good enough for her son as I wasn't from Cornwall! I came to realise it was her way of telling me I was 'one of them' now. Thank you, Dale, for all your love, support and the champion-ing of my books (apologies to Andrew at Waterstones in Truro!)

I have the most patient family and friends. Thank you all for understanding when I'm off in my own world, when I miss birthdays and nights out. The uni girls, the school mums, and all my other lovely friends have been so supportive by pushing my book in the faces of their friends. My mum and my hus-band have absolutely no shame when it comes to promoting my books and I'm sure have hand-sold hundreds of copies. Though it embarrasses me hugely, don't ever stop. I love you.

I couldn't have written this book without the support of my husband. Thank you, James, I'm so lucky to have you in my life. Finally for my sons, to whom this book is dedicated.

I didn't know how much it would mean to me to have you be so proud of your dear old mum. I know you hate it when I get gushy in public, but tough! ALEX AND DANNY, I BLOODY LOVE YOU! I will do everything in my power to help you follow your dreams, just as you inspire me to follow mine.

Love, always x

JO JAKEMAN

Jo Jakeman was the winner of the Friday Night Live 2016 competition at the York Festival of Writing. Born in Cyprus, she worked for many years in the City of London before moving to Derbyshire with her husband and twin boys.